D0857424

Literary Structures
Edited by John Gardner

THE
DOOMED
DETECTIVE

The Contribution of the Detective Novel
to Postmodern American and Italian Fiction

STEFANO TANI

SOUTHERN ILLINOIS UNIVERSITY PRESS

Carbondale and Edwardsville

Library of Congress Cataloging in Publication Data

Tani, Stefano, 1953–
    The doomed detective.

    (Literary structures)
    Includes index.
    Bibliography: p.
    1. Detective and mystery stories, American–History
and criticism.   2. Detective and mystery stories, Italian
—History and criticism.   3. American fiction—20th
century—History and criticism.   4. Italian fiction—20th
century—History and criticism.   5. Literature, Comparative—American and Italian.   6. Literature, Comparative—
Italian and American.   7. Postmodernism.   I. Title.
II. Series.

PS374.D4T36 1983   813'.0872'09   83–10233
ISBN 0–8093–1148–8

In memory of
John Gardner
and of my father,
Giorgio Tani.

—And Nicole?

—She is gone, but we still remember her because of what you wrote on her.

—On her? I never wrote on her. . . .

—In this case, my friend, you didn't know what you were doing, just like the hound chasing a quarry and barking at the moon.

(*A Faint Stone*)

Contents

Acknowledgments

There are four persons without whom this book would not exist:

Gaetano Prampolini, Professor of American Literature at the Università degli Studi di Firenze, Italy, who first recommended this topic to me, carefully read the manuscript, and offered many helpful suggestions.

The late John Gardner, who gave me encouragement and advice the very day I was about to drop this project. The many stimulating conversations we had, his brilliant comments and his generous help in revision made this work possible. To his memory I owe my great debt and gratitude.

Susan Strehle, Professor of American Literature at the State University of New York at Binghamton, who read the first draft of the manuscript in progress, offered a flow of wonderful ideas, and gave cheerful moral support.

Rudolph Bell, Professor of History at Rutgers University, who assisted me at the final stage of this work. His editorial comments and guidance have proved to be invaluable, and I owe to him my overcoming the paranoia of the publishing process.

My sincere appreciation goes also to Julio Rodrigues-Luis, Professor of Comparative Literature at the State University of New York at Binghamton, whose insightful criticism and encouragement have been of great help. In addition, I want to thank Kay Glasgow and Cheryl Spiese of the Glenn G. Bartle Library of the State University of New York at Binghamton, who took generous care of my many requests for hard-to-find articles. I owe valuable information about Italian cinema to the kindness of Guido Fink, film critic and Professor of American

Literature at the Università degli Studi di Bologna. Elisabeth Tricomi, Brendan Dooley, Frank Mormando, Thomas Mueller, Julia Hunt, and Iliana Perini read the manuscript and gave many useful suggestions. Louise Barnett, Professor of American Literature at Rutgers University, helped me solve quite a few problems.

It is a pleasure to acknowledge that parts of chapter 4 and the conclusion of this book appeared in the form of an article, "The Dismemberment of the Detective," in *Diogène* no. 120; I am very grateful to the editors for granting permission to reprint it. Finally, I want to give my thanks to Southern Illinois University Press, and particularly to Director Kenney Withers, who believed in this book.

Introduction

From its beginnings down to the 1950s, the detective novel was considered a negligible form of fiction. Almost as soon as detective fiction appeared, with the publication of Poe's "The Murders in the Rue Morgue," "serious" writers began to make use of the devices of detective fiction—Dickens and Dostoevski, for example—but the "real" detective novel, with its indifference to deep characterization and significant theme, never pretended to be—was never viewed as—art. It served, in one way or another, as popular entertainment, either as elegant puzzle matter (the English school) or as macho escapism (the later "hard-boiled" American school). Then, with the rise of French existentialism and its World War II burst of popularity—a time when there was practical value, especially in the French underground, in the belief that a man is free to define or redefine himself at any moment (assert his "essence"), that is, when he might become whatever he chooses or needs to become in an inherently absurd universe—the private detective, or rather the mythic private detective conceived by such writers as Dashiell Hammett and Raymond Chandler, suddenly became the intellectual's hero: a creature capable of dealing efficiently with a disorderly and dangerous world. He was, in effect, the hero who took the place of the soldier. The moment of this emergence into respectability is significant, coincident as it is with the time of war disillusionment in the late forties (when Jean Paul Sartre fixed on him as the "existential hero") and the early fifties, when for Americans the glory of World War II—itself already beginning to seem dubious—had decayed into the dull nightmare of the Cold War. The private detective no longer has an army working with him, at any rate no army he can trust, and he no longer has a high moral cause: his business is simply to stay alive and figure out who committed the crime, whether or not he approves of the laws that have been violated.

Though the mythicizing existentialists who seized on him did not at once notice the fact, the private detective became the model of middle-class enterprise. Relying only on his personal resources, he could beat an army of thugs. In effect, he avenged middle-class humiliation and loss of identity at the hands of what, by 1961, even president Eisenhower was decrying as "the military-industrial complex." The middle-class ethos is based on faith in private enterprise, and the detective is the response of private enterprise to the police as state-run system, reminiscent of the by-now discredited army as state system. (For an impression of the general climate of the times, think of *The Naked and the Dead* and *Slaughterhouse Five,* and of films like *The Bridge over the River Kwai.* America's needless firebombings, not to mention the strategically dubious atomic bombing of Hiroshima and Nagasaki, were by this time well known.) And so by the 1950s and thereafter, the detective novel in its hard-boiled American form rose to literary prominence. Dashiell Hammett became a major literary figure, and undeniably "serious" young novelists like John Hawkes, in *The Lime Twig* (1961), began to turn the private-eye vision into one form or another of ironic, complex literary art. By the early sixties scholars were starting to study detective fiction as if it were important, and not long thereafter, though the true detective novel is almost always a work of ingenious craft rather than authentic art, the mechanics of detective fiction were beginning to serve as a normal platform for more ambitious, more "literary" fiction.

I choose the detective novel as the object of this study because it was changed radically both in structure and inner significance by the postmodern sensibility. As we will see in the following chapters, two of the most unquestionable features of postmodernism are that it is de-structuring and asymbolic, so that it finds in the highly structured and symbolic detective novel the traditional genre that most needs its intervention and that potentially gives the plainest evidence of the changes this intervention would initiate. Thus the "something else" into which the detective novel is turned by postmodernism provides a perfect way to see postmodernism finally at work rather than as a catchy and elusive theoretical definition—in this way its preoccupations gain in intensity and are further clarified through application.

The present study attempts to establish how recent serious novelists take advantage of detective fiction conventions to write something quite different from detective fiction, and how this "something else" fits into the literary panorama of postmodernism. To make my case, I begin by trying to clarify what a detective novel is formally and socially, how it evolved, and what it seems to be further evolving into. I briefly examine the history of detective fiction so that we can better understand recent developments, and I examine apparent patterns and styles connecting the old detective novel and the new.

In this context the United States and Italy represent a very rewarding choice for the study of the mutation and ultimate inversion of the detective novel. I choose the United States because it is the acknowledged homeland of the genre and, even more than Britain, the country where the tradition went through all its historical developments (Poe, the classical ratiocinative detective novel from Van Dine to Ellery Queen, the hard-boiled, the recent popular fiction-degeneration such as the thriller, the crime story, the spy-novel). On the other hand, Italy seems a good selection for the opposite reason; in this country the detective novel was an imported genre that began to be published in a distinctive fashion only in 1929, but eventually the Italian production gave, as the American one, some of the most interesting examples of the postmodern mutation of the genre. Let us see how this happened.

Until 1929 in Italy the notion of detective novel did not exist. A few British mysteries had been published in serials by pulp magazines or disguised as "adventure-stories" by second-rate publishers, but only in 1929, when a large and prestigious publishing house—Mondadori—tried officially to launch the British mystery on the Italian market, can we talk of a recognition of the genre as such by a wide and educated readership. While the British mystery became very popular in the thirties, the American hard-boiled detective story was subjected to a literary embargo, as was most American fiction in that time. Finally, from 1941 to 1943, Fascist censorship first restricted and then prohibited the circulation of any kind of detective novel. As a consequence of all this, the greatest part of American hard-boiled detective fiction arrived in Italy only after World War II. Thus Italy was exposed only very late to the detective novel, and almost exclusively to the British tradition, which was in turn the elaboration of the straight and ratiocinative Poesque detective story. As a result, it is mainly with that tradition that Italian writers identified the detective novel since the hard-boiled, which came later and with very distinctive characteristics, was justly considered a different thing, an American derivation. This is why, when they recently started to write "literary" detective fiction, Italians had as a model not so much the hard-boiled as the solid and traditional British mystery.

In my examination of literary or postmodern detective fiction I include a brief history of the Anglo-American detective novel to provide groundwork for the analysis of the Italians' redefinition of the form, then present an outline of the origins and development of the Italian detective novel. I do not discuss the development of detective fiction in France because French writers were from the beginning and in general are still interested in the hard-boiled detective novel and its "existential" derivations (e.g., the fiction of Hemingway). Italian writers, on the other hand—such writers as Sciascia—assume and manipulate that ratiocinative and "Poesque" kind of detective fiction that became very popular in Italy in the thirties and that now leads directly to postmodern or metafictional styles. I argue, in short, a connection between the Poesque detective story and the Italian writers' subversion of the rationality celebrated by Poe. The Poesque detective story and the British elaboration of that form (the old-style mystery as written by, for example, Agatha Christie), which the existentialists and others tended to consider a rational game of self-limiting conclusions, proves to be very much alive, since from its basic pattern, shrewdly manipulated, comes some of the best contemporary fiction of Italy (Sciascia's *A ciascuno il suo,* Eco's *Il nome della rosa*) and, in broader terms, one of the most important literary movements now visible: postmodernism in the fashion of the ironic intellectual fiction of writers ranging from Borges and Barth to Calvino.

Italian fiction, thanks to the pioneering contribution of Gadda (*Quer pasticciaccio brutto de via Merulana,* 1946) and, more recently, of Sciascia, Eco, and Calvino, seems today the spearhead of what we have temporarily called "literary" detective fiction, a postmodern form or variety of forms that reshape the seeming dead-end rationality of the British mystery into an original "something else." This something else is what I will describe as the anti-detective novel, a high-parodic form that stimulates and tantalizes its readers by disappointing common detective-novel expectations. I am interested in pointing out how widespread the recent anti-detective-fiction phenomenon is and how it comes to involve writers of a country—Italy—that has a very limited tradition in detective fiction and, just because of it, fastened and worked on the Poesque model with quite surprising postmodern results.

Thus both the United States and Italy—the former as the ultimate result of a long tradition in detective fiction, the latter just because of the lack of such a tradition—came to produce anti-detective fiction, notwithstanding those macroscopic differences between them that at first sight seem to forbid any kind of close tie in the literary field. All this should not surprise us, since these novels are directly related not only to national situations, but also to the sense of crisis and disorder common in Western culture after World War II. In the fifties during the Korean War and the sixties during the Vietnam war and the beginning of economic recession, the United States experienced an identity crisis of sorts; it is to that time that I trace the first American examples of the anti-detective novel. Just as it occurred in the case of the British detective novel (which was imported into Italy when in the United States it was about to be supplanted by the hard-boiled novel), the economic boom and a short period of general stability and welfare started in Italy (the Italian *miracolo economico* of the early sixties) when the same things began to be questioned in the United States. This moment of welfare of course did not last, and Italy in this sense also soon caught up with the United States. The 1968 socio-political crisis and the general recession of industrialized societies hit Italy perhaps more than any other Western country; the widespread sense of uneasiness and disorder typical of these years was elaborated by some enlightened writers in the post-modern fashion of the anti-detective novel.

A study of American and Italian anti-detective fiction thus offers the advantage of linking the detective-novel tradition and literary postmodernism through two countries that, although having very different backgrounds in the field of the detective novel, came to a similar result, featuring anti-detective fiction as a form of postmodern expression. This shows how wide-spread postmodernism is and suggests that it may not be limited to any single national literature. Never as in the last twenty years have we seen such a koine, both in literature and mass culture, unifying in taste and thought all Western countries.

Anti-detective fiction thus becomes a crossroad of multifold preoccupations: tradition and postmodernism, mass culture and high culture, Italy and United States, Italy-United States and Western societies. The sense of an ending or of a new beginning, the twilight zone between the nuclear age and what comes after it, between rationality and mystery, can be clarified through a study of anti-detective fiction, the crossroad where unsolvable mysteries and doomed detectives meet with a less optimistic but clearly more mature sense of man and his limits.

1

The Development of the Detective Novel and the Rise of the Anti-Detective Novel

The origins of the detective story have been traced to the Oedipus myth, Greek tragedy, the Bible, and Egyptian tales; but if a genre is a form aware of itself and of its own conventions, the life of the detective story begins officially in April 1841 with the publication, in *Graham's Magazine*, of Edgar Allan Poe's "The Murders in the Rue Morgue," followed shortly by the "The Mystery of Marie Rogêt" (1842) and "The Purloined Letter" (1845). Rather than harken back to the biblical Daniel for the detective story's origins, it seems more profitable to identify two main eighteenth century literary currents[1] that merge in Poe's creation and remain fundamental in every further development in the genre. We may refer to them, broadly, as the intellectual and the popular impulses as these are reflected, respectively, in works like Voltaire's *Zadig* and the typical Gothic tale, the one generally static, ratiocinative, and philosophical, the other adventurous, atmospheric, emotionally suspenseful. Intellectual and "popular" currents have always been present in literature, often in the same work; but for an understanding of the rise of detective fiction, it will be most fruitful to concentrate on the rational period *par excellence,* the Age of Enlightenment, a period shot through with the cultural paradox of fascination with the rational and a keen interest in madness, a paradox frequently expressed in single individuals, as in the case of Dr. Johnson. The second half of the eighteenth century is the age of both French encyclopedism and the Gothic novel, of both Kantian intellectual idealism and *Sturm und Drang.* In 1748 Voltaire published *Zadig,* presenting in the character of

Zadig himself a sort of protodetective, since by mere reasoning
he is able to describe a horse and a bitch dog though he has
never before seen either. In 1776 Beaumarchais introduced a
similar example of reasoning in a letter he wrote to the editor of
the London *Morning Chronicle.* After a ball, he found a lady's
cloak and, by examination of the garment was able to give in his
letter a remarkably complete description of the unknown lady,
whom he asks to come and collect it. One of the basic assumptions of the Enlightenment was of course that everything should
be explainable by the power of reason. Voltaire and Beaumarchais epitomize the triumph of Enlightenment rationality and in
their playful examples of "inductive reasoning"[2] foreshadow
the detective's role.

On the other hand, in 1764, at the height of this rational
period, Horace Walpole published his fantastic *Castle of
Otranto,* the novel that sets off the tradition of the Gothic tale.
Walpole's *The Castle of Otranto* was followed by Ann Radcliffe's
The Romance of the Forest (1791), *The Mysteries of Udolpho*
(1794) and *The Italian* (1797). In the plots and settings of these
novels, irrational elements—the furniture of nightmares and the
unconscious: oppressive skies, mysterious noises, and uncanny
occurrences—weigh down and darken reality as surely as do the
ancient castle or monastery settings; and though all oddities may
be explained away at the end of the novel, the overall effect is
unmistakably one of bafflement and unease.

And alongside the rise of Gothicism we notice another phenomenon, which will in time evolve into literary irrationalism.
During the first half of the eighteenth century, it was common
among the chaplains on the staff of English prisons to collect
oral confessions from criminals about to be executed and to
have them published at the time of the criminal's death. These
publications, among them the famous *Newgate Calendar,* are of
course both realistic and fictitious, vivid in their details and
highly rhetorical in style, but not always honorably researched.
They narrate, as they claim to do, real life stories, but the
stories are romanticized, filled with gruesome and sensational
material—murders and wild adventures designed to appeal to

the popular taste. They initiated a literary connection between the rational (the "realistic," the claim that this is a "true story") and the irrational or nightmarish (the morbid indulgence in violence and mystery). They blend opposites to satisfy a hunger for "sensation" in the drudgery-burdened lower-class audience, and they sold like hot cakes.

Evidence of this interest in the lives of adventurers can be traced at least to the end of the sixteenth century, where we find it in biographies of popular rogues, such as *La Vie Généreuse des Mercelots, Gueuz et Bolmiens* (published at Lyons in 1596), in picaresque novels like *Gil Blas* by Le Sage (1735), and in tales of the careers of criminals and legendary outlaws like Robin Hood, who was famous well before Shakespeare's time.[3] But in publications like the *Newgate Calendar*, the attitude of writer and reader toward the felon changes from open admiration to moralistic condemnation,[4] a change allowing into play darker psychological elements—the good Christian's morbid fascination with the sordid, his sentimental inclination toward pity, given the criminal's realistically reported "sad story," and his delicious shudder at the recognition that, were he not so lucky and virtuous, he might have made the same mortal mistakes.

Not surprisingly, very good writers soon picked up the fashion and made more cunningly artistic use of it. Daniel Defoe (1659–1731) wrote accounts of the careers of such criminals as Jack Sheppard, Jonathan Wild, and the pirate John Gow (1724); these were more glamorous "journalistic" versions of the *Newgate Calendar* reports. He also created his fictitious lady criminal *Moll Flanders*. By the early nineteenth century this impulse toward popular adventure evolved into the formula of the crime-memoir genre, of which an early example is the one published in 1828 by Eugène François Vidocq, first a criminal, then later, after his reformation, chief of the first modern police force, the French *Sureté*. This genre evolved, too, into increasingly sophisticated versions of the biographical crime novel on the pattern basically established in *Moll Flanders*.

The revolutionary achievement of Edgar Allan Poe (1809–

49) was his fusion of the rational and the irrational literary currents in his first three detective stories, especially in "The Murders in the Rue Morgue" (1841). In this tale, rightly one of Poe's most famous, we encounter a passage that has not received the attention it deserves. It is the narrator's description of his friend M. Dupin when he is exercising his "peculiar analytic ability":[5]

> *His manner at these moments was frigid and abstract;* his eyes were *vacant* in expression; while his voice, usually a rich tenor, rose into a *treble.* . . . Observing him in these moods, I often dwelt meditatively upon the old philosophy of the Bi-Part Soul, and amused myself with *the fancy of a double Dupin—the creative and the resolvent.* . . . What I have described in the Frenchman, was merely the result of an *excited,* or perhaps of a *diseased intelligence.*[6]

Uncannily, here, in the first true detective story, we find an intimation of the double current, irrational and rational, that will become typical of the genre. Duality is the basic principle of detection, since the sine qua non requirements of the detective story are a detective and a criminal. Whatever the source of Poe's "old philosophy of the Bi-Part soul," that philosophy grounds and prepares Poe's "fancy of a double Dupin—the creative and the resolvent." In these words are suggested a mine of information about Poe and his ideas concerning the detective and detection.

It should go without saying—though later we will find the idea more significant than it at first appears—that Dupin is an essential Romantic hero, the absolute individualist, almost a divinity through the power of his double gift, imagination and reason. His reason (or judgment) is almost preternaturally developed, and through imagination, or an intensely active kind of fancy—a sympathetic gift reminiscent of Wordsworth's notion that a man can learn dignity from sympathetic apprehension of mountains—he can intuitively feel out the universe. But he is not an innocent Romantic hero. His imagination, like Roderick Usher's, and perhaps his reason as well, are somehow "diseased." Let us put all this back into Poe's own language, a terminology which avoids identification of the Bi-Part Soul with either eighteenth- or nineteenth-century systems.

The "creative" Dupin thinks so intensely of the crime-puzzle to be solved as to obliterate his usual personality ("his manner"). He "empties" himself to be able to "receive" and reconstruct the origins of the puzzle: in some passive way he realizes, almost psychically, what must necessarily have happened, namely that the crime cannot have been the work of a rational personality. The adjectives here used by Poe emphasize cold impersonality ("frigid"), detachment from the self ("abstract"), a certain psychological emptiness ("vacant"). Dupin, in other words, temporarily sets aside his own psyche, much in the fashion of a medium at a seance (note the strange "treble" voice), to allow in something outside himself, presumably the nature or personality of the criminal. This is the "creative" side of the double Dupin's process of detection, a first step in the process, to be followed by activation of the "resolvent" side, the psychological state in which Dupin makes the necessary connections and finds a harmony in apparently disparate clues. (Neither eighteenth-century creativity theory, involving "fancy" brought to order by "judgment," nor early Romantic theory, involving "imagination" and "reason," quite account for the psychology here, though either one might have served as Poe's point of departure.) If Dupin talks "at these moments"—in the "creative" period—his voice rises unnaturally "into a treble" because he has still to recollect his own (mature and male) personality. As we have said, the duality represented by "the creative and the resolvent" is by no means a harmonious fusion, but rather results in an "excited, or perhaps diseased intelligence," a vampiresque schizophrenia by which the creative side lures in a fanciful range of possibilities that the resolvent side then sorts and applies to the case.

In fact Poe, like Dupin, often strikes us as two personalities at war with each other, one creative, the side that writes "The Raven," and one resolvent, the side that writes "The Philosophy of Composition" in order to explain the writing of "The Raven."[7] The resolvent seeks to claim priority over the creative, that is, to rationalize inspiration. In fact, in "The Philosophy of Composition" the "resolvent" Poe claims that he wrote

"The Raven" by a prior rational, almost cynically success-oriented process in which inspirational creativity had very little part. This is of course a ploy that, quite sensibly, Poe does not even try to maintain in his detective story, although, as we shall see, Poe's ambivalent love-hate attitude toward art is clearly expressed in his theory of crime detection. After Dupin's "creative" process, the "*re*solvent" necessarily follows as *re*collection and *re*connection, a logical assimilation of the data and clues evoked or composed by the creative exercise. The "creative" and the "resolvent" exist in a relationship as troubled as that obtaining between the two fundamental characters in detective fiction, the criminal and the detective. Each depends upon the other for his existence. As Dupin conjures up fanciful possibilities—ultimately the murderer personality—the murderer, in effect, "invents" the detective who must necessarily follow (and chase) the murderer; in other words the detective exists—is made possible—because the murderer exists. The criminal is simply "creative"; the detective both stifles and, ironically, *realizes* the criminal's creativity by bringing to light the full nature of the criminal act and then imposing on the criminal the detective's "resolvent" power, defusing creative anarchy with common-sense morality.

It is striking to notice how the first murderer in the first detective story is not a "Jack-the-Ripper," as the reader at first imagines, looking at the bloody mess made of Madame L'Espanaye and her daughter, but instead an animal, an orangutan. Frightened by the screams of Madame l'Espanaye, the ape reacts with spontaneous physical force, and then, when he sees the horrified face of his master, the sailor, looking at him from behind the windowglass, labors comically and contritely to clean the mess by throwing the old lady's decapitated corpse into the courtyard and shoving her dead daughter up the chimney.

Two points seem especially worthy of note here: the creativity of the murderer is accidental (the ape creates unconsciously, setting up a misleading and puzzling problem for the detective) and the murderer's creativity is morally neutral; the orangutan is not good or evil but simply "natural." The first murderer in detective fiction, in other words, is a natural force that gets out of control (the ape escapes from the sailor's closet—he is the "skeleton in the closet"), an accidentally creative outburst the detective exploits for his success—"explains" and brings back into the rule of the law. Poe does not present good defeating evil but rationality exorcising the irrational, the "ape in the closet."

Thus we have a set of clashing forces: Poe the logician or critic seeks always to "explain" away Poe the poet, and ultimately Poe's nineteenth-century detective story, conceived in the spirit of the French Enlightenment and motivated by a deep personal need for order, struggles to exorcise through reason the ghost of eighteenth-century Gothicism. The restoration of order and rationality is never complete in Poe's fiction—or in his life, for that matter—because each term inevitably evokes its opposite. In fact, as we will see, the two impulses, rational and irrational, are always present in the development of detective fiction, just as the detective-criminal duality, a game of opposites reluctantly restrained in the same persona, presents a recurrent pattern throughout. An *ante litteram* Jekyll-Hyde situation[8] (expressed, for instance, in Poe's "William Wilson") seems to be at the base of the whole genre, but, unlike Stevenson's Jekyll, Poe's Jekyll (the detective, "the resolvent") does not consider committing suicide to kill his Hyde (the criminal, "the creative");[9] in fact, Poe's criminal in "The Murders in the Rue Morgue" does not even go to jail. As we will see concerning "The Mystery of Marie Rogêt," there may well lie profound reasons for Poe's choice never to jail his culprit; but let us now turn to his less problematic third detective tale.

In "The Purloined Letter" (1845), Poe openly plays with the duality hidden in "The Murders in the Rue Morgue": the Minister D—— who stole and hid the letter is both "poet and mathematician,"[10] and thus he is similar to Dupin, who combines both creative and resolvent parts of the mind. In this tale the whole problem becomes one of "an identification of the reasoner's intellect with that of his opponent."[11] The Minister

D———, in hiding the letter that compromises the honor of "a personage of most exalted station"[12] (likely a royalty, perhaps the queen) for the purpose of blackmailing, acts selfishly and antisocially. The French Prefect of Police, knowing the content of the letter, seeks to recapture the letter for the common good (and, of course, for the reward), but after repeatedly searching the Minister's house, can find nothing. When Dupin is called into the case, he easily finds the hiding-place of the stolen letter. It is, in fact, the most visible, "innocent," obvious place in the house. In the mental duel between Dupin and the Minister, Dupin's mind defeats the Minister's because his mind is so similar to the Minister's that it can parasitically identify with the Minister's way of thinking and thus arrive at the puzzle's solution (the "resolvent" moment). While in "The Murders in the Rue Morgue" Dupin had to "look for" the personality of the unknown criminal, to "create" it and then "resolve" the mystery, here, since the identity of the criminal is well known (Minister D——— is actually an acquaintance of Dupin), the creative moment is substituted by the moment of identification, which leads almost automatically to the solution. Thus the process here lies in controlled psychological *identification* made possible by the acquaintance and odd affinities between Dupin and the Minister, not in medium-like *evocation* through psychophysical vacancy—which was, however, the only way to get the "criminal" in "The Murders in the Rue Morgue," as nothing was known about him. Here as in "The Murders in the Rue Morgue," the detective is theoretically bound to be a repressive force, yet ironically he cannot serve that function. As he earlier imposed restraint on nature (the ape) but could not jail the offender, he now imposes collective morality (as represented by the Prefect of Police) on the individual immorality (of the Minister D———), yet he must let the Minister off. Poe is obviously aware of the irony and highlights it, showing his culprit, in "The Murders in the Rue Morgue," as an innocent animal misbehaving because frightened by the sailor's whip and, in "The Purloined Letter," by portraying an amusing and crafty blackmailer, who, by the authority of his social role (a minister)—

and because of society's need to keep things secret (the "personage of most exalted station" 's honor)—cannot be made to stand trial.

The only one of Poe's criminals who might ordinarily be expected to end in jail, the killer of Marie Rogêt ("The Mystery of Marie Rogêt," 1842) is evoked and reconstructed by analyzing the several reports of the mystery in the newspapers, but not caught and imprisoned, at least within the limits of the story. (Note that the solution obtained by the analysis of the newspaper accounts of the murder was beginning to be developed already in "The Murders in the Rue Morgue" since, in this tale, Dupin draws from the disagreeing published reports of the witnesses the necessary conclusion that the "gruff voice" of the killer could not possibly belong to a foreigner but, rather, to an animal.) It is easy to give superficial reasons for Poe's having left the conclusion of "The Mystery of Marie Rogêt" unresolved. One may argue that Poe is interested in abstract detection and in abstract characters, and that a killer in jail would make both sordidly realistic. (Poe's removal of the actual case, the Hudson river murder of Mary Rogers, to a more Romantic setting, Dupin's Paris, suggests this tendency in Poe's thought.) Or one might argue that a realistically enfleshed killer might overburden a literary form Poe considers essentially a game. But from what we have seen already of Poe's way of working, his treatment of detective and criminal as conflicting elements of one personality, the creative and resolvent sides of Dupin's mind, or indeed of Poe's own, we may suspect that something more basic is involved. Poe's wish, however conscious or unconscious, is to exorcise one half of the "double Dupin," the creative, not to annihilate it. The relation between the terms of the duality is in the detective stories playfully vampiresque, not mortally vampiresque as in darker, more serious tales—"Ligeia," "The Fall of the House of Usher," and "William Wilson."

In Poe's detective stories there is no fully rounded, "realistic" criminal and thus no room for the tragic implications of crime. In these stories, characters always stand for ideas; the form itself is not emotional but ratiocinative. Dupin is a double mind, "the creative and the resolvent," he exists only in his role as detective. The orangutan is only an orangutan; though Poe was a master of vivid detail, his ape here has no smell, no particularizing characteristics, only his theoretically necessary handling of the razor and fear of the whip. The Minister D——, the playful mirror image of Dupin, is as fleshless and intellectual as Dupin is; Marie Rogêt is only a name, a corpse, her killer a ghost evoked through detection. For all Poe's widely recognized imaginative power, nothing in these tales is vividly imagined or meant to be. In the Poesque conception, detection is a game of clashing but interpenetrating ideas in which the characters are reduced to their essential functions; as in a chess game, every piece is capable of only certain moves. There is, we begin to see, a good deal of truth in Krutch's observation, "Poe invented the detective story in order that he might not go mad."[13] In Poe's hands, the detective story is a formalization of the conflict between irrational and rational forces wherein the latter is always the winner, exorcising the former. Thus the detective and the rational operation to which he subjects reality symbolically order an external chaos that reflects an inner chaos, that of the divided mind.

In his essay on Poe in *Studies in Classic American Literature* D. H. Lawrence writes that Poe "is rather a scientist than an artist. . . . This is why Poe calls his things 'tales.' They are a concatenation of cause and effect. . . . He never sees anything in terms of life."[14] For reasons we have seen, Lawrence is basically right in his observation. Poe's characters, at least in the detective fiction, are mere ideational pawns. The detective himself is especially lifeless. Like numerous later detective logicians—Borges' Isidro Parodi (who is actually in jail) and Rex Stout's Nero Wolfe, among others—Dupin rarely leaves his house, leads an ascetic life, and is interested only in the puzzle.

In the character of Dupin, Poe invented not only the stereotype of the classical detective, but the first literary detective himself. In the 1840s even the police force had only recently been established: *La Sureté* in Paris had been founded by

Vidocq in 1811, and the London Metropolitan Police was organized only in 1829. Poe, besides pioneering a genre, introduced into literature a characterization of the detective profession and a professional (scientific) way of dealing with crime. His invention comes at the philosophically appropriate moment, corresponding to the nineteenth-century rise of the scientific and optimistic attitude of positivistic philosophy towards reality and human control of reality through the development of technology, the attitude seminally expressed by Auguste Comte (1798–1857). Dupin's "technology" is the passage from "the creative" to "the resolvent" moment, whose result imposes rationality on the apparent irrationality of the case.[15]

This is not quite to say, even in the detective fiction, that Poe's attitude was essentially optimistic. The idea of divided heart (or soul) that we have seen operative in his detective stories can be traced back to Poe's famous earlier tales, such works as "Ligeia" (1838), "The Fall of the House of Usher" (1839), and "William Wilson" (1839). Though these are not, of course, works of detection in the ordinary sense, they show the intensity of Poe's ambivalence concerning the "creative" and the "resolvent" forces and may help to clarify the paradox destined to inform detective fiction from Poe's time to the present. We have said that Dupin's process of detection recalls nineteenth- or perhaps eighteenth-century creativity theory, with its emphasis on imagination and reason, or fancy brought to rule by judgement. Poe was, of course, far more a late-Romantic than a man of the Enlightenment, and his attitude toward the creative process was a good deal more gloomy and uneasy than the attitude of, say, Alexander Pope. On the level of allegory, "Ligeia" is the story of an artist's revitalization of the past by murder of the present. The narrator's early description of Ligeia—whom in many respects he can barely remember—identifies her with things ancient, primitive, Romantic: he associates her with some old city near the Rhine, with the Homeric epithet "hyacinthine," with the graceful medallions of the Hebrews, the "gazelle eyes of the tribe of the valley of Nourjahad," and so forth; in other words, she represents for him the long ago, the perhaps already-long-decayed youth of the world as well as his own youth, now all but lost. After her death he is disconsolate; and though the narrator seems not to know it himself—behaving in a kind of trance throughout—when he marries his second lady, Rowena, we gradually come to realize that it is for the purpose of an act of unconscious witchcraft. Befuddled by opium, that favorite quickener of the Romantic imagination, he enacts a ritual—ostensibly to make his Rowena more healthy—in which mysterious drops fall into her wineglass; her spirit sinks, and at last she is literally replaced by the narrator's lost Ligeia. Unless we want to believe what the narrator tells us—that Ligeia is indeed reincarnated in Rowena's dead body—we come to realize from many hints planted in the tale that he poisons Rowena to prompt the resurrection of Ligeia, which, of course, does actually occur only in his imagination deranged by opium. Ligeia is not resurrected. Whichever the interpretation, what the allegorical tale suggests, of course, is that art's process is as much destructive as constructive: to bring back childhood's sense of innocence, beauty, and wonder, to give substance to the artist's dim intuition of what might be or might once have been, the artist violates and destroys what *is*.

In "The Fall of the House of Usher" Poe presents an even darker view of the artistic process. The narrator of the tale, a reasonable and orderly man who, on the level of allegory is a representative of what Pope would call "judgment" (reason), performs, with the hypersensitive Roderick Usher, representative of fancy (imagination), an act of witchcraft (though neither man is quite conscious of the fact) designed to bring back to life Roderick Usher's dead—or presumably dead, she suffers from catalepsy—sister, Madeline, whose figurative role is parallel to that of the lost Ligeia; she represents, that is, the lost beauty which it is the business of art to recapture. The ritual process is more elaborate and subtle here than in "Ligeia." The narrator reads an old romantic tale (Poe's suggestion is that one of the ways in which art performs its magic is by imitation of earlier art), and as the tale reaches its dramatic climax, a climax reinforced by the increasing ferocity of the storm outside, terrible noises are heard in the house (earlier identified as oddly like a skull with a crack in it) and the apparently dead sister bursts into the room, not fully and beautifully rejuvenated, but horribly battered and bruised. As in the case of "Ligeia," clues planted throughout the narration make us entertain the possibility that the final apparition of the lady is the fruit of Roderick's diseased and haunted imagination (very likely he buried her alive) and of the narrator's collapsing "judgment," impaired by self-suggestion. The poisonous exhalations of the "minute fungi" covering the exterior of the house, the reading of "Mad Trist" (note the ominous title), the storm, and the noise certainly contribute to the final hallucination and may explain how both Roderick and the narrator experience it at the same time. Note that the narrator has only a visual experience of Madeline entering the room—and quite a quick one, as he escapes immediately—and that there was no way Madeline could leave the locked dungeon in which she had been entombed, even in the case that she had been buried alive—unless we want to leave the ground of rationality and consider the tale as supernatural. Whichever our personal stand concerning the interpretation, Poe's conception of art seems to be here even darker than in "Ligeia"—not only does the artist "murder" to create, he creates only a monstruous approximation of what is hoped for.

In "William Wilson," finally, the double nature of the artist becomes the central dramatic device in Poe's fiction. The narrator of the story, who asks us—rather mysteriously—to call him, for the moment, William Wilson, tells of a student who looks like him, who blames him repeatedly for his evil acts, and who also carries the name William Wilson. The "good" William Wilson becomes, in effect, the indignant pursuer of the "bad" one, who reacts by killing his benign double. With his last breath the "good" Wilson tells the "bad" one—who perhaps is simply seeing his own image in a mirror—that, in killing him, he kills himself. Also in this case, Poe's allusive language leaves enough clues to cause reasonable doubt as to whether the double ever existed. Significantly, no other student except the narrator ever noticed the striking resemblance the "bad" Wilson claims; no one actually ever noticed the "good" Wilson at all; besides, at the beginning, we are warned by the evil narrator that he is the descendant of a race remarkable for "imaginative and easily excitable temperament." Mirror images abound throughout the tale; the "bad" Wilson drinks heavily, and, by the end, the alert reader necessarily wonders whether the always whispering and admonishing good doppelgänger is the product of the diseased imagination of a drunkard haunted by remorse for his profligate and amoral life.

In all three of these stories Poe is in one way or another dramatizing what he sees as the paradox of creativity, the psychological fact that creation implies destruction, ultimately destruction of the artist himself. To bring back Ligeia, the narrator must get outside himself by means of opium and, in this "vacant," "abstract," morally "frigid" state violate the very life principle he means to serve, that is, must commit murder. The mad narrator parallels the "creative" Dupin; his "crime" is detected by the reader, who plays the part of Dupin's resolvent side. In "The Fall of the House of Usher," the narrator and Roderick Usher function together to enact the "crime." As he reads the old romance, the narrator means to be calming and helping his hypersensitive friend, and ironically, when at the end of the story the narrator escapes, he does not realize the extent to which he has played accessory to the "crime" and helped bring about the family catastrophe—the destruction of the skull-like house and death of the Ushers. In these early tales, the interdependence of the creative and resolvent faculties is complete: the resolvent faculty does not yet work as a repressive force but is integral to the crime. The inherently restrictive quality of order helps to cause the anarchic creative outburst. And in "William Wilson" the two impulses, irrational and rational, creative and repressive, are so completely one that the death of the latter automatically condemns the former, at least in the moral sense: for all practical purposes, the tale is narrated by a dead man, or at very least by a man whose hold on identity is momentary and feeble. Poe's ambivalence about art, shown first in these three tales and then in his ambivalence about the detective and the criminal, eerily foreshadows postmodern developments of the detective-story genre—especially what I will define as the metafictional anti-detective novel—and directly prefigures certain twists of the British detective novel, notably Agatha Christie's *The Murder of Roger Ackroyd*, a novel in which we at last discover that the narrator is the murderer. His most immediate effect on the genre, however, was less complex. He established two basic principles: first, that the detective genre should be stylized, "lifeless," ritualized, essentially a rational exorcism of irrationality, a conflict between logic and multiform, mysterious reality; and second, that the two fundamental terms of the conflict, the criminal and the detective, "the creative and the resolvent sides of the double Dupin," should function as doubles, each a negation of the other.

It was not entirely by chance that Poe situated his Dupin tales in Paris. France generally—and Paris as its capital in the 1840s—epitomized reason and a certain elegant nonchalance, which is part of Dupin's appeal in solving the cases; but Paris also represented for nineteenth-century Americans the opposing impulse we have noted in Poe's fiction: irrationality, mystery, dark creativity. It is the city of Balzac and Eugène Sue, and of the eerie proto-Romantic composer Daniel François Auber, whom Poe mentions in "Ulalume."[16] In France some characteristics typical of the detective story were at this time independently germinating in the popular feuilleton, a form of novel published in episodes in daily newspapers, each episode ending with a sudden twist of suspense designed to induce readers to keep buying the paper. Unlike Poe's detective fiction, the feuilleton characteristically presented a blunt opposition of good and evil in a simplified, popular vision of reality. Melodramatic conflict was the earmark of the feuilleton.[17]

While Poe's detective story was a highly structured, intellectual genre, the feuilleton had labyrinthine plots and appealed to a broad audience, especially the lower levels of the middle class and literate workers. It featured surprise revelations, panting suspense, murders, and violence, particularly violence done to virgins; in short, it was designed more to attract and titillate readers than to achieve such aesthetic ideals as elegant structure and plausibility of denouement. Indulgence in the sensational and in gruesome detail, and an ambivalent treatment of the horrid and the merely sensual put the feuilleton in the tradition of Gothic tales and *Newgate Calendar* reports, that is, located the feuilleton on the "irrational," or at least intellectually easy side of the Romantic double impulse. The readers of the feuilleton wanted "realistic romances," stories that had the easy comprehensibility of realism and the glamour and adventure of romance. Again, as in the *Newgate Calendar,* we have the formula of sensation in everyday life, along with a bit of stereotypic and harmless socialism (the rich and wicked ones come off badly). When the detective story structure as established by Poe comes together with the feuilleton genre, the hybrid result will be an enriched form, the detective novel (intellectual, objective) expressed in the emotional and vividly elaborated terms of the feuilleton.

So it comes about that a French feuilleton-roman writer, Emile Gaboriau (1832–73), transforms Poe's formula into what is generally considered the first detective novel, *L'Affaire Lerouge* (1863). Gaboriau's novel is economically plotted around a murder and its detection—the standard form for detective novels to follow in the future—though a few pages before the solution a gratuitous flashback produces almost a novel within the novel, paying cumbersome tribute to its origin in the feuilleton style.

For the novels of authors such as Balzac, Dickens, and Dostoevski, the feuilleton is the evolutionary source in its handling of plot and atmosphere. As the Italian Marxist thinker Antonio Gramsci (1891–1937) points out, the feuilleton "shows how certain cultural currents (motives and moral interests, sensibility, ideologies, etc.) can have a double expression: the merely mechanical one of sensational intrigue (Sue, etc.) and the 'lyrical' one (Balzac, Dostoevski and partly V. Hugo)."[18] As we shall see, the whole detective novel genre is split between a popular and mass-produced current (the mechanical one, in Gramsci's terms) and an intellectual current (the "lyrical"). These two movements correspond to those we have traced as irrational and rational.

Five years after publication of *L'Affaire Lerouge*, Wilkie Collins (1824–89) published *The Moonstone* (1868, first in serial form in Dickens' magazine *All the Year Round*, then, during the same year, in three volumes, as it was normal custom when the serialized version proved the novel to be a successful enterprise). *The Moonstone* is the first British detective novel and, like *L'Affaire Lerouge*, merges mystery (the loss of "the Moonstone," a splendid and cursed Indian diamond) and the account of a rational detection into the vivid atmosphere of the society it portrays (aristocratic Victorian England).

In December 1887 Arthur Conan Doyle (1859–1930) published, in *Beeton's Christmas Annual*, "A Study in Scarlet," the first Sherlock Holmes story. Sherlock Holmes is the natural development of Poe's Dupin. Dupin's rationality, with all its mystical overtones—vacancy, abstraction, frigidity—becomes in Sherlock Holmes the partly deductive, partly ecstatic method, which is, in its rational element, an application of the technique used by the British medical doctor Joseph Bell (one of Doyle's professors in medical school) to formulate diagnoses. Holmes' method relies heavily on a knowledge of chemistry, anatomy, and botany—sciences that help him achieve scientific detection—but Holmes' personality is not exclusively rational; it is in fact an exaggeration of Dupin's personality, combining ratiocination and a touch of divine madness. Holmes is a misanthrope who lives exclusively for, or in view of, his extraordinary cerebral performances; he kills the time between bursts of logical energy by playing the violin, composing, or drugging himself with cocaine.[19]

Part of Doyle's success arises from the fact that, like Poe, he manages to create in Holmes a conflict between the rational (the positivistic) and the irrational, in Doyle's case influenced by literary decadence as expressed by Rossetti, Wilde, and their respective circles. Holmes is the triumph of Victorian positivism

in his cerebral performances, but is at the same time decadent
in his habits, even, finally, his intellectual habits, since he con-
trasts markedly with the gentle and essentially intelligent humanist Watson. His vices along with his rational but almost
superhuman abilities help to create around him an appealing
halo of mystery and glamor. Dr. Watson is a late-Victorian
version of the narrator and friend in Poe's Dupin stories, the
stereotypes for all the detective's intellectually ordinary friends
to come, the sidekick who reflects and verbalizes the puzzle-
ment the reader feels as the story unfolds.

The conventions, indeed the whole machinery of the detective novel, are definitely set by Doyle. In early works Doyle
indulges in feuilleton intermissions à la Gaboriau by interposing
before the end of the fiction a gratuitous flashback diversion
which comes close to creating a novel within the novel (*A Study
in Scarlet*, 1887; *The Sign of Four*, 1889). Yet in *The Hound of
the Baskervilles* (1901) and all following works (except for *The
Valley of Fear*, 1915, resorting again to the intermission), he
sheds the superflous and freezes the British detective novel into
a model that will be imitated by a horde of later writers. This
model will achieve its chief success in the fiction of Agatha
Christie (1890–1976) and will begin to disintegrate in the fiction
of Dorothy Sayers (1894–1957), when the detective novel becomes a novel of manners (the Lord Peter Wimsey stories), a
sentimental portrait of a declining British aristocracy, fiction
wherein murder and detection are little more than plot excuses
for sociological nostalgia.

Meanwhile in the United States the detective story genre
does not find any significant writer able to work by the standard
set by Poe or to inject new life into the form. Although in
Cooper's *The Ways of the Hour* (1850), in Hawthorne's *The
House of the Seven Gables* (1851), and in Melville's *Benito Cereno* (1855) traces of a detective plot can be recognized,[20] Poe's
model of the ratiocinative, tightly structured detective story
wins no followers. Poe's form is replaced in the 1880s by a mass
publication phenomenon, spurred by the process of industrial-
ization that is changing the country after the Civil War: the

"dime novel," cheap hybrid of the adventure novel in the feuilleton fashion and the detective story, holds the field. For roughly three decades teams of professional hack writers successfully grind out thousands of flat stories according to a never-changing scheme whereby the entirely good guy fights and secures to justice the entirely bad guy after various adventures and a good deal of chasing in which the brain gets very little play. The most popular hero of the dime novels, Nick Carter, is a kind of scout-crime fighter who is a late "industrialized" version of Cooper's Natty Bumppo and of characters celebrated in the French feuilleton. He makes very little use of the detective process; he is too busy—a man of action.

The years between World War I and World War II have been called the Golden Age of the detective novel. The period was one we may characterize as both an elaboration of the Poesque ratiocinative tradition (in England) and an introduction of anti-Poesque innovation (in the United States).

In England the highly rational and stylized detective novel in the Poesque tradition had by now become a classical genre, thanks to the steady, high-quality work of puzzle-makers like Agatha Christie, E. C. Bentley, Margery Allingham, and Cecil Day Lewis. As Marjorie Nicolson writes in her charming essay "The Professor and the Detective" (1929), the British-style detective story is a leisurely reading particularly in vogue among academics for its escape "not from life, but from literature."[21] The novel-of-manners quality typical of British detective novels of the Golden Age represents a "return to the novel of plot and incident,"[22] to a nostalgic and entertaining kind of "nineteenth century" reading in an age when all certainties are, in the work of "serious" modern writers, called into question. As Michael Holquist puts it,

> What is difficult about a Mann novel . . . is . . . its unsettling message: all the certainties of the 19th century—positivism, scientism, historicism—seem to have broken down. Dangerous questions are raised, the world is a threatening, unfamiliar place, inimical more often than not to reason. Is it not natural to assume, then, that during this period when rationalism is experiencing some of its most damaging attacks, that intellectuals, who experienced these attacks

first and most deeply, would turn for relief and easy reassurance to the detective story, the primary genre of popular literature which they, during the same period, were, in fact, consuming?[23]

A characteristic of the twentieth-century British detective novel is the "utter unreality"[24] of its murders—chess moves on the chess board of a story that, according to the rules of "fair play" (the writer cannot hide from the reader anything that the detective knows), is a thoroughly amiable "battle of wits" between the author and the reader.[25] Julian Symons pointed out in 1962, when detective fiction had come to be taken seriously as a cultural phenomenon, that the codification of rules for the writing of detective stories (Ronald Knox in England, S. S. Van Dine in the United States) and the foundation of a "Detection Club" among British writers of detective stories (in 1928) to enforce these rules are "the proof that in the twenties the detective story was a rational game, something almost scientific."[26] We may go further: the rules are the swan song of old-style middle-class fiction, an attempt to freeze the last literary remains of the nineteenth-century novel wherein order is, in the end, always restored.

In the twenties and thirties art historian and critic William Huntington Wright, who took the nom de plume S. S. Van Dine (1888–1939), imitated in the United States the classical British detective story, translating its conventions to suit American experience. His detective Philo Vance is a dandyish and conceited version of Agatha Christie's Hercule Poirot. In the thirties, Van Dine's experiment was extended by the "Ellery Queen firm" (the result of the cooperation between two cousins, Manfred B. Lee and Frederic Dannay), which for forty years produced British-style detective stories set in the United States and adjusted to meet the taste of the American audience. Writers like "Ellery Queen" seem to have tried in their oceanic production all of the possible combinations offered by the logic-puzzle and finally to have exhausted it in endlessly varied repetition of the same themes.

The classic British detective story pushes to extremes the rational trend of the Poesque duality and evokes in the reader two basic feelings, both largely unconscious. One is a sense of escape from reality, since the story is stereotypic (the characters are chess-pawns, the murder a bloodless excuse for a cerebral game, and the environment is safely remote, some beautiful country house in Britain). The other feeling evoked in the reader is a sense of reassurance, since the detective's rationality restores the order violated by the murder (the culprit is discovered and punished and the status quo reestablished; the mystery can be understood and solved, if not prevented). The British detective story, which Marjorie Nicolson among others has described as "the fairy tale of the Golden Age," is a conservative genre primarily enjoyed by upper-middle-class readers (professionals, academics). The outside threat is resolved in an exorcising and entertaining ritual, consumed in two hours of escape from everyday cares in the "den" of a comfortable house.

Walter Benjamin in "Paris, die Hauptstadt des XIX. Jahrhunderts" ("Paris, Capital of the XIXth Century"), typifies the house and its objects as containers of bourgeois life and dreams, and traces the importance of physical possessions in the development of the classical detective novel:

With the Revolution of July the bourgeoisie fulfilled the goals of 1789 (Marx).
For the private citizen the space in which he lives enters for the first time into contrast with the one of daily work. The first becomes the *intérieur*. The office is its complement. The private citizen, who keeps account of reality in the office, demands that his *intérieur* entertain him in his illusions . . . The *intérieur* is the refuge of art . . . The *intérieur* is also the "container" of the private citizen. To inhabit means to lave traces which acquire, in the *intérieur*, a particular importance. A profusion of covers and cases, sheaths and boxes is invented where objects of everyday use impress their traces. Even the traces of the inhabitant impress themselves upon the *intérieur* and from them is born the detective story, which goes after these traces. "The Philosophy of Furniture," along with his detective stories, proves Poe the first physiognomist of the *intérieur*.[27]

Exactly against this bourgeois pattern of reassurance and escape from reality, typical of the British form and of its American imitators, a new school of detective story writers arose in

the United States, the so-called "hard-boiled school." It re-
volved around *Black Mask* and other "pulp" magazines in the
late twenties and thirties and found its chief spokesmen in
Dashiell Hammett (1894–1961) and Raymond Chandler (1888–
1959). In his famous essay "The Simple Art of Murder," Chandler explains concisely (in a typically hard-boiled way) the innovations in the genre traceable to Hammett:

> Hammett took murder out of the Venetian vase and dropped it into
> the alley . . . Hammett gave murder back to the kind of people that
> commit it for reasons, not just to provide a corpse; and with the
> means at hand, not hand-wrought dueling pistols, curare and tropi-
> cal fish. He put these people down on paper as they were, and he
> made them talk and think in the language they customarily used for
> these purposes.[28]

This rage for realism coincided with the rise of Naturalism in
American literature, a movement which represented the
struggles of the lower classes in even their most unpleasant
aspects and denounced social injustice. W. M. Frohock remarks
concerning James M. Cain's *The Postman Always Rings Twice*
(1934): "The historical importance of books like *The Postman* is
that they were the ultimate exploitation of the climate of sensibility which also produced the best novels of . . . Hemingway . . . Steinbeck, Farrell, and Dos Passos,"[29] that is, the novels of American Naturalism. Critics still question how much of
his style Hammett borrowed from Hemingway, and how much
of the borrowing may have been the other way around.

Chandler's creed was of course the exact opposite of that
expressed by Marjorie Nicolson. The Naturalistic detective
novel, which delighted in the unpleasantly realistic, was thus a
major break with the Poesque tradition. It changed drastically
the familiar form and purpose, instituting a new manifestation
of the genre.

American city wastelands replace the idyllic countryside setting of the British detective novel, and the hard-boiled dick, a
lonely hero who clings to a personal moral code, no matter how
absurd his devotion to it may seem, takes the place of Dupin
and Sherlock Holmes. Though the hero of hard-boiled detec-

tive fiction is normally unmarried as are Dupin and Holmes, he is far more a flesh-and-blood character. He likes liquor and women, but his periods of incontinence seem to be the necessary preamble to the "ascesis" of detection, since any ascesis (solution) implies a previous fall.

Chandler writes that the hard-boiled detective story "is this man's [the detective's] adventure in search of a hidden truth."[30] In fact the detecting process is no longer only the solution of a riddle, but a quest for truth in a reality far more complex and ambiguous than in the stereotyped "fairy tales" of the British tradition. Steven Marcus in his introduction to a collection of Dashiell Hammett's stories writes:

> What he [the detective] soon discovers is that the "reality" that anyone involved will swear to is in fact itself a construction, a fabrication, a fiction, a faked and alternate reality—and that it has been gotten together before he ever arrived on the scene. And the Op's work therefore is to deconstruct, decompose, deplot and defictionalize that "reality" and to construct or reconstruct out of it a true fiction, i.e., an account of what "really" happened.[31]

The detective is no longer a logical mind in a positivistic world as he was in Poe's tales. His attempts to unravel the mystery often clash against his own impulses and against a "reality" which is no longer explained and constricted within the optimism and rationality of nineteenth-century positivism but rather has been reinterpreted in a questioning fashion by the then recent theories about relativism and the unconscious. This new notion of reality of course defies the neat solutions and the simple truths of the too logical and too artificial British detective novel.

Dashiell Hammett is very aware of this fundamental change and, in the thirties, already senses the postmodern mutation that will start after World War II. For example, *Red Harvest's* (1929) Continental Operative almost anticipates the "doomed detectives" of innovative anti-detective fiction. The Op is called to purify Personville, a town dominated by crime and corruption, but ends up by being driven by its bloodlustful atmosphere into illegal forms of detective work. The Op's aplomb and ability to settle the matter are deeply shaken, but eventually he gets hold of himself and leaves Personville in a better shape than he had found it, although the town is potentially "ready to go to the dogs again."[32]

An important connection between *Red Harvest* and the novels of what I will call innovative anti-detective fiction is that in both, the solution, although still present, is ambiguous and partially unfulfilling. Yet the intentions in Hammett's work are radically different from those of anti-detective novels. In fact, although Hammett believes in a more realistic detective novel and becomes the leading figure in a new manifestation of the genre (the hard boiled), he still operates within it. The detached awareness of the postmodern writer who plays with the rules and the techniques of detective fiction from *without*, to obtain programmatically something else, is not yet found in Hammett. Simply, he is a professional detective novel writer who deeply innovates the rules and setting of the game by making them more credible and by tuning them up with that sense of uneasiness and relativism that all gifted modernist writers experienced in the same period. If in doing so he intimates and even anticipates features of that "something else" that will turn out to be the anti-detective novel, still he operates in the field from *within*. He has not the impious awareness of Pynchon or Calvino, who resort to detective novel techniques to write something that is no longer a detective novel but rather a deliberate negation of the fundamental purposes of the genre.

The predilection of the hard-boiled detective novel for "realistic" setting and details generally demythicizes the detective character. By now the detective is no longer a genius as Dupin and Sherlock Holmes were, but a normal man with a hangover the next morning, a jaw that really hurts. He is above all a man who accepts and endures absurdity, the sudden twists to which an unpredictable reality subjects him in his unrewarding job, which he sticks to anyway, Sisyphus-like.

As Edward Margolies puts it, the hard-boiled detective's relentless and risky search for truth goes beyond mere job routine and implies a "moral, if not metaphysical quest." Margolies continues, "Thus it may be that the ancestors of M. Dupin derive from the rationalists of the Enlightenment while the ancestors of the hardboiled private eyes derive from those legendary medieval knights who most Americans first got to know via the novels of Scott and nineteenth century gothic romances."[33] In fact the hard-boiled school, emphasizing realism and committed to a social and moral message (the corruption of society and the importance of the individual stand against it, no matter how ineffectual) creates a late disguised form of romance in which the hero must be idealistic and "tough" as well, because that is what is required of him by the corrupt society in which he operates. The idealistic motive (the professional high-mindedness of the hardened but good "knight" who fights within a corrupt society) is more nearly connected to the "irrational" current of the genre, including the degenerate "dime novel" and the tangential feuilleton, than to the line that runs from Poe to the British cerebral game. Hard-boiled detective fiction recalls not the ascetic's cool deductions but the oppressive and obsessive emotions of the Gothic tale, the *Newgate Calendar,* and the medieval romance, all forms of intensified reality, overheated imagination, where the irrational (the dense, nightmarish, fantastic) plays an important role.

In the United States the post-World War II period had much the same effect on detective fiction as the post–Civil War had had eighty years before: mass production and a decline in quality, a general sense of moral disorientation, and a spiritual void that not even the tough and knightly detective of the hard-boiled school was able to overcome. It is thus not surprising that after World War II the tough guys typical of the fiction between the two wars become supertough, inclined to gratuitous violence, and that the duality in the detective hinted at in Poe becomes dramatically visible. By now the sleuth is no better than the murderer he is chasing. He is simply covering the opposite job. The switch from one role to the other comes easily if adequately rewarded, and the methods of detective and criminal are exactly the same. The strain of the Cold War and the hysteria of McCarthyism make detective fiction a sneaky and popular form of propaganda—Mike Hammer, the "hero" of Mickey Spillane, hates "the Reds and the niggers" and his moral commitment is "to mop them out of America." Part of this involution is motivated also by the competition of other media grown quickly after World War II: television, radio, comic strips, cinema are detective fiction's powerful opponents in the grab for the American market. These media exploit and merge adventure and detective plots in the way the Nick Carter dime novels did in the Gilded Age, updating everything with the new sex-and-violence formula. Detective fiction conforms to survive and thus turns into kitsch or, at its best, self-parody. The almost surreal, self-mocking hero of the glamorous sixties comes to life: Ian Fleming's James Bond, in whose stories blatantly fantastic action, outrageous luck both with women and with killers, and thoroughly improbable feats of nerve, supported by spectacular gadgets, overwhelm any serious need for detection. The detective novel becomes a secret agent story (spies, glitter, fast action, self-consciously cheap suspense) or "thriller," also known as a "crime story," in which the murderer often is known from the beginning and suspense degenerates into the author's bushwhacking the reader—unexpectedly killing off some beautiful female character or the hero's best friend—shocking him with an overload of violence and almost invariably stirring his childish love of novelty with some ingenious variation of the classical chase. At the same time the vaguely sentimental and existential tough dicks of the hard-boiled school enter the repertoire of the nostalgia industry—passé kind-hearted guys of the good old days. Superman, the farm-bred American hero from another planet, a being gifted with supernatural powers, is the strip-counterpart of 007; he mediates the fantastic and the realistic in adventure stories in which his flying intervention rids society of some banal Evil and restores order. His ancestors are easily traced: Nick Carter and the heroes of the feuilleton.

Other manifestations of the new emotional frenzy, exploited by both fiction and movie industries, are the Mafia story (e.g., *The Godfather*) and the gangster story (e.g., *Bonnie and*

Clyde), which have their common cinematographic ancestor in films such as *Scarface* (1943), in which the story is seen from the point of view of the villain. It is easy to see a connection between these mass phenomena and that current, opposite to the Poesque tradition, that includes the dime novel, the feuilleton, the *Newgate Calendar,* and the Gothic tale. The appeal to the emotions rather than to the intellect of the reader, the emphasis on the business side of the enterprise and on the sensational in a realistic context, the fond indulgence of violence and sex, the stereotyped opposition of good and evil characters are, *cum grano salis,* typical of the whole current. In recent years of course there also have been authors who hold themselves to the classical conventions of the hard-boiled school (Ross Macdonald, Robert B. Parker) or cling to the conventions of the British style (P. M. Hubbard) peppered with self-parody. Other authors have found a personal compromise between detective fiction and fiction in general, focussing on the everyday milieu and the relationship between ordinary life and routine policework, an approach that generates at last a sort of epiphanic detection, as in the novels of Georges Simenon.

As I mentioned in the introduction, the detective novel in Italy has long been an imported genre, and even as such, during the second half of the nineteenth century it was practically nonexistent. There is some intimation of detection in *La cieca di Sorrento* [The blindwoman from Sorrento], a feuilleton by Francesco Mastriani (1852), and there actually is an "inverted detection" in *Il cappello del prete* (1888) [The priest's hat] by Emilio De Marchi (the reader knows who killed the priest; the "detective" is a judge made suspicious by the behavior of the murderer), but this particular form of detection does not become so crucial and important in the story as to fill its plot and allow us to characterize it as a detective novel. Rather, the emphasis is on the remorse of the culprit, who is eventually "betrayed and punished by his own conscience." The detective form officially entered Italian culture in 1929 when the Mondadori publishing house began printing translations of British and

American—but mostly British—detective fiction in a special collection called "*I libri gialli*" [The yellow books] in which the adjective "*giallo*" refers to the unusual color of the covers contrived to catch the attention of the reader. "*Giallo*" soon became a familiar noun to define the genre, replacing in everyday usage the English "detective novel" and the French "*roman policier*." Beginning in the thirties, Italian writers "tried out" the detective novel in a noncommittal and often parodic way, since the genre was a foreign one and the importing publisher left very little space for homemade imitations. Besides, a snobbish and elitist concept of literature descended from the Italian classical tradition and exacerbated by the genre's connotation of escapist fiction, did not help to elevate the opinion of "serious" writers with regard to the *gialli*. The serious literary artist might write one, but only to amuse his audience, and very likely with a falsely modest preface explaining the writer's lapse of taste and slyly encouraging the reader to notice the writer's versatility. Fascist censorship, which went so far in its attempt to portray a "happy nation" as to eliminate the crime page from the newspapers, of course did not care for detective novels, a "fictional relative" of the abolished crime news.

Notwithstanding these biases, a few professional writers did involve themselves with the genre following the bloodless formula of the British detective novel and adding to it a touch of Italian irony. Alessandro Varaldo (1878–1953) made an effort to adapt detective novels to the Italian setting and "offered a model for the *giallo* which is bloodless and adventurous, alien from the macabre and all the extremes."[34] In fact the Latin indifference to Gothic tradition and a certain natural sense of measure (suspended, of course, for opera) favored an ironic and parodic approach over indulgence in the murder or any gruesome aspects of the narrative.

In *Quaranta milioni* [Forty million, 1931] Arturo Lanocita (1904–83) twisted the stereotypes of the detective story and poked fun at the "British rules," emphasizing the comic side in the mechanism of the *giallo,* creating, instead of detectional suspense, a sort of comedy of errors. Luciano Folgore (1888–

1966) made of *giallo* conventions an almost surreal, fantastic game, *La trappola colorata* [The colored trap, 1934]. Other writers, such as Pietro Zampa and Armando Comez, instead of treating the form playfully, used the *giallo* as a means of organizing realistic portraits of Italian provincial life and society. In the thirties, Ezio D'Errico (1892–1972) created Richard, an intellectual and withdrawn Paris policeman reminiscent of Simenon's Maigret. In a series of novels Augusto De Angelis (1888–1944) tried for the first time to portray, without parodic self-mockery, an Italian detective, for which purpose De Angelis recast and developed Richard's character into De Vincenzi, a pensive commissioner gifted with a poetic sensitivity who reads Freud and Oscar Wilde. From his Milan police office he gets the criminal by trying to understand his soul through a process which includes—as Dupin's included, much less noticeably—something extrasensory and nightmarish.

In 1941 the sale of detective novels was restricted and in 1943 officially prohibited by the Fascist regime on the moralistic grounds that such fictions were apologias of crime,[35] and for a long time after World War II any possible Italian detective novel production was discouraged by the flood of American thrillers that had piled up and were finally ready to be translated after the years of Fascist censorship.

A few authors, such as Franco Enna (b. 1921) and Sergio Donati (b. 1933), tried a compromise between the fashionable hard-boiled novel and the post-war Italian *neorealismo,*[36] but the available audience was much too engrossed with the American model to care about Italian attempts. In the sixties the time was at last ripe for an Italian version of the Chandler and Hammett approach, and the Giorgio Scerbanenco (1911–65) transposed the American hard-boiled genre to a Milan by now grown, thanks to the economic boom, into a European New York. The Italian reality had unfortunately caught up with its model: organized crime, United States style, was fiction no more.

After Scerbanenco, the Italian "hard-boiled" genre evolves into a sort of social detective novel trying to stay in touch with reality and the problems of industrialized Italian society (i.e., crime, kidnapping, strikes, political and administrative corruption, internal immigration, and drugs), easily finding its inspiration in the newspapers.

Among the other Italian media, film began exploring the possibilities of detective fiction when directors Mario Bava and Riccardo Freda in the sixties and Dario Argento in the seventies started a kind of Italian cinematographic thriller that has its formula in an heavy use of camera-eye technique (the murderer's eye), and—especially in the case of Argento—in a detached and detailed filming of violence in an urban tentacular landscape that enhances the nightmarish atmosphere of the movie. But while these directors still deal, although in an original way, with the thriller formula, Michelangelo Antonioni (b.1912) has been showing since the early fifties a keen interest in the most puzzling aspects of the detective novel and can justly be recognized as the cinematographic founder of anti-detective fiction: think of the ironic sense of fatality already present in *Cronaca di un amore*, 1953, and of *L'avventura*, 1961, in which the girl who disappeared is a haunting presence throughout the movie. An interest in detection as existential discovery and the use of long silent shots emphasizing objects—perhaps reminiscent of the *nouveau roman*—has constantly been present in his recent films (*Blow up*, 1966; *Professione: reporter*, 1975) and especially in *Identificazione di una donna* (1982), in which we can only try to guess the mystery behind Maria Vittoria's sudden attempt to escape her lover, since the tantalizing episodes characterizing their affair lead to no final explanation.

Some serious Italian writers (Landolfi, Buzzati, Piovene, Sciascia, Eco) have sought to exploit the British-style detective-novel techniques for higher artistic purposes, and in the wake of these writers a significant recent trend in the Italian publishing world has been the presentation of new collections of detective novels in which the suspense plot simply forms the scaffolding for fiction definitely characterized by a literary commitment.[37] Techniques borrowed from the detective novel are seen as antidotes to the boredom the reader may experience when reading novels with a more traditional structure. The "literary detective novel" is written not by professional detective-novel authors trying to write "better" detective novels (a kind of writer almost nonexistent in Italy anyway), but by established serious writers, some of whom—as in the case of Leonardo Sciascia and Oreste Del Buono—have written essays on the detective novel genre and know very well what they are doing when they borrow plot and technical devices from it.

In Italy an extraordinarily well-written detective novel by one of the few professional writers of the genre will always remain "only a detective novel," while even a mediocre novel with a detective structure, if written by a traditional "serious" writer (i.e., Michele Prisco), has every chance of coming to be considered by critics a valuable innovative novel.

The Italian *giallo* of the thirties, since in large part derivative from the British detective novel, never split into the two definite currents we have noticed—the Poesque and the non-Poesque, the "rational" and the "irrational"—but rather assumed only those individual, stylistic qualities expressive of the personalities of particular authors—a taste for the parodic and comic side of the foreign genre, as we have seen, or an adaptation allowing the form to focus less on crime detection than on a portrayal of Italian life and society. But when we come to present-day detective fiction, the situation changes. If there ever have been two separate trends in Italian detective fiction, it is now when, as in the United States, we find a mass market and a multimedia low-quality detective production on one hand and, on the other, a literary detective novel mostly reminiscent of the British mystery, which had been in Italy *the* detective novel until World War II. The new popularity of this fiction is everywhere evident. Reprints of the "classics" (Christie, Doyle, Van Dine, even Chandler and Hammett) are now in fashion as never before. This testifies in Italy, as elsewhere, to a nostalgia for the genre as it was in the secure good old days and also, of course, to an evident pause in the evolution of mainstream detective fiction, a pause that has lately pushed to extremes the form's two currents, turning fiction either very commercial or very literary.

The literary detective novel, in both Italy as in the United States, is nowadays written, generally speaking, by people who are not primarily detective writers, but who assume the structure and techniques of the genre for a different end. The foregoing historical outline has, I hope, established the standard styles against which we may measure literary innovations or exploitations after World War II, artistic experiments contemporary with mass media commercial exploitation. We are still dealing with that phenomenon described by Gramsci as a double expression of the same cultural trend: the "merely mechanical" expression (the recent mass media exploitation) and the "lyrical." In our time the second expression emerges in the highbrow literary detective fiction of Borges, of Nabokov, of the *nouveau roman* and of all the even more recent writers (Pynchon, Gardner, Hjortsberg) who achieve innovation in the genre or else exploit it—we shall need to determine which—imposing upon it new forms and intentions. It will be useful to pause briefly over a few examples of the new highbrow movement, for the sake of getting a very general sense of what has happened to the familiar old genre.

In "La muerte y la brújula" ("Death and the Compass"), published in 1942, Jorge Luis Borges (b. 1899) narrates the story of a criminal who sets up three murders to lure a detective into a mortal trap. In fact the detective reconstructs the clues left by the assassin and shows up in the place where he knows the fourth murder should occur, only to be the victim. The battle between the detective Lönnrot and the murderer Red Scharlach, named also "Scharlach the Dandy," is a "battle of wits" according to the classic detective story tradition, but it ends in a highly untraditional way. Their names, which have almost the same meaning (*Scharlach* in German=scarlet; *rot* in German=red, *lönn* is perhaps a distortion of *lohn*—reward—so that Lönnrot is "red reward," the bloody and fatal "reward" he gets from Scharlach for his flawless detection), seem to parody the self-destructive detective-murderer duality that is the pivot of the story. At the same time, the nickname "Scharlach the Dandy" emphasizes the aesthetic game that, according to Philo Vance and, before him, Thomas De Quincey ("Murder Considered as One of the Fine Arts," 1827), must be present in a perfect murder if it is to be considered a "work of art." Even in the title, "La muerte y la brújula," the stress is on the duality of annihilation and logic or annihilation as logic, that is, death as detection—murderer equals detective. The story is a perfect example of sophisticated reexamination of traditional detective narrative; all of Borges' typical games (playful logic, mirrors, labyrinths) converge to reverse the detection.

Another such reexamination is *Les Gommes* (*The Erasers*), published in 1953 by Alain Robbe-Grillet (b. 1922), the main theoretician of the French *nouveau roman*.[38] Robbe-Grillet narrates the story of a detective who knows that a murder will be committed in a certain place at a certain time and gets there to prevent it, but then is himself the one who shoots the victim.[39] Here as in "La muerte y la brújula," the detective plot turns against its "orderer," the detective, who becomes the victim of his detection ("La muerte y la brújula") or the murderer himself (*Les Gommes*), fulfilling the Poesque duality of detective-murderer. Poe's ambivalence about the creative and the resolvent, most darkly expressed not in the Dupin stories but in his earlier tales, has at last reached its logical fruition in a version of the genre it originally set off.

In *The Real Life of Sebastian Knight* (1941) by Vladimir Nabokov (1899–1977), the half brother of a dead novelist (Sebastian Knight) "writes" the book to refute a misleading biography of Sebastian. Also, he tries to explain to himself and to the reader who Sebastian really was and what his fiction (which often used detective fiction plots) was about. We get, of course, a portrait of Sebastian that is even more misleading than the biography it was intended to refute, while the clumsy detective-like attempts of Sebastian's half brother to discover Sebastian's "real life" provide ironic literary interaction with the dead novelist's "detective" fiction.

These works, among many others—such as *Quer pasticciaccio*

brutto de via Merulana (*That Awful Mess on Via Merulana*), published in 1946 by Carlo Emilio Gadda (1893–1973)—definitely wreck that pattern of mannerly order and reassurance characteristic of the British detective novel and already cracked by the hard-boiled American (and French) school. But it is a wreckage coming not directly from the detective tradition itself—whatever its prefiguration in Poe—but from the outside. Borges, Robbe-Grillet, and Nabokov are by no means professional detective-story writers like Hammett or Chandler; they intermittently use detective conventions with the precise intention of expressing the disorder and the existential void they find central to our time in a genre designed to epitomize the contrary. What they write is thus best described as a form of anti-detective novel.[40]

The conventions of the detective novel are more exploited than renewed by these writers, who deconstruct the genre's precise architecture into a meaningless mechanism without purpose; they parody positivistic detection. They dismantle the elegant engine Poe constructed, pulling apart the once functional machinery and removing its pieces (now the plot, now the suspense technique, now the clichéd detective) to do different things with them. Todorov writes in *Poétique de la prose,* "detective fiction has its norms; to 'develop' them is also to disappoint them; to 'improve upon' detective fiction is to write 'literature,' not detective fiction."[41] Serious novelists do not even try to "improve upon" detective fiction but rather use the form as a scrapyard from which to dig out "new" narrative techniques to be applied to the exhausted traditional novel; the detective novel clichés are like the spare pieces of an old car that cannot run any more but, if sold as parts, can still be worth something. Let us turn now to an examination of which "spare parts" serious contemporary writers are using and how.

2

Toward a Definition of the Anti-Detective Novel

We have seen that from the nineteenth century to World War II the detective novel developed in two parallel, sometimes interflowing currents: the Poesque (or British), which is rational, static, and intellectual, and the non-Poesque (hard-boiled American), which is nonintellectual, adventurous, and popular; and we have seen how the literary detective novel after World War II acquired such definite characteristics at the hands of authors of various nationalities and cultures (Borges, Robbe-Grillet, Nabokov, Gadda) as to stand out not only from the popular non-Poesque current but also from its own nearer tradition, the Poesque intellectual detective novel as it had endured until World War II. It seems useful to call this kind of post-World War II literary detective novel "the anti-detective novel" since its characteristics, although certainly more related to the Poesque tradition than to the hard-boiled one, deeply subverted the former and showed a great difference from the latter.

At this point the natural questions are, first, how does it come about that authors so distant in space and culture as Borges, Nabokov, and Gadda, among others, write in the forties the same kind of "different" (anti-) detective novel setting an example for another generation of writers? Second, what exactly does the anti-detective novel borrow from conventional detective fiction? And third, how does the former differ from the latter? Answering these questions should allow us to formulate a definition—however tentative and provisional—of the anti-detective novel and consequently to perceive important differences among anti-detective novels themselves.

As we have seen, every innovation in the detective story genre has occurred in reaction to the current that had long been the dominant one and that later seemed closed to variation. The British detective novel, which took up the Poesque inheritance, reached fulfillment between World War I and World War II, mainly at the hands of Agatha Christie. During its expansion period the English model came to be imitated in the United States, but during the same period the more important American contribution was the reaction of the hard-boiled school to the British detective novel's aristocratic leanings, if not "imperialism."

This kind of action-reaction (tradition-innovation) process is of course nothing new; it has always played a part in the evolution of literary genres. We find it explained in "Literaturnyj Fakt" ["The Literary Fact"], an essay written in 1924 by the Russian formalist critic Jurij Tynjanov (1894–1943). To the literary current dominant at any given time, developed by writers in all its possible variations, he gives the name "automatized constructive principle" and points out that "in the analysis of the literary evolution we meet the following stages: 1) an opposite constructive principle [in the case of detective fiction, urban environment in the adventurous detection] takes shape dialectically versus the automatized constructive principle [stereotypical countryside in the static detection—the British detective novel]; 2) the opposite constructive principle looks for the easiest application [the "hard-boiled" formula of chase rather than careful deduction]; 3) it extends to the widest range of phenomena [the mass media inflation and degeneration of the hard-boiled school after World War II]; 4) it gets automatized [worn out] and triggers opposite constructive principles [the anti-detective novel]."[1]

While in the early hard-boiled formula the stress was on the socially realistic environment where the detection is performed (a tentacular Los Angeles, the daily dingy routine of the detective in Chandler's stories), after World War II, as the hard-boiled school degenerated, what mattered was no longer the environment and its social and existential implications, which were taken for granted, but rather the adventurous and sensational—and generally easy—solution. In fact in the late epigones of Chandler (Cheyney, Spillane) the stories become almost entirely chase and capture, with very little real mystery involved. Thus a stress on the solution was the automatized principle of the hard-boiled formula against which the anti-detective novel shaped itself, reacting by its opposite constructive principle, that is, the suspension of the solution. The evolution of the two currents is parallel and almost never independent; a change in one comes generally in reaction to the other as, indeed, in the nineteenth century, Poe's detective story was an intellectual reaction to Gothicism, and the first detective novel (Gaboriau's *L'Affaire Lerouge*) was a mediating reaction of the loose feuilleton mode to the challenge of Poe's more tightly structured and rational detective story.

By the time the anti-detective novel and its frustrating nonsolution (or parodic solution) comes to be exploited by the media, if it ever is (we will perhaps see an even bigger, more competent Kojak scratching his bald head over an unsolved mystery while the "*the end*" passes across his face), its constructive principle (the suspension of the solution) will already have readjusted its aim in the later phase (automatization) and will be exhausted, ready to be replaced by some opposite constructive principle, if any remains.

As Tynjanov's essay shows, the Russian formalists seek to apply a scientific evolutionary method to the explanation of literary developments. Thomas Kuhn's *The Structure of Scientific Revolutions* (1970),[2] in which a method similar to Tynjanov's is applied to explain progress in the sciences, tends to confirm Tynjanov's procedure. Kuhn describes his concept of "paradigm" as an accepted model or pattern over which scientific research is built and which is eventually replaced by another paradigm capable of solving problems the old one could not solve. Likewise, Tynjanov's opposite constructive principle (e.g., the suspension of the solution in the anti-detective novel) slowly grows against the weaknesses of the automatized one (e.g., the "sensational solution" in the degeneration of the hard-boiled detective novel), that will be depleted through repetition and eventually replaced by the opposite. The new opposite constructive principle, like the new paradigm, is incompatible with the old (nonsolution vs. solution) and is full of potentialities that remain to be articulated and developed (e.g., the variety of possibilities present in the anti-detective novel).

The similar concepts of constructive principle and paradigm serve our purposes here, answering at least in part our first question—how could authors so distant in space and culture as Borges, Nabokov, and Gadda subject the detective novel in the forties to the same mutation. These writers, it seems, sensed the inadequacy of the by then worn out stress on solution in the detective novel and the necessity for a change reflecting the wider alterations taking place in the cultural climate of the twentieth century, the passage from modernism to postmodernism. The shift within detective fiction corresponds perfectly to a shift without, in the general literary and cultural atmosphere.

It is of course hard to say exactly when postmodernism took the place of modernism. The process is too contemporary for us to have a clear perspective, as is suggested by the fact that the very term *postmodernism* was coined a posteriori, at the end of the sixties. Modernism and postmodernism overlap and blend; there are recent authors who contributed to both of them (Virginia Woolf, Gertrude Stein),[3] contemporary authors who have written like early modernists (the late John Cheever, John Updike, William Styron),[4] and others who in the forties had already acquired a postmodern sensibility (Borges, Gadda, Nabokov). It is perhaps sufficient to leave the matter vague, considering some anti-detective fiction by those writers (Nabokov's *The Real Life of Sebastian Knight,* 1941; Borges' "La muerte y la brújula," 1942; Gadda's *Quer pasticciaccio brutto de via Merulana,* 1946) as the approximate watershed. There are, indeed, critics who claim the existence of an atemporal postmodern sensibility present everywhere in literature and make Sterne's *Tristram Shandy,* if not Apollonius Rhodius' *Argonautika,* a perfect example of postmodern concerns.

In order that later lines of argument may be clear, it will be worthwhile to pause here for a brief reexamination of postmodernism as opposed to modernism and to ask why writers who wrote anti-detective novels should be described as postmodernists, or at least as having postmodernist tendencies. Needless to say, we are now on mined ground. Numerous critics have distinguished (or tried to distinguish) postmodernism from modernism[5] and, while their opinions are similar, they never agree totally, as one should expect when dealing with issues so contemporary as to make objective critical perspective difficult.

The beginning of modernism in literature is normally identified with the turn of the century and the accelerating decline of the old European order; and, since that time modernist literature (Joyce, Kafka, Woolf, Yeats, Eliot, Pound) has been characterized by a will to surpass or to escape the middle-class ethos and literary taste. These writers attacked the typical nineteenth century realistic, easily accessible novel by writing learned, technically innovative, and sometimes obscurant works in which psychoanalysis and classical mythology, even languages only available to scholars, were the instrument for a discovery of the self and of the new symbolic possibilities of meaning. The modernist author was still in command of his fiction (part of the so-called Western logocentric tradition), *at the center* of the mythical and symbolical universe he created; but his work already stressed the position of the artist as a man alienated from society (Mann's *Tonio Kröger*, Joyce's *A Portrait of the Artist as a Young Man*, Kafka's *Ein Hungerkünstler*).

The rise of French existentialism[6] and the harsh reality of World War II caused the constructive principle of modernism (Symbolism, the discovery of the self through myth and psychoanalysis) to seem inadequate and worn out (automatized), and existentialism, the dramatization of a human condition refusing any system or *telos*, became the new "opposite constructive principle" behind postmodernism.

The main difference that separates postmodernism from modernism, then, is postmodernism's lack of a center, its refusal to posit a unifying system. Postmodernism's new awareness is the absence of a finality, a solution. This is exactly what the anti-detective novel is about.[7] As William V. Spanos writes in "The Detective and the Boundary," "the most immediate task . . . in which the contemporary [postmodern] writer must engage himself . . . is that of undermining the detective-like expectations of the positivistic mind . . . by evoking rather than purging pity and terror—anxiety."[8] The detective novel, a reassuring "low" genre that is supposed to please the expectations of the reader, thus becomes the ideal medium of postmodernism in its inverted form, the anti-detective novel, which frustrates the expectations of the reader, transforms a mass-media genre into a sophisticated expression of avant-garde sensibility, and substitutes for the detective as central and ordering character the decentering and chaotic admission of mystery, of nonsolution.

Of course postmodernism does not mean only "lack of a center," and postmodernist authors do not write only anti-detective fiction, but this is the aspect of postmodernism that concerns us at the moment, as other aspects have concerned a number of critics. Especially in the last fifteen years, critics have, in fact, labeled and articulated distinct facets of the postmodern imagination. So we read about "black humor," "new gothicism," "new fiction," "metafiction," and "fabulation,"[9] all cryptically attempting to serve as the American answer to the *nouveau roman,* the French postmodern chief exhibit during the fifties and early sixties. These different critical labels express slightly different aspects of the same thing, a complex literary and cultural movement which, fittingly enough since it distrusts "systems," resists systematization.

If the anti-detective novel is basically an inverted detective novel, should the anti-detective novel still be considered an integral part of the detective fiction genre and not merely its exploitation? The point may be of only theoretical importance; but since the detective story as a genre has evolved into a tightly structured system of rules obeyed by professional writers exclusively devoted to detective fiction, it seems most reasonable to view the anti-detective novel not as a continuation of the genre but as a transgression of it, or as a mutation. A new use of old techniques can lead not only to the renewal of a genre but also to the constitution of another genre, or, as I think the case is here, to a phenomenon that still maintains visible connections with the detective novel (the literary and intellectual anti-detective novel is mainly in the stream of the rational Poesque and British tradition even though it offers no solution) but has a basically new meaning.

In his essay "Literaturnyj Fakt," Tynjanov writes that "a [literary] epoch always selects its necessary materials, but it is the use of these materials that specifically characterizes the epoch . . . the whole essence of a new construction can be in the new use of old techniques, in their new constructive meaning."[10] One can examine in this light the detective fictional techniques used in the anti-detective novel; it is actually how they are used and, indeed, which of them are used that clarifies the meaning of the new fictional form and creates distinctions among the anti-detective novels themselves.

A conventional detective story is a fiction in which an amateur or professional detective tries to discover by rational means the solution of a mysterious occurrence—generally a crime, usually a murder. This definition implies the presence of at least three invariable elements: the detective, the process of detection, and the solution. Besides these basic elements other characteristics typical of detective fiction and useful for definition of the anti-detective novel are: a mystery or a crime to unravel; suspense (the interaction between detection and solution as it plays with the expectations of the reader); delay of the solution (normally caused by a first false solution planted by the criminal or caused by a mistake on the part of the detective). For our present purposes, however, the crucial elements of the genre are detective, detecting process, and solution; they are chronologically sequential in the fiction and can change or subvert its meaning if used in a new way. The solution is the most important element since it is the final and fulfilling link in the detective novel's sequence, the one that gives sense to the genre and justifies its existence. So it is to the solution that the anti-detective novelist devotes his attention; he anticipates the solution in the narrative sequence (Gardner's *The Sunlight Dialogues*), fulfills it only partially (Sciascia's *A ciascuno il suo*), denies it (Pynchon's *The Crying of Lot 49*), nullifies it (Hjortsberg's *Falling Angel*), or parodies it (Calvino's *Se una notte d'inverno un viaggiatore*).

The twist of the final element is prepared for by an elaboration of the two others (detective and detection), which does not thoroughly follow the rules of the conventional detective novel yet does not subvert the meaning of the fiction either. The detective of the anti-detective story no longer has the detachment of a M. Dupin. Unwillingly, he gets emotionally caught in the net of his detecting effort and is torn apart between the upsurge of feelings and the necessity for rationality (Laurana in *A ciascuno il suo;* Oedipa in *The Crying of Lot 49;* Clumly in *The Sunlight Dialogues;* Harry Angel in *Falling Angel*). The detective's relationship with the mystery or with the crime cannot be impersonal any more, suggesting that something unexpected (not an unexpected solution) awaits the reader at the end of the fiction. In the hard-boiled school, detection could become a personal existential quest, but not to the point of being unfulfilled (as it is in *The Crying of Lot 49*) or fulfilled in a thoroughly unconventional way ("La muerte y la brújula," *Les Gommes*).

It is the more or less radical treatment of the solution that distinguishes different kinds of anti-detective novels; the treatment of the old form creates the new content. All the other elements must seem apparently unchanged so that the fiction at the beginning can be identified by the reader as a detective novel and reveal itself as a negation of the genre only at the end. Thus what in an anti-detective novel seems suspense that promises fulfillment actually proves unfulfilled suspense by the end of the reading, while the delay of the solution becomes nonsolution; even the nature of the crime or mystery often acquires during the development of the detection disturbing and unusual connotations, as in *The Crying of Lot 49*. Conventions hence become deceitful clues planted by the writer to rouse the attention of the reader before disappointing his expectations; conventions are paradoxically functional in the disintegration of the genre.

We can distinguish three different techniques for handling the solution; these techniques correspond to three kinds of antidetective fiction.

1) *INNOVATION:* an early solution disappoints the reader and then an unexpected final one puzzles him (*The Sunlight Dialogues*), or a solution does not imply the punishment of the culprit (*A ciascuno il suo*), or a solution is found by chance (*Il nome della rosa*). These novels are characterized by a social preoccupation related to the crime and its causes. This social preoccupation is totally foreign to the "British" kind, but is already present in the hard-boiled school. In general, the conventional rules of detective fiction are freely used or twisted but not subverted; some partially satisfying solution is still present.

2) *DECONSTRUCTION:* the opposite constructive principle is fulfilled; instead of a solution there is a suspension of the solution. The novel frustratingly ends a few pages before the denouement, after having teased the reader into a wild goose chase throughout the fiction by planted and inconsequential clues (*The Crying of Lot 49*); the suspension of the solution can leave the reader in total darkness (*The Crying of Lot 49*), or intimate a solution (Sciascia's *Todo modo*), or give a mocking solution that is rationally unacceptable (Hjortsberg's *Falling Angel*). The crime is seen as a conspiracy by a secret organization ruling and perverting society; the investigation is experienced by the detective as an existential quest; both are emphasized at this level—the truly postmodern one that subverts the conventional detective novel's rules. Here the postmodern imagination often plays an important part in the form of "black humor" and "new gothicism."

3) *METAFICTION:* these novels are only in a very general way anti-detective novels. They emphasize that "book-conscious-of-its-bookness" aspect typical also of the puzzle-like British detective fiction. Here the detection is present in the relation between the writer who deviously writes ("hides") his own text and the reader who wants to make sense out of it (who

"seeks" a solution). A similar "hide-and-seek" relation corresponds within the fiction. In fact *Se una notte d'inverno un viaggiatore* (*If on a winter's night a traveler*) by Calvino presents a relation between writer and reader outside and within the fiction: 1) writer (Calvino) deviously writing (hiding the solution of) the text and real reader trying to make sense out of it (seeking the solution); 2) fictional "writer" (Marana, the translator-forger) forging and interrupting the texts within the text (hiding their conclusions) and two fictional readers trying to make sense out of them (seeking their conclusions). These relations can also be simplified by the absence of fictional readers as in Nabokov's *Pale Fire*: 1) writer (Nabokov) deviously writing (hiding the solution of) the text and real reader trying to make sense out of it (seeking the solution); 2) fictional "writer" (Kinbote, the commentator-distorter) distorting the text within the text (the poem "Pale Fire") by his comment. Parody and "intertextual detection," a metafictional preoccupation that has been lately predominant in the growth of the postmodern imagination,[11] are typical of this third and very flexible kind of anti-detective novel.

These categories are intentionally overlapping and by no means rigid and definitive. It is obvious that a novel that is primarily deconstructive, such as *The Crying of Lot 49*, in which there is no solution, is also a novel that neither implies the punishment of the culprit nor the triumph of justice; in this sense it also satisfies some features of innovative anti-detective fiction. Characteristic features themselves may vary in intensity within a category; for example, *The Crying of Lot 49* is much more a deconstructive anti-detective novel than *Todo modo*, as in the former there is a total suspension of the solution, while in the latter some hint is given. Likewise, the relation criminal-detective/writer-reader typical of the metafictional anti-detective novel is present in any text where there is a "dialogue" (implicit or not) between reader and writer (for example, in the famous Ellery Queen's interruptions, in which he challenged the reader to find the solution before the end of the novel as by that moment he had all the elements in hand). Thus one of *The*

Crying of Lot 49's metafictional hints resides in its third-person narrator who reminds us continuously that it is not Oedipa who is telling her story but someone else who could even be the Tristero (if we like to remain within the fiction) but who is actually Thomas Pynchon (who is anyway for all of us a name as mysterious and unsubstantial as Tristero itself). The fact is that the voice narrating *The Crying of Lot 49* plays with us, as does any other third-person narrator; this in other cases would be an obvious fact, but in a complicated novel like *The Crying of Lot 49* it adds a further dimension to its imperviousness. At any rate, it should by now be clear that any category "implies"—although with an intensity varying according to the novel concerned—quite a few characteristics of other categories.

What also connects innovative, deconstructive, and metafictional anti-detective novels is a teasing, puzzle-like relation between the text and the reader, which gets more overt and sophisticated as one goes from the first to the third treatment of the solution. This relation replaces and changes the function of the conventional suspense, since the reader gets involved in the mystery and in the detection to be only partially or not at all rewarded by a plausible denouement.

Just as these anti-detective modes renew the conventional use of solution and suspense, they also alter the relation to time, which in traditional detective fiction is repetitive and predetermined, but in some deconstructive anti-detective novels is non-repetitive and open.

The traditional detective novel presents a reconstruction of the past and ends when this reconstruction has been fulfilled. To reconstruct the past is to go back to a point (the one of the crime) about which the detective is concerned. There must be a fixed point; otherwise the regression in time would be infinite. So to go back in time is equal to finding a criminal, to unravelling a mystery.[12]

There is no free time in a detective novel: the present is employed to explain the past, the past has already happened before the story started, and the future is not even taken into account. The detective "wins" the past, unravels it, but only to be doomed to go backwards in time in the next story. If it is a detective-fiction serial, he must repeat the same process over and over, and it is perhaps because of his continuous frequenting of the past, because of his living in the past, that he never ages in the present. Nero Wolfe and Hercule Poirot are always the same, impervious to passing time. Their next victory, which is by no means unexpected (the reader knows from the beginning that they will eventually solve the mystery), represents just a slight variation in a repetitive formula; victory is private and ephemeral since it concerns only a few people and never transcends the puzzle-like ratiocination of the case. Neither Nero Wolfe nor Hercule Poirot, however, can refuse to win, since the solution is fundamental to the genre in which they are imprisoned; they cannot lose as they cannot have a complete and final victory.[13] Like Sisyphus, they are doomed to roll the stone of detection up to the top of the hill over and over. To have to repeat the discovery ultimately means that no discovery is final, no discovery is a solution but rather a tendency, an approximation, since the past is full of unsolved mysteries waiting for their detective.

By contrast, in the deconstructive anti-detective novel, the inanity of the discovery is brought to its climax in the nonsolution, which unmasks a tendency toward disorder and irrationality that has always been implicit within detective fiction (i.e., both parallel and intersecting Poesque and non-Poesque currents). The detective in the deconstructive anti-detective novel does not solve the mystery and so avoids the trap of repetition (serialization). The anti-detective is like the Kierkegaardian ironist who knows that the only way to remain free (not imprisoned in the fiction and its serialization) and somehow superhuman is to choose not to choose (not to solve the mystery), since choice is a limitation of freedom and of the power of creativity as it turns the potential into the actual. To choose not to choose is the widest choice the anti-detective can make, because to let the mystery exist does not restrict his freedom to a single choice and, at the same time, potentially implies all solutions without choosing any. The anti-detective arrives reluctantly at this nonsolution, however, forced to it by the proliferation of meanings (clues) in the events he goes through; at the same time, even if unwillingly, he or she (Oedipa Maas in *The Crying of Lot 49*) still transcends in a single sweep the honorable but limited victories of an endless career (Poirot), since here, too, not to choose is to allow all outcomes.

It is interesting that the detective's discovery is about the past, while we think of discovery always in terms of the future, as giving us a knowledge that will make us progress into the future. This is what we think in relation to scientific discoveries. The detective is supposed to use a scientific method, but he applies it to a discovery in the past. The point is that a discovery is not about finding something really new but, rather, about finding a missing link, something that already existed and we did not know about (or about which we had only a vague notion). America had always been there, waiting for a Columbus. Ultimately, both for some detectives and anti-detectives, to discover is "to recollect in tranquillity" their double's emotions, to find out about their own past, of which they are not aware (Hjortsberg's *Falling Angel*). Even for a serialized detective like Maigret, to find a criminal means to identify with him, to drench himself in the environment of the murder and wait patiently for an epiphany that will solve the mystery.

The detective is a scientist, but a particular kind of scientist, a humanist, an archeologist. In fact both the detective and the archeologist "dig out," and their reconstruction is only partial, limited to *what is left after* (after the end of a civilization, after a murder). The detective can discover why Mrs. Smith killed her husband, where and how, but, of course, he will never be able to stop Mrs. Smith because the murder has already happened.

It is now possible to see how a set of elements typical of mythology (mirror, labyrinth, and map) recurs both at a literal and at a symbolic level in some early anti-detective fiction (especially in Borges' stories such as "La muerte y la brújula" and in the French *nouveau roman*) and how it contributes to relate time to the development of the detecting process. In fact, if the detective is an "archeologist," he is also a map-maker, a maker of meaning (of solution), who turn into rational symbols something that he cannot take hold of, because he cannot relive the past, but only piece together what is left of it, which can be cigarette butts, overthrown furniture, a corpse in the living room. Objects are important to him, as they are all potential clues.

Theseus, the map-maker, went through the labyrinth Daedalus made. Getting through the labyrinth and finding the exit was to Theseus what finding the solution, making sense out of the past in the flowing of time, is for the detective. If the detective is the map-maker (the maker of a solution), the present time is the mirror-maker, since every present moment flows away from the time of the murder, changes and distorts the image of that past: a cigarette butt is kicked away by someone who perhaps is also busy setting back the overthrown furniture or moving the corpse. The labyrinth of the past "mirrored" (distorted, changed, removed) in the present is the best ally of the murderer. The murderer was not the maker of the labyrinth (the maker of the labyrinth is of course the flowing of time which, as it makes things past, I will simply call "the past"), but he gave it a dimension; freezing a point in time by the murder, he fixed how far in "mapping" the past the detective must go.

It seems hardly necessary to stress the importance of mirrors, labyrinths, and maps in Borges' fiction.[14] The *nouveau roman* also contains this pattern, although it declares itself antisymbolical and antimythological. This pattern relates detecting process and time: the detective tries to map the labyrinth (the mystery, the murder) fighting through the distorted view available in the present (the mirror). The novel is thus simplified in a tension between the distortion of the past due to the flowing of present time (mirror) and the mapping of that past attempted by the detective. The flowing of present time (present=mirror-maker) makes occurrences past, that is, mysterious and irretrievable (past=labyrinth-maker); the silent presence of things, witnesses of the mystery, may help the detective, the map-maker, to "map" the labyrinth (the mystery, the crime), to find a solution (solution=map) by following an Ariadne's thread, a lead, throughout the labyrinth. These mythical symbols work at more than one level.

The mirror that the detective has to crash through to get to the past is also the prefiguration of the "double," the detective's reflection who is the criminal he is looking for (Poe's "William Wilson," Hjortsberg's *Falling Angel*, Robbe-Grillet's *Les Gommes*, Butor's *L'emploi du temps*). The mirror is also the deceiving reproduction of multiform reality, and, as such, it appears as a forewarning in the first lines of *L'emploi du temps*: "[T]he dark windowpane [of the train compartment was] covered on the outside with raindrops, myriad tiny *mirrors* each reflecting a quivering particle of feeble light that drizzled down from the grimy ceiling."[15]

An actual map as a symbolic and objective representation of the place where the anti-detective novel is set (and the prefiguration, ironical or not, of the success of the detective as "map-maker," maker of a solution) is often offered to the reader in the first page of the novel as it often used to in the old-style British mystery (Robbe-Grillet's *La Jalousie*, Butor's *L'emploi du temps*, Ollier's *La Mise en Scène*).[16] The novel setting objectively represented in the map is often opposed to a "mirror." I call the "mirror" the distortion of the novel setting by the narrator. This occurs no matter how objective his narration appears (the obsessive camera-eye description of the house where the action takes place by the third person narrator of *La Jalousie;* in *L'emploi du temps* the narrator's description of Bleston, the mapped town, as an evil, eerie place). In Borges' "La muerte y la brújula," the map of the city is a crucial element in the fatal detection performed by Lönnrot (the detective as "map-maker"). More generally, many of Borges' titles emphasize the shape (the "mapping") of objects or of environments: "Las ruinas circulares" ("The Circular Ruins"), "El jardín de senderos que se bifurcan" ("The Garden of Forking Paths"), "La forma de la espada" ("The Shape of the Sword").[17]

Time itself becomes a mirror-image, emphasizing specularity and repetition; everything ends (almost) as it has started (Butor's *L'emploi du temps*, Ollier's *La Mise en Scène*, Robbe-Grillet's *La Jalousie* and *Dans le labyrinthe*)[18] while the static plot and the detailed, obsessive descriptions of the objects as surfaces in the environment give the reader an objective correlative of patterned, impenetrable repetition, that is, the sense of the labyrinth (*L'emploi du temps, La Mise en Scène, La Jalousie, Dans le labyrinthe*). Labyrinths are present in Borges' "detective" stories; an actual one in "Abenjacán el Bojarí, muerto en su laberinto" ("Ibn Hakkan al-Bokhari, Dead in His Labyrinth"),[19] and a literary one in "El jardín de senderos que se bifurcan" ("The Garden of Forking Paths").

The narrator of *L'emploi du temps,* Revel, burning the map of Bleston, the town locus of the novel, gives himself up to the inscrutable labyrinth Bleston represents for him. The detective novel he has been reading, *Le Meurtre de Bleston* (*Bleston Murder*) perfectly mirrors something that is going to happen to him: an occurrence in which he is the unaware (but to what degree unaware?) accomplice of an attempted murder he describes in his journal. The journal in the novel and the detective novel (*Le Meurtre de Bleston*) in the novel are interacting and so are the time in which the journal is written and the time of the occurrences it describes, and we have again a game of mirrors.

We will see how also in some recent anti-detective novels the elements of the labyrinth-mirror-map pattern can be traced either at a symbolic or at a literal level. In Sciascia's *Todo modo* the "mirror" is symbolic for the detective-murderer duality, while there is an actual drawing, a "map," which leads the narrator to the solution of the mystery. In Eco's *Il nome della rosa* (*The Name of the Rose*) all three elements are actually present and also stand for the chronological development of the detecting process: labyrinth=the mystery to unravel; mirror=the distortion, the false solution; map=the solution. The three elements—especially the map—may be found even in traditional detective fiction, perhaps because they are generally evocative of mystery.

All these terms, of course, can be undermined or perverted—a fact of which Poe seems to have had at least an inkling. In

"The Murders in the Rue Morgue" it turns out that there was not, technically, a murder; in several of his nondetective tales, as in "Ligeia," the narrator leaves us with a false solution; and in the detective story-like tale "William Wilson" the seeming solution destroys the solver, while in *The Narrative of Arthur Gordon Pym of Nantucket* the solution of the (nondetective) mystery is withheld. But since Poe's time the world has changed. The madness and self-contradiction of the narrator has become general, a quality of the universe in which the detective struggles.

3

The Innovative Anti-Detective Novel

The three anti-detective novels examined in this chapter, Leonardo Sciascia's *A ciascuno il suo,* John Gardner's *The Sunlight Dialogues,* and Umberto Eco's *Il nome della rosa,* all have in common an unfulfilling solution. The first two are characterized by detectives who cannot maintain their detachment (Laurana in *A ciascuno il suo;* Clumly in *The Sunlight Dialogues*). The sleuth in these novels is no longer the perfect detective; his human nature dooms him (Laurana) or saves him (Clumly), independently of the results of his own investigative work. *A ciascuno il suo* and *Il nome della rosa* stress the possibility of human error in the detecting process; Laurana warns us that the detective can push himself to believe something (the widow's innocence) which his rationality doubts, and the Holmesian William of Baskerville in Eco's novel imposes his professional logic on facts that are only casual. Both portend a main problem of deconstructive anti-detective fiction—the relation between the detective and the means of communication, between the detective and reality. The detective can find a solution, but is it only the projection of his desires, one of the multiple solutions that a puzzle may have, or the *real* solution? Who is the detective to impose one meaning on a reality that is ambiguous and multiform per se? Oedipa Maas (Pynchon's *The Crying of Lot 49*) and Harry Angel (Hjortsberg's *Falling Angel*), detectives who coped with this problem, are discussed in the next chapter.

In innovative anti-detective fiction a solution is still present, although partially unrewarding. In fact in *A ciascuno il suo* and in *The Sunlight Dialogues* justice does not triumph as we automatically expect when the solution is discovered. By now rationality (solution) and humanity (justice) do not coincide any more. The rational detective or the tough policeman who enforces the law seem unable to make the step from effective rationality to justice, that is, to civil commitment and human compassion. Yet we still have a detective who performs a detection and musters together a more or less stammering solution. Rules are not subverted, but rather put in a dubious light, which foreshadows the more radical operations of deconstructive anti-detective fiction.

Leonardo Sciascia's
A ciascuno il suo

Leonardo Sciascia is one of the most interesting living Italian writers. Born in 1921 in Racalmuto, a small town in Sicily, he was from 1949 to 1970 a grammar school teacher, rarely leaving the island that is often the source and the setting of his fiction. He seems to have been influenced by Pirandello in his perception of the ambiguity of reality and by Manzoni in his use of irony and of a masterful plain style. In the late thirties his literary interests took shape as he began to read the French rationalists of the Enlightenment (Voltaire, Diderot) and then American fiction writers such as Dos Passos, Caldwell, and Steinbeck.[1] These two trends in his early readings developed later in his literary career, on the one hand, into a rational and critical preoccupation with the moral and political state of Italy, a preoccupation that becomes civil commitment, *littérature engagé* in the French pamphleteers' tradition (historical investigations such as *La scomparsa di Majorana*, 1975; satirical novels such as *Candido*, 1977; the pamphlet *L'affaire Moro*, 1978) and, on the other hand, into an interest in a realistic novel of action with social concerns, which is apparently regionalist (the Sicilian setting) but actually a metaphor for a wider reality (novels such as *Il giorno della civetta*, 1961; *A ciascuno il suo*, 1966; *Todo modo*, 1974).

An early expression of these rational and realistic interests was his study of the detective novel genre. In 1954 Sciascia published a long article on the genesis and history of detective fiction; he stated therein how "the recent involution of the genre [Spillane] shows the 'Gothic' nature of the detective novel—its descent from the eighteenth century Gothic novel,"[2] and he regretted the end of "British" puzzle-like detective fiction that required an almost "philological reading" in order to discover the solution. Two short essays, one on Simenon's Maigret as a successful compromise between the traditional detective novel and "serious" literature,[3] the other on the degeneration of recent American detective fiction further clarified Sciascia's personal interest in the genre. In the latter essay, he wrote:

> Technically, the good detective novel concurred, and by a remarkable contribution, in the evolution . . . "toward a novel which is all narration, an endless flow of narration." Even in its limited existence as a by-product, the detective novel has followed the development of contemporary fiction, and often by an exchange of elements which would be interesting to detect.[4]

Further on in the essay, he added, "it is certain that novelists such as Hemingway, Faulkner and Cain have learned a lot from detective fiction: and not only in a technical sense."[5]

Perhaps by writing these essays Sciascia realized the artistic potential of detective fiction and the ease with which the rationality inherent in its structure could convey that clear-cut social indictment he wanted to express. This critical awareness was soon absorbed by Sciascia the writer, since most of his fiction has a detective-novel plot adapted to his new purposes (e.g., *Il giorno della civetta*, 1961; *A ciascuno il suo*, 1966; *Todo modo*, 1974). Sciascia's main purpose is to paint a critical portrait of the sad state of Sicilian (and, generally, Italian) affairs, a portrait of the social and political condition of his island ruled by a secret power (the Mafia) which has corrupted the official power (the state) so deeply that by now the two are nearly identical. In an island that has been dominated and exploited by all the civilizations in the Mediterranean basin (Greeks, Romans, Arabs, French, Spaniards), a sort of conspiracy, a network of secret solidarity among the inhabitants, was first a necessity in order to survive and to resist the rulers, but it became a means of local power used by Sicilians themselves against each other when, after the Italian unification, Sicily was no longer a conquered land but, at least on paper, part of Italy, with equal rights and equal duties.[6]

At the present time, in Italy, the aim of the Mafia is not to subvert the state by overthrowing it, which would be utopian in the twentieth century, but parasitically to take advantage of its inefficiency by infiltrating the state organization and by establishing illegal connections between the state administration and the industrial and financial world. The network of "favors" and the complicity between political and economical powers become so intricate that eventually no one has any interest in raising a scandal that would damage both sides.

A longer digression about the Mafia would not be pertinent to this work, but rather to a sociological study. One characteristic of the "Honored Society," however, is important to understanding the novel (*A ciascuno il suo*) I am going to examine: the Mafia, like any "secret society," is based on a "conspiracy of silence" (the so-called *omertà*). If someone rebels against the network of imposed "favors" and is murdered, even though everyone knows who killed him, no one talks because of fear and because of an automatic complicity which may come from a material personal interest as well as from a general and secular mistrust for the police and the laws, still viewed as oppressors and exploiters.

This situation created by the Mafia looks like the perfect ground for a detective story or a crime story, as fictions more sensational and less honest in intentions than Sciascia's have shown by romanticizing the American branches of the Sicilian Mafia (Mario Puzo's *The Godfather*). Instead, Sciascia's insight in the Sicilian situation is detached and glamorless, often bitterly ironical and never collusive.

He creates an anti-detective novel in which rational method and social discourse coincide and clarify each other in a realistic and yet symbolic indictment of the Sicilian situation. He says in an interview, "I have used Sicily as a metaphor, so to speak, of the world. My books would have not attracted any attention out of Sicily, if they had not been read in such a way. . . . The problems of the Sicilian microcosm are the ones which can kill the world."[7] Sciascia's intentions and literary talent transcend the limits of detective fiction's conventions and yet he freely uses the genre's rules to fit his purposes. As usual, the detective character and the denouement are the crucial issues of this experiment, the ones that justify my considering *A ciascuno il suo* (1966) a literary and innovative anti-detective novel.[8]

The quotation from Poe's "The Murders in the Rue Morgue" following the novel's title ("Let it not be supposed . . . that I am detailing any mystery or penning any romance")[9] is a "statement of purpose." *A ciascuno il suo* holds no unsolvable mystery (at the end there is a denouement, although unrewarding and unconventional), as the reality of the Mafia's power in Sicily is no mystery and no romance. In *Le parrocchie di Regalpetra* Sciascia wrote, "I believe in human reason, and in the freedom and in the justice that from reason arise."[10] Hence Poe's epigraph seems to be also a proof of Sciascia's belief in the Poesque concise and rational story as the perfect literary vehicle to denounce lack of freedom and justice in society.

The analogy between Poe and Sciascia, however, is limited to conciseness and rational method. In fact Professor Laurana, the amateur detective of *A ciascuno il suo,* does not have M. Dupin's detachment; rather, he finds himself emotionally involved in the mystery he unravels and becomes the victim of his inability to take a moral stand. Besides, while in the Poesque detective story the solution automatically implies the punishment of the criminal, in *A ciascuno il suo* everyone knows who the culprit is, but no one even thinks of breaking the conspiracy of silence (the *omertà*). *A ciascuno il suo* is not a "fiction," but rather a charge against a real state of affairs; as such it cannot afford a reassuring and happy denouement in the tradition of the utterly unreal "fairy tales of the Golden Age."

Before examining more closely the detective character and the denouement, it is worthwhile to comment on the title, which, like the epigraph, is significant. "A ciascuno il suo" means "to each his own" and is the Italian translation of the Latin saying *unicuique suum,* which is part of the subtitle in the heading of *L'osservatore romano,* the official daily newspaper of the Roman Catholic Church. In the context of the Catholic daily, the subheading "unicuique suum" stresses a sense of justice and rightful retribution; that is exactly what is lacking in the novel. The protagonist of the novel, Paolo Laurana, catches a glimpse of the word "unicuique" through the back of an anonymous minatory letter composed with newspaper cuttings and sent to the pharmacist of the village where he lives. He immediately associates the "unicuique" with the heading of *L'osservatore romano* and, after the pharmacist and the village's doctor, Doctor Roscio, have been found shot dead in the countryside where they had gone hunting, he starts to inquire on his own about who in the village buys the Roman daily. Thus "to each his own" is also a clue, and epitomizes the logical, "Poesque" sequence followed by Professor Laurana in his investigation: to each clue its own explanation. The title is also a comment on the lives of the suspects for the murder who, protected by their respectable personae, do what they want. Referring to the Sant'Anna's parish priest and to the archpriest, Laurana ironically thinks, "how well one does in the church and in the rectory . . . they really do live well, *each in his own way.* Or perhaps, believing what people say, both of them in the same way, differing only in appearances."[11] The pharmacist and Doctor Roscio also receive "their own" for a reason that Professor Laurana tries to discover, and Laurana himself is murdered at the end of his too-successful investigation for not having minded his own business.

Hence the original meaning of the Catholic newspaper's subheading is totally subverted: from stressing justice it ends up signifying the Mafia's vendetta. Somehow, the novel is the progressive undermining of the sense of justice emanating from the words "unicuique suum," and it ends as the priest of the village, referring to the dead Laurana and his vain investigation, says "he was a fool," and Laurana receives again "his own" *ad memoriam* from a corrupted representative of "divine justice."

In *A ciascuno il suo,* epigraph and title are especially significant because they are elements of an anti-detective novel, which is generally more allusive and complex than the solution-oriented conventional detective novel. In Sciascia's case, the anti-detective novel becomes a multiform and a bitterly ironic indictment of a society in which appearances and reality never coincide.

It is not accidental that Laurana's first clue comes from a newspaper, a means of communication, and that almost everyone of the eighteen brief chapters in the novel is partly or entirely occupied by a "casual" conversation between Laurana and a suspect or someone who can given give him useful information. This narrative structure makes the novel's pace interesting and dynamic but, more than that, tells us something about a particular concern of detective novels in general and of anti-detective novels in particular: the problems of communication (think also of Pynchon's *The Crying of Lot 49*). The detective, Laurana, is the man who finds the hidden message among reticent words, who makes the implicit and accidental communication (the clue, e.g., the "unicuique suum") explicit, clear. He is a "maker of meaning"; as such he can solve the mystery, but the solution is no longer the point. Rather, the point is that the detective may be a victim of the signs he tries to interpret and of the ambiguity of reality. Sometimes it is easier for the detective to find a meaning in an accidental series of events (William of Baskerville in *Il nome della rosa*) than to face the fact that perhaps there is no meaning or that the ultimate meaning he imposes on reality is actually a distortion of communication, the pernicious result of his involvement with a suspect that he is no longer able to consider as such (Laurana and the widow in *A ciascuno il suo*). In other words, the first thing to question is no longer the mystery, but the detective. Laurana's solution of the mystery is ultimately useless because he does not have any social or moral stand to counterpose to the "morality" of the conspiracy, and he does not have one precisely because of the virtues that allow him a perfect detection. In fact Professor Laurana, the intellectual far superior in culture to anyone in the village, is an alien, a displaced man who has little contact with the other people, who daydreams and is basically dominated by a powerful mother,[12] but, more than this, whose "intellect" has left him with no belief to rely on. Detecting for him is only a pleasure of the mind, and his death shows that in the second half of the twentieth century it is of no avail to be *only* a Dupin. The rational and well-read man who naively escapes real life out of intellectual spite is going to be easily manipulated by more mundane people (the sensual and wicked widow of Doctor Roscio), especially if his rational and abstract faculties limit his ability to a merely technical detection and prevent him from taking a clear moral stand—in fact from knowing what a moral stand is. The following passage well explains Laurana's way of thinking:

> [H]is curiosity concerning the motives and the mode of crime . . . was merely intellectual and somehow born out of stubborness. . . . In fact the idea that the solution of the problem would lead . . . to the deliverance of the culprits to justice, and thus *tout court* to justice, didn't even flash through his mind. . . . His own had been a human and intellectual curiosity, which neither could nor must be confused with that of those whom society, the State, paid to reach and hand to the revenge of law the persons who transgress or infringe it.[13]

Hence Laurana's indifference to human laws and justice does ultimately play the game of the Mafia, which many Sicilians do not necessarily consider a criminal organization but, paradoxically, a "moral code," a way of acting and thinking that, as such, permeates Sicilian society and influences even people who think themselves to be beyond it:

> And part of this obscure self-respect of his was the centuries of infamy that an oppressed people [the Sicilians] . . . had burdened on the law and on those who were its instruments; the belief not yet extinct that the best right and the rightest justice, if someone really cares about them, if he is not willing to leave their fulfillment to destiny or to God, can only come out of the barrels of a gun.[14]

Laurana's is the failure of the intellectual to live and act effectively in everyday reality; it represents the problem of the "ivory tower." At the end of the short novel, his fellow citizens consider dead Laurana a fool because they, too, had performed their own private detection, discovering that lawyer Rosello, cousin of Doctor Roscio's wife Luisa, Luisa herself, and their uncle the archpriest had organized the double murder and sent the minatory letter to the pharmacist to direct to him the attention of the people and police. The others' investigation had been silent, however, carried out through cautious village gossips without letting the murderers know that they knew, that is, respecting the law of silence (the *omertà*). Laurana, instead, had not done things cautiously enough (Rosello knew that he knew) and, even in Mafia's terms, his major mistake had been his refusal to take a stand. He did not accept powerful Rosello's offer to do him favors (i.e., to buy his silence) out of a moralistic spite that was not, however, strong enough to overcome that intellectual spite that made him discard the idea of cooperating with the police. Thus he was "a fool with no place to go" and, as such, extremely vulnerable. At the end of the novel, Roscio's beautiful widow, Luisa, to whom Laurana is very attracted, pretends to be uninvolved in the murder of her husband and to have recently discovered Rosello's responsibility. When she asks if he would go to the police with her, she is simply testing the soundness of his present immobility between the two stands he could take. When Laurana says he would go along with her, he dooms himself, taking the right stand with the wrong person. Lack of "mundanity" and naive sexual desire blind him, though his rationality still warns him that something is wrong with the widow. Luisa does not show up at the night rendezvous they had planned in the county seat to decide what to do; disappointed, Laurana walks toward the railway station to catch a train and go back to the village when someone who looks familiar offers him a ride. He accepts and the car ominously "[takes] off in a rush."[15]

Like Lönnrot in "La muerte y la brújula," ultimately Laurana is killed because he has performed the most perfect, the purest detection, that is, detection for its own sake, beyond any moral or material purpose—something that not even M. Dupin, who gladly accepted the Prefect's check, used to do.

Shortly after Laurana's disappearance, lawyer Rosello, a powerful politician and Mafia leader with a respectable legal practice as a front, and his longtime lover, Dr. Roscio's rich widow, throw a party in the archpriest's house to celebrate their engagement, which perfectly represents the collusion among religious, political, and economic power. In fact the archpriest Rosello gives his blessing to the engagement between the two cousins, which is questionable practice for Roman Catholics, so that the widow's money can remain in the Rosello family rather than being snatched away by some other husband. The three characters are tied by the murder of Roscio and by bonds of blood and of economical and legal relations. The three corrupted powers they represent may very well stand for the state, slowly taken over by the Mafia conspiracy, which is careful enough to leave it a front of respectability.[16]

As we can see, the detective plot in *A ciascuno il suo* is ultimately a device to hold the reader's attention and to convey a social indictment in a concise and rational way. Ironically, Sciascia never mentions the word "Mafia" in the whole novel; the Mafia is the conspiracy of silence and of course none of the characters involved in it mentions his own sin.

The use of a third-person omniscient narrator conveys a sense of detachment, permits the use of irony and allows some anticipation, which gives the story a bitter sense of inevitability (e.g., "This small decision had to have, in his [Laurana's] life, the role of fatality. . . . Chance, for the second time: but this time pregnant with mortal fatality").[17] Another example of the effective intrusion of the omniscient narrator comes at the end of chapter 17, following the chapter in which Laurana accepts the ominous ride. Chapter 17 is devoted to the police's vain effort to discover what happened to Laurana; ironically the commissioner ends up believing that shy and withdrawn Laurana at last eloped with a mysterious lover. It is worth noticing that, until the end of the chapter, the reader knows only that Laurana had accepted a ride and that the car "[had taken] off in a rush,"[18] which is more than the commissioner knows but, still, no certainty about Laurana's destiny. The last three lines of the chapter, however, represent a dry and sudden turn from the farcical suspicions of the commissioner and confirm what the reader had very likely already guessed about Laurana's disappearance: "But the professor lay under a heavy heap of residue, in an abandoned sulphur-mine, midway as the crow flies between his village and the county seat."[19]

As the novel-focus, Laurana, "disappears," the third-person narrator becomes a necessary and perfect medium for reproducing the village gossipers who, like the travesty of a Greek chorus, end the novel commenting on the truth behind the engagement and branding dead Laurana as a fool.

In *A ciascuno il suo* the rules of detective fiction are freely used to unravel not so much a solution as the mechanisms of power and corruption. Two elements especially, the detective character and the denouement without punishment of the culprits, become warning symbols for, respectively, the professional middle class's growing apathy concerning the administration of the state and for the disastrous but inevitable outcome of such an attitude.

John Gardner's *The Sunlight Dialogues*

John Gardner's *The Sunlight Dialogues* (1972) is also concerned with the relation between the individual and the law, which appears in *A ciascuno il suo* as Laurana's failure to grow from an intellectual interest in the murder to a civil commitment against the Mafia. But, while in *A ciascuno il suo* the salvation of Laurana would come from understanding and following the laws (e.g., to report Rosello), in *The Sunlight Dialogues* Chief of Police Clumly gains his salvation by learning to depart from them. Clumly ends up not understanding laws any more, lets his prisoner the Sunlight Man escape, and is at last saved by the elemental virtue of compassion. The Sunlight Man challenges the injustices of Western society and, paradoxically, is killed by a policeman as he tries to surrender to "law and order." Hence the terms of the problem are here inverted: while in *A ciascuno il suo* an understanding of the law and a civil commitment would save the alien, in *The Sunlight Dialogues* the "alien"[20] finds his identity and social commitment through human compassion and individual freedom, that is, by going beyond the stifling strictures of "law and order."

In both novels the main character is an alien, a man who does not share the values of society and the common perception of reality. In *A ciascuno il suo* the intellectual Laurana is out of touch with the real world, and in *The Sunlight Dialogues* the Sunlight Man is a misfit whose way of facing reality ranges from conjuring to mysticism. His opponent, Chief Clumly, is so appalled and at the same time attracted by him that he progressively becomes an alien himself, losing his aplomb and all his certainties concerning the system he is supposed to enforce.

These two different messages come from two countries both in crisis at the end of the 1960s, but for opposite reasons: Italy because of not enough (and sound enough) state power, the United States because of too much of it, with all the drawbacks related to their wearing commitment as "watchdog of the Western World."

Like *A ciascuno il suo*, *The Sunlight Dialogues* can be considered a novel that uses detective techniques as a device in an innovative way. It plays on the relation between policeman and criminal and also on detective fiction expectations. It anticipates and thus diminishes the solution of the mystery concerning the Sunlight Man's identity, and offers at the end a denouement (the "criminal" shot, the policeman announcing his death and explaining what happened) which is conventional only at first sight. In fact, Clumly's raving "powerful sermon" at the Dairyman's League has nothing to do with the reassuring and rational Holmesian explanation of the solution to Watson and clients in the cozy Baker Street apartment. In his confused speech, he must admit that "justice didn't triumph, in a way"[21] while he is overcome by grief and tears.

To find out who committed the crime is what the detective job is about. In *The Sunlight Dialogues* this basic concern of detective fiction is ridiculed and reduced. The ludicrous crime of the Sunlight Man is to have painted the word "love" across two lanes of Batavia's Oak Street, while here the policeman's job is not to find and catch who committed the "crime," but, literally, to find who this person is, his identity, since the Sunlight Man managed to let the police catch him immediately.

The mystery of the Sunlight Man's identity is proposed in the first 100 pages of the novel as the potential leitmotiv of the whole fiction, but, at the end of the second chapter, one of the Sunlight Man's jail mates, the thief Boyle, has already recognized him as Taggert Hodge, the man who was his lawyer the first time he had been arrested.[22] Afterwards, Taggert Hodge is silently recognized by all the members of his family, one by one (Will Hodge, Sr., Ben Hodge, Will Hodge, Jr., Millie Hodge, Luke Hodge), until toward the end of the novel even Chief Clumly recognizes the Sunlight Man.[23] The reader is "cheated" in his expectations by all the characters.

In *The Sunlight Dialogues* all of the reader's expectations for a detective novel are in fact doomed to end up in soap bubbles, in nothing. Gardner teases the reader by neatly building up a typical detective-fiction situation only to let it afterwards deflate in a false alarm. There are many examples of unjustified suspense: one night, going back home, Clumly has the feeling, first, that someone is in the back seat of his car; secondly, that someone may be ambushing him in his garage or on the premises.[24] Another time, at night, "he [is] absolutely certain that there was someone in the house."[25] These are all wrong hunches which, however, show the orderly world and beliefs of Clumly quickly breaking down under the pressure of the Sunlight Man's ideas, which threaten him even at home. Gardner employs a similar device also in *Nickel Mountain* in which, as in *The Sunlight Dialogues,* George Loomis' sensation that someone is in his house spying upon him emphasizes the loneliness and inner insecurity of the character.[26] When the police inspect Luke Hodge's house, where the Sunlight Man and Nick Slater hide themselves, Millie, Luke's mother, "[tries] to think of some way of signalling to them [the police]."[27] Suspense builds up while the reader expects something to happen; but nothing happens, the police leave and Millie and Luke remain prisoners of the Sunlight Man.

The same frustration of expectations characterizes the short episode of the bleeding Negro woman who arrives at the police station: "She came through the door, and Tommy [the son of the policeman Miller] turned his face away. Her forehead was torn open. She took a deep breath. 'I killed a gentleman,' she said."[28] At the moment, the reader supposes that this murder is somehow connected with the Sunlight Man, but, instead, the Negro woman is never mentioned again. Other "soap bubbles" include the tension that builds up at a night rally in Buffalo and seems to be about to explode into a riot but does not,[29] and Will Hodge, Jr.'s fears of being assassinated by the crooked businessman Kleppman when he accepts his invitation and flies to St. Louis to visit him at night in a remote area.[30] Kleppmann is to the honest lawyer Will Hodge, Jr., who is going through a private and family crisis, what the Sunlight Man is to Chief Clumly: an "opposite" to whom he feels uncannily attracted because he represents the freedom from that law that Will Hodge serves by now in a very disillusioned way. Kleppmann seems to Will to be the ultimate threat to his beliefs and, at the same time, the possible source of an alternative; this is why Will, Jr., as a lawyer specializing in collections, hounds Kleppmann relentlessly just as the policeman Clumly pursues the Sunlight Man. The old Poesque duality detective-criminal is present even here.

The labyrinthine plot of *The Sunlight Dialogues* also includes the episode of thief Boyle-alias-Benson's discovery of his wife's affair with the activist Nuper. Benson thinks of killing Nuper on the spot with a two-by-four piece of wood he finds on his back-porch steps. He ambushes his wife's lover but, when he is about to club him down, Nuper, who is carrying a box, shifts it to his head and "Benson, in confusion, [ducks] back into hiding."[31] Benson's subsequent attempts to "vindicate his honor" have no better luck. The tragicomic episode sometimes acquires thriller-like connotations because of Benson's murderous intentions, whose results are, however, anticlimactic; they somehow parody and redeem the banality of the stereotypical triangle situation. Eventually, while spending a night in a barn during his vain pursuit of Nuper, Benson catches a bad cold and discovers the emptiness and failure of his life. Also in this case, there is a "game of doubles" as well as a pursuit (Benson-Nuper) but, unlike the situations of Clumly-Sunlight Man and Will Hodge, Jr.-Kleppmann, here the double is "interiorized" (the double is Boyle, the other identity of Benson), and thus does not correspond with the pursued (Nuper). So in this case the existential conflict started by the chase (the pursuit of Nuper) does not concern only the ideological clash between the pursuer (the middle-class Benson) and the pursued (the activist Nuper) but rather focuses on the inner conflict between Boyle the professional thief and Benson the middle-class "salesman," that is, between the character's two identities and personalities, which finally face each other and "trigger" an unpleasant existential discovery during the night spent in the barn. Hence one could say that in *The Sunlight Dialogues* the conventional problem of the physical identity of the criminal (the "whodunit," or, better, the "where is the one who did it?") is restricted to the problem of his official identity (the Sunlight Man is in jail, but who is he?) or turned into the problem of the existential identity of his pursuer, who goes through self-discovery and transformation during the chase (Clumly, Will Hodge, Jr., Benson-Boyle).

In *The Sunlight Dialogues* there is no real detective story plot but, rather, a crime story plot, for when instead of an unfulfilled suspense there is at last a murder, we know or we see who commits it. Such is the case for Nick Slater, who progressively slides from accidental murder to cold-blooded assassination: "The first [murder] completely by accident, the lady in the car. Then the next one a little less by accident [Mrs. Palazzo]. Then last night the third one, only just barely by accident [Hardesty, the neighbor of Luke Hodge]."[32]

A partial exception is Clive Paxton's death, which for the reader is a mystery almost until the end of the novel. In fact at his funeral Clumly suspects that he did not die of natural causes and, after a visit to the widow and her lover, he seems to have understood what happened, but the reader's curiosity is left unsatisfied. Much later, the mystery is revealed to the reader, not by Clumly but directly by the murderer, the Sunlight Man, who is Paxton's son-in-law. In fact he remembers that the night before he painted "love" on Oak Street, he went to visit his father-in-law to make peace with him, but "at last, he . . . [put] his hands around Clive Paxton's throat. It was all he could remember, but he knew it was not an illusion."[33]

At this point we can readjust the terms of our connection between *A ciascuno il suo* and *The Sunlight Dialogues* in order to better justify the techniques (i.e., a very rational and concise detection in *A ciascuno il suo;* unfulfilled suspense in *The Sunlight Dialogues*) that the two novelists employ to reach their goals.

Sciascia suggests that rational detection (Laurana) devoid of civil commitment is finally ineffective; Gardner implies the same for "law and order" (Clumly) devoid of compassion, but his vision is ultimately affirmative, while Sciascia's novel has a pessimistic ending. Both writers seem to stress society as a community of human beings rather than as a depersonalized structure.

Sciascia shows a detection that is sound in its course but ineffective in its outcome since Laurana is not going to be changed by it; he remains an alien and an intellectual with no civil commitment and eventually dies as a consequence of his displacement. Gardner instead shows a detection that is already ineffective in its course, since he wants to show Clumly's progressive transformation from policeman with a heart as cold as steel[34] into compassionate man. Unconsciously Clumly does not want to catch the escaped Sunlight Man because he knows that through his "dialogues" with him he is going to learn something that will explain the personal crisis about "law and order" which he is already experiencing. He chases the Sunlight Man as Ahab chases Moby Dick,[35] because he thinks he can find in him the answers to his problems; he wants to talk to him, not catch him, because the message he wants to hear is about individual freedom, which represents the opposite of his official function, catching the criminal.

Thus, Clumly's progressive acceptance of life's blessed disorder is prepared for by the disruption of the connection cause-effect, clue-deduction. The reader of detective fiction, a Pavlovian dog who salivates because he expects a certain food (murder) when hearing a certain sound (suspense), is going to drool in vain in *The Sunlight Dialogues,* in which all moments of suspense are inconsequential. The fact is that the disconnection in the narrative "timing" of the novel corresponds to twentieth-century man's awareness of a wider disharmony, of his centerlessness in the disorder of an entropic universe. As a minor character in *The Sunlight Dialogues* puts it, using words of Hamlet in a context that reduces them to a comment on ordinary life, "The times are out of joint,"[36] and thus the order to be looked for is no longer the cause-effect connection in the outside world, but, more humanly, personal harmony, the inner order of the self, which, as Clumly shows, is eventually evoked just by the failure of the detective expectations and by the inadequacy of "law and order."

Umberto Eco's *Il nome della rosa*

Il nome della rosa (*The Name of the Rose,* 1983), published in Italy in 1980, is a hard-to-classify anti-detective novel. To examine it will help me to reconsider my taxonomy and, in particular, to see the interrelations existing among the three types of anti-detective fiction I distinguished.

Il nome della rosa starts with a preface entitled "Naturalmente, un manoscritto" ("Naturally, a manuscript") in which the author states he has translated the text into Italian from a French nineteenth-century book that was itself the reproduction of a seventeenth-century Latin edition, which was in turn the printed version of a fourteenth-century Latin manuscript written by Adso of Melk, a German monk who is the actual writer and protagonist of the adventures related in *Il nome della rosa.* The "translation" by Umberto Eco tries to maintain in Italian the rhythm of the "original" Latin with its long sentences, which have an archaic flavor but, still, are pleasant to read.

The text is the narration in first person of a week in November, 1327, when Adso, at that time a novice Benedictine, and his mentor, the Franciscan William (Guglielmo) of Baskerville, stayed in an abbey in Northern Italy. There William had to mediate a meeting between the leader of a supposedly heretical fringe of the Franciscans and the emissaries of Pope John XXII.

The medieval setting is carefully detailed and the reader is plunged into the struggle for power between the wicked Pope and Ludovico the Bavarian, successor to the throne of the Holy Roman Empire. The descriptions of life at the monastery, the rationally and theologically oriented discussions among the monks, the sense of crisis in the monastery caused by the economic rise of the city-states, and the Inquisition's persecutions of the heretics are some of the factors that contribute to the recreation of the medieval atmosphere and that hold the interest of the reader.

Brother William of Baskerville had been an inquisitor, but gave up the position because he felt he could not distinguish any more between good and evil, true faith and heresy. The inquisitor is, of course, the perfect protodetective and the English William of Baskerville (whose physical description and whose name, evocative of *The Hound of the Baskervilles,* remind us of Sherlock Holmes) makes his debut in the novel by describing to the abbot a horse he has never seen. This is a typical Voltairean enterprise (think of Zadig), which can be well performed by a monk who is friend of the best rational minds of the Middle Ages, the philosophers Roger Bacon and William of Occam.

Also the narration is rationally articulated: seven chapters correspond to the seven day time-span it covers, and each chapter is divided in parts according to the day's "liturgical hours," the prayers that regulate the monks' life. In fact, very rational and allegorical structures are typical of medieval works (e.g., Dante's *Divina Commedia*).

When William and Adso arrive, the abbey has just been upset by the mysterious death of a monk. William's efforts to solve the case constitute the main part of Adso's narration; Adso is a "Watson *ante litteram*," narrator of and assistant to his mentor's detecting. The first death is followed by others. Homosexual affairs and power struggles among the apparently holy monks who died and a mysterious book in which all of them were interested are the clues followed by William and Adso. Throughout the narration they try to disentangle the intrigues and to find the book, which may be concealed in the monastery library, a frightening (Borgesian) labyrinth where only the librarian is allowed, but where they make illicit nocturnal trips. William and Adso manage to find the logical key to the labyrinthine library (which is also equipped with distorting mirrors to frighten trespassers) and draw a map of it that helps them to locate the secret room where they discover the mysterious book is hidden. Here the labyrinth-map-mirror pattern I pointed out at the end of the second chapter is present at a literal level,[37] and also reflects the three stages of detection: labyrinth=the mystery to unravel; mirror=the distortion, the false solution; map=the solution. Eventually William discovers that the book contains the section on laughter from Aristotle's *Poetics*, which had been presumed lost since the classical age. The recovered section considers laughter as a saving attitude that exorcises unreasonable fears; Jorge, one of the oldest and most severe monks, deemed this view a threat to his lugubrious and repressive conception of Christianity. Thus he drenched the pages of the book with a powerful poison and hid it in the library so that every monk greedy for knowledge who succeeded in stealing it died by thumbing through it. Chased through the library-labyrinth, Jorge manages to wrench Adso's lamp out of his hands and to throw it away. The lamp falls on a pile of books and the whole library is set afire and burns down. William accidentally finds the right solution through the wrong "clues," as he connects irrelevant and casual elements that he thought had been planted by Jorge. Significantly, he says in his last grieved conversation with Adso, while the abbey is ablaze:

> I arrived at Jorge through an apocalyptic pattern that seemed to underlie all the crimes, and yet it was accidental. I arrived at Jorge seeking one criminal for all the crimes and we discovered that each crime was committed by a different person, or by no one. I arrived at Jorge pursuing the plan of a perverse and rational mind, and there was no plan, or, rather, Jorge himself was overcome by his own initial design and there began a sequence of causes, and concauses, and of causes contradicting one another, which proceeded on their own, creating relations that did not stem from any plan. Where is all my wisdom, then?[38]

Thus William must confess his defeat, his new awareness that "there is no order in the universe"[39] and that disorder is part of God's will, of His freedom from human concerns.

Even from this outline, we can see how difficult it is to define this text without pigeonholing it. The title itself is hard to explain, unless we consider it an epitome for an impossible definition, for the lack of a real correspondence between name (symbol) and thing (rose), which implies a "void" in between the two and stresses the fact that their relation is only symbolical; the thing we name "rose" could be designated by an endless number of other names. In other words, William discovers that the neat puzzle he pieced together was mostly accidental; the relation between signs can be causal but also casual, the "rose" (there is no mention of any actual rose in the novel but in a Latin line ending the book) has many names.[40] The line in Latin—which is taken from the medieval poet Bernard de Morlay and ends "Adso's manuscript"—seems to go along with this interpretation: "It is cold in the scriptorium, my thumb aches. I leave this manuscript, I do not know for whom; I no longer know what it is about: *stat rosa pristina nomine, nomina nuda tenemus.*"[41] In fact the translation from Latin could be: "the ancient rose stands (i.e., exists) [only] in relation to its name, we hold [only] bare names." A dead thing (the ancient rose, "rosa pristina") can be considered still existent (stands, exists, in Latin, "stat") because of its name, not because of its reality. There is a fracture between the signifier and the signified, between the ancient name "rosa" and the actual rose. The name can be more powerful than the thing itself, the language "creates" (stands for) reality, but only in an unsatisfactory, limiting way (we hold only "bare names"), as reality and its "solution" cannot be held by descriptions, by names. The mystery remains; Adso's account is only an attempt to tell the truth (to explain the mystery), as language is only an attempt to represent reality.

On the whole I would say that *Il nome della rosa* is mainly an innovative anti-detective novel; there is an original setting, a somehow parodic protodetective, a free use of conventional rules, which are transposed in a predetective fiction time, and even a social and ironical preoccupation with the portrayal of a medieval time which seems so close to our own in terms of struggles for power and the sense of crisis. The solution, although satisfying from a rational point of view, however, is partly casual and at the end the "detective" feels so discomforted as to state, very postmodernly: "I behaved stubbornly, pursuing a semblance of order, when I should have known well that there is no order in the universe."[42] At any rate, there is a solution; a culprit is found, although he is not directly responsible for all the deaths. Hence we have only a hint of the deconstructive anti-detective novel in William's postmodern awareness of the centerlessness of the universe, just as we have in *The Sunlight Dialogues*. Rather, there is a stronger accent on the metafictional aspect of anti-detective fiction since the book we read is, supposedly, the translation of a translation, the detection in the book mainly concerns a mysterious book that cannot be found, and the reader is often named and questioned by the narrator (Adso). So we have a "book conscious of its bookness" and an "intertextual detection," which remind one of Calvino's *Se una notte d'inverno un viaggiatore*. Calvino's novel and *Il nome della rosa* have in fact similar relationships between writers and readers outside and within the fiction: 1) writer (Eco) deviously writing (hiding the solution of) the text and real reader trying to make sense out of it (seeking the solution); 2) fictional "writer" (Jorge, the monk) hiding the book (the mysterious book whose content—poison—*is* the cause of the deaths and thus the solution of the mystery; hence Jorge hiding the book in the library actually corresponds to the writer hiding the solution of the text in the text) and two fictional "readers" (William and Adso) seeking it.[43]

The book hidden in the library-labyrinth as the solution of the text in the text is clearly a Borgesian parody, as it reminds us of Borges' "La biblioteca de Babel" ("The Library of Babel"),[44] in which, in a library-labyrinth crowded with indecipherable and perhaps meaningless volumes, men look for the "total book," which should be the key to all the other books, the solution. In a similar way, the lugubrious monk Jorge, as blind custodian of the book-solution, is also a parody of his illustrious namesake, Jorge Luis Borges, blind creator of erudite mysteries. In addition, it is worth noticing that the abbey is another good readaptation of the typical "microcosm-setting" (the countryside cottage) of the British mystery, while the "fireworks"-ending (the burning of the abbey) is a modern concession to the spectacular ending typical of the mass-media decadence of the irrational current (think of the usual apocalyptic ending of most James Bond movies, in which the secret lab-in-the-island-of-the-evil-scientist explodes while the scientist himself—Jorge in Eco's novel—perishes in the fire).

At the end of his narration of that week in November 1327, Adso remembers how, a long time after his adventure, he went back to visit the ruins of the burned monastery. As he searched among the debris of the labyrinthine library, he found shreds and fragments of parchment:

> [The fragments] had survived like treasures buried in the earth; I began to collect them, as if I were going to piece together the torn pages of a book. . . . [and now] I have almost . . . the impression that what I have written on these pages, which you will now read, unknown reader, is only a cento, a figured hymn, an immense acrostic that says and repeats nothing but what those fragments have

suggested to me, nor do I know whether thus far I have been speaking of them or they have spoken through my mouth.[45]

Thus the narration acquires at the end an even more composite, symbolical meaning, and becomes almost an archeological reconstruction of the (bookish) fragments of the past.

A text like *Il nome della rosa* prompts a few considerations: 1) A contemporary literary detective novel is almost necessarily an anti-detective novel, especially if its author is self-consciously aware of his place in the postmodern trend. Sometimes it has elements of all three of my categories, which blend and resist systematization. 2) I got through the 500 pages of Eco's novel because of its detective plot, because I wanted to know who the culprit was. The beautifully reconstructed medieval atmosphere, the brilliant philosophical discussions among the monks contributed to hold my interest, but my attention as a reader had its prime motive in the "whodunit," no matter how literary. 3) Only after I finished the novel and satisfied my curiosity did the novel start to assume a different aspect. Thinking again of it, I do not especially care for the detective features that "helped" me through its 500 pages (e.g., the mechanics of the plot, the detection, the suspense, that is, the looking forward to the solution) but, rather, for all the literary qualities that during my reading may have appeared collateral (e.g., the reconstruction of the Middle Ages' mentality, the atmosphere of the monastery, the characters, the brilliant writing, etc.) and that now become my main recollection of the novel. This is the difference between a conventional detective novel and a literary anti-detective novel: the former is finalized in the mechanics of plot and in the solution, and once read it is consumed and forgotten; the latter instead, is mainly a portrayal of characters and of social background,[46] is not finalized in the solution (that is partially inverted or totally eliminated), and thus, once read, is not yet consumed, forgotten as is the conventional detective novel. I could say that while in detective fiction end and solution coincide and the purpose of the work is in the last five pages, in the anti-detective novel the purpose is beyond the reading (the end of the novel) and the "solution" is the "working out," the assimilation of the novel's ingredients in the mind of the reader. Ultimately, the difference is the one between ingenuity (craft)[47] and creation (literature), which also implies craft but goes much beyond it.

4

The Deconstructive Anti-Detective Novel

In comparison with innovative anti-detective fiction, which undermines conventional detective fiction by arriving at solutions without justice and by social criticism, deconstructive anti-detective fiction is basically characterized by a more ambiguous perception of reality from the point of view of the detective. The detective is unable to impose a meaning, an interpretation of the outside occurrences he is asked, as a sleuth, to solve and interpret. Reality is so tentacular and full of clues that the detective risks his sanity as he tries to find a solution (Oedipa Maas in *The Crying of Lot 49*). At the end he (or she) quits sizing up clues and admits the mystery: he discovers that in the meanwhile, even if he has not found an objective solution, he has at least grown and understood something about his own identity. In a very Poesque way, the confrontation is no longer between a detective and a murderer, but between the detective and reality, or between the detective's mind and his sense of identity, which is falling apart, between the detective and the "murderer" in his own self.

Reality is ambiguous and devil-ridden; in his (or her) attempt to solve the mystery in it, the detective "splits," and we have again the creative and the resolvent sides of M. Dupin (the painter in *Todo modo*, Oedipa in *The Crying of Lot 49*, Favorite and Angel in *Falling Angel*). The detective creates, evokes the mystery more than solving it (Oedipa, Angel). If he solves it, he keeps the solution for himself, because, perhaps, he is the criminal, and his murder is strictly tied to his creativity. Perhaps it is an act of identity and the proof he exists in a corrupted and alien society (the painter in *Todo modo*). The detective tries to simplify the ambiguity of reality in an almost "medieval" way: reality is elusive, un-catchable, and thus bad, evil, actually devil-ridden. Strangely enough, the devil is quite similar to the detective himself, who sometimes gets rid of the "devil" (the painter and don Gaetano in *Todo modo*); or perhaps the devil is a projection of the detective's hallucinations (Oedipa Maas and the Tris-tero); or, ultimately, in a crescendo of abandonment to dark-ness, the devil does exist and tricks the detective, who has always been devil-ridden without knowing it (Angel).

In his vain quest for a solution, the detective discovers his double (the devil) and thus himself (the painter and don Gae-tano; Angel and Favorite). Detection becomes a quest for identity, which can be "solved," while the "outside mystery," reality, is never solved. For example, like Clumly in *The Sun-light Dialogues,* Oedipa grows and finds her identity thanks to her pursuit of the ambiguous identity of "mystery" (the Sun-light Man in *The Sunlight Dialogues,* Tristero in *The Crying of Lot 49*), which finally leads to human compassion (Clumly's "powerful sermon"; Oedipa hugging the old sailor with dt's). To accept the mystery "outside" somehow releases the mys-tery inside the detective. One could even say that white magic (the Sunlight Man), hypnosis (don Gaetano), an indistinct blurring between reality and hallucination (Tristero), black magic (Favorite), ultimately all the fantastic forms that mys-tery may assume, "refract" the detective's investigation from the mystery outside to the mystery inside his own person. Angel's discovery of the mystery inside himself is a disturbing one: he is possessed by the devil (his double, Johnny Favo-rite). The painter in *Todo modo* may kill the "devil" (his double, don Gaetano) and affirm his own identity but, in do-ing so, he seems to have become as inhuman as the devil himself. "Whoever fights monsters," writes Nietzsche, "should see to it that in the process he does not become a monster."[1] The painter becomes a monster through his possible victory over the devil (don Gaetano); Angel fights the monster (Cyphre, the devil) only to realize that he is a monster as well, since his soul belongs to Satan. His defeat makes him more human than devil-ridden, however, as he is painfully aware of being doomed.

The mystery of reality cannot be solved, so the detective must accept the mystery and its epitome, the prince of darkness, the devil. The irrational side of the Poesque duality reflourishes in contemporary anti-detective fiction.

In deconstructive anti-detective fiction, justice is not even an issue any more, since there is no solution. The social indictment I pointed out in the innovative category (*A ciascuno il suo*, *The Sunlight Dialogues*) may be still present (*Todo modo*), but it is overwhelmed by the pervading sense of a conspiracy of power and evil (*Todo modo*, *The Crying of Lot 49*, *Falling Angel*) against the detective (the painter, Oedipa, Angel) and what he stands for. The conspiracy cannot certainly be stopped by social criticism; thus the detective adequates himself to it (the painter), or gives herself up to it (Oedipa), or fights it and is defeated (Angel).

Leonardo Sciascia's
Todo modo

Proof of how flexible and various is the relationship between a writer and anti-detective fiction is *Todo modo* (1974), another novel by Leonardo Sciascia which falls into the kind I named "deconstructive" and shows that the same author can range from modification to subversion of the structure in his borrowing of detective fiction material. In the case of *Todo modo* I can use the term "deconstruction" because the traditional expectations of detective fiction are "taken apart," betrayed one by one: there is a teasing and progressively growing cluster of clues that leads us nowhere; the unfulfilled suspense we saw in *The Sunlight Dialogues* becomes in *Todo modo* suspension of the solution, that is, negation not only of justice (as it was in *A ciascuno il suo* and in *The Sunlight Dialogues*) but even of a logical denouement. All the reader can (and perhaps should not) do is to try compulsively to make sense out of the clues in a second reading of the novel and fabricate his own solution, not forgetting that, in doing so, he may end up reconstructing accidentally a "right solution" (but who could ever tell him that it is the right one?) out of casual "clues," as William of Baskerville did in *Il nome della rosa* or, worse, finding even a totally wrong solution in order to nurture in some way his now battered reassurance.

The words "todo modo" (from a corruption of Spanish and Latin, meaning "in all possible ways," "by all means") are from St. Ignatius of Loyola's prescription of spiritual exercises as "by all means" the best way to approach Catholicism—an unquestioning remittal to the divinity through penitence and meditation. As in *A ciascuno il suo,* the irony of the title is soon clear as the reader realizes that the novel is mainly about the ideological confrontation between an agnostic painter (the narrator of the story) and a worldly, brilliant priest, don Gaetano, who runs a monastery-hotel where the very unorthodox "spiritual exercises" are performed.

The novel opens as the painter (who never mentions his own name) is giving himself a vacation by driving randomly through Sicily, striving for a total freedom:

> [While I was driving I had] no uneasiness, no apprehension. Except the ones, obscure and irrepressible that I always had, about and because of life . . . but slight and slightly stunned ones, as if I were inside a *game of mirrors,* not obsessive but luminous and quiet as the time and the places which I was driving through, ready to repeat, to multiply, when would spring, when I would decide to let spring, *my act of freedom.*[2]

At an intersection he sees a sign: "Zafer's Hermitage, [kilometers] 3"; and, since the *two* words are followed by the number 3 and he is afflicted by a "small but stubborn . . . neurosis of trinities,"[3] he decides to stop and visit the place.

The painter is basically an alien who "understood the game" and accepts being integrated in the "industrial" business of art. Out of mere technique, he can paint two or three paintings per day and is rich and established. His submission to the hypocritical consumer society in which he plays the role of the artist, however, is "by all means" limited to practical advantages, and he preserves consequently some freedom from needs and routine. Thus he maintains the awareness of his compromise as well as a sort of detached ironical vision of society, power, and its games. He also exercises his rational detachment through a curious hobby: writing detective novels, which he publishes under a pseudonym.

Don Gaetano is another product of the compromise, the filtration of two thousand years of Christianity that, in order to survive, learned to reconcile opposites, often finding its drive just in denying the principles it was supposed to stand for. For example, don Gaetano says paradoxically that "the good priests are the bad ones. . . . It is behind the image of imperfection that the idea of perfection lives: the priest who violates sanctity or, in his way of living, even devastates it, actually confirms it, enhances it, serves it."[4]

His "hermitage" is the symbol of the collusion between power and religion, an ugly and luxurious hotel where Christian Democrats,[5] politicians, a state secretary, bank presidents, chief executives of state-run industries, and cardinals gather for a week during summer, using as their excuse the performing of "spiritual exercises" (retirement and meditation) under the guidance of don Gaetano. Of course, the spiritual exercises are "by all means" only a way to meet and divide even better the "pie of power": "They felt on vacation: but a vacation which allowed them to tie again fruitful relations, to hatch plots of power and wealth, to reverse alliances and return treasons."[6]

The painter approaches don Gaetano and asks him permission to stay for a couple of days, before the arrival of the first shift of powerful guests. (There are four summer shifts.) The permission is extended, and the painter remains and satisfies his curiosity about don Gaetano and about the unusual spiritual exercises performed at Zafer's hermitage. This is how the priest appears to him the first time:

> Tall in his long black gown, motionless; his eyes having a faraway look, staring and lost . . . his right hand big and almost diaphanous on the chest. He seemed not to see me, but he came towards me.

And still not seeing me, giving me the curious sensation, close to hallucination, that he was splitting visually, physically, in two halves—the one motionless, cold, properly unpleasant, which was rejecting me beyond the horizon of his stare; the other one full of fatherly benevolence, welcoming, fervent, thoughtful—welcomed me to Zafer's hermitage.[7]

As we saw from the inclusion of Poe's epigraph in *A ciascuno il suo* and from his articles, Sciascia knows Poe and detective fiction in general very well and here he shows he is well aware of the main theme in the genre, the theme of the double, to which he now connects a "problem of vision." Don Gaetano seems to have always a vitreous, absent look (which reminds me of "creative Dupin's" "vacant eyes")[8]and sometimes wears pince-nez glasses, which are exactly like the ones worn by the devil in a painting, "Tentazione di sant'Agostino" [Temptation of St.Augustine] by Rutilio Manetti, a bad copy of which is preserved in the crypt of the hermitage. The copy is by a Sicilian painter whose name is evocative of the devil, Buttafuoco [Flamethrower], and don Gaetano is "the copy of the copy," the ultimate replica of the devil, whose temptations in the twentieth century are no longer overt and threatening, but diluted and ambiguous. So too, the fascinating culture of don Gaetano and his wry taste for paradoxes are ambiguously tied with his manipulation of political and religious power. The devil's temptation of St. Augustine (of the legendary monk Zafer in the copy by Buttafuoco) is the offering of the pince-nez. They would enable the almost blind holy man to read without effort the Christian texts which, however, through the distortion of the devil's lenses, would turn into the Koran. The devil is thus connected with sight and distortion, two crucial points in the painting's craftmanship. In fact, don Gaetano always seems out of focus (a composition of doubles) and appears and disappears almost magically throughout the whole novel.

> Don Gaetano materialized on the threshold. But perhaps he was there before . . . when he [don Gaetano] had already left, his image persisted . . . so that it was impossible to distinguish the precise, real moment in which he went away. That was, altogether, an effect consequential to that kind of splitting into doubles I was trying to

describe. The fact is that being with him established something like a sphere of hypnosis. But it is hard to express such sensations.[9]

Don Gaetano's (the devil's) eyeglasses impress and disturb the painter so much that he finds himself drawing them: "[I]t came out a field of eyeglasses like watermelons: big, small, barely outlined, some without lenses, others with lenses; and some having the lifeless eyes of don Gaetano behind them."[10] As the devil proposes to Zafer, don Gaetano proposes to the painter a utilitarian and paradoxical "view" of Catholicism, but he does not convert him to his "optics"; rather; he establishes with him a complicity, as he subtly makes fun of the crass and stupid retainers of power, his guests, who are subjected to his manipulative charisma.

The ambiguous complicity that both the characters share with the Italian establishment (and, consequently, with power and success) certainly makes the complicity between the two of them easier, a complicity between two cynical and unconforming intelligences, both despising a hypocritical and obtuse ruling class. However, although the painter seems to have nothing (certainly neither faith nor moral principles) to lose in his collusion with don Gaetano, he is attracted and repelled by him at the same time. Perhaps out of intellectual hostility for a mind as brilliant as his own, if not more so, he continuously confronts the view (the "lenses") don Gaetano offers him.

Besides the embodiment of the theme expressed in the painting, the two characters represent a game of opposites having the same persona. Don Gaetano and the painter are in fact basically the same character, the cynical alien who is both victim and victimizer of a society he condemns and takes advantage of at the same time. Hence ambiguous complicity and compromise defile their nonconformity, which is ultimately ineffective.

The fruitful vacation at Zafer's Hermitage is upset by a murder that occurs when all the guests are saying the rosary at night, walking up and down the area in front of the hotel in a square-shaped formation led by don Gaetano. A gunshot kills an ex-senator, Michelozzi, who had become the chief executive of an important state-run industry. A police commissioner and the district attorney Scalambri (an old high-school mate of the painter) arrive and try to reconstruct the position of every single person in the square-shaped group. The aim of this attempt is to find out who could have left his position and sneaked close to Michelozzi in order to shoot him. Lawyer Voltrano says he has been on the left of Michelozzi who, in turn, was on the left of don Gaetano in the squared formation. The lawyer had "the impression that he didn't always have him [Michelozzi] at his side,"[11] that is, that someone slid in between, perhaps the killer. The next day Voltrano is found dead, thrown off a terrace from the eighth floor of Zafer's Hermitage. The district attorney and the painter-narrator of the story tease the reader with their hypotheses about the two murders. Perhaps Michelozzi, who, it is discovered, used to bribe almost all the guests in the hotel, had been killed by one of them over money, and Voltrano had pretended to know who the killer was, by saying he had been next to Michelozzi, in order to blackmail the killer. The night after the second murder, the painter goes to don Gaetano's room and talks with him. Back in his room, he draws a design he had promised to Scalambri:

> And thus, by drawing the nude for Scalambri, I developed an hypothesis that I had made after the first murder; I developed it, I mean, as Monsieur Charles Auguste Dupin develops his own in Poe's tales. While my hand and my eyes wandered on the sheet, my mind wandered on the ground in front of the hotel, a half-circle extending one hundred meters toward the woods. . . . I stopped drawing when it seemed to me I had solved the problem. Overdrawn, heavy and a bit tinseled, the design; but the solution of the problem precise and almost obvious: very similar to the one in "The Purloined Letter" by Poe. And postponing until tomorrow the verification [in the woods], I went to bed and fell asleep almost immediately.[12]

It is altogether normal for the detective-novel reader to know that the detective (in this case the painter) knows—or perhaps will know before the reader does in the detective's fair competition with him—the solution of the case; but here the situation is much more frustrating, since the reader is not going to share with the detective any solution in the last pages of the novel. The reader is tantalized in vain.

The next day the painter goes "to do the research which [he] had designed, so to speak, the day before."[13] Then he has lunch with don Gaetano, Scalambri, the commissioner, the state secretary, and the bank president:

> [The state secretary and the bank president] laughed. They were still laughing when we left the table.
>
> I went back to the hotel in the late afternoon; and proceeded directly to my room, because I had an idea about the Christ [the drawing] I had promised to don Gaetano. Not exactly promised: but by now I could consider it a promise to keep.[14]

After he has been drawing for a couple of hours, he is informed that don Gaetano has been found killed in the woods, lying against a stone of the old ruined mill, in the place where the priest had had a conversation with him after the first murder. The narrator goes there:

> It did not greatly impress me to see him again dead. Death, which confers solemnity even upon fools, had subtracted some from don Gaetano . . . one's eye, at least mine, lingered then on the glasses which, from the string tied to his chest, had slid on a root and stayed there in a curious angulation in relation with a ray of sunlight that, among the leaves, fell on them . . . At a short distance from his left hand, there was a handgun, a revolver.[15]

The district attorney seals the hotel in order to avoid other murders. Scalambri, the painter, and the commissioner try to reconstruct who could have possibly reached don Gaetano in the woods and killed him when all the exits of the hotel were watched by policemen. Scalambri concludes:

> "Now, you see: the policeman [watching the door] must have fallen asleep . . . when the assassin sneaked out. There is no other explanation, if we want to remain within the limits of reality, of common sense. If we want to go beyond it, we can arrive where we want: we can even think that one of the three of us [Scalambri, the commissioner, the painter]. . . . Here: you [the commissioner] say you stayed here, to take a nap; but you are the one who says it. . . . And you—to me [the narrator, the painter]—you say you went. . . . Where did you say you went?"
>
> "To kill don Gaetano"—I [the painter] said.
>
> "You see where one ends up, when he leaves the road of common sense?"—said Scalambri triumphantly—you, myself, and the commissioner become as liable to suspicion as these crooks [the guests of

the hotel], and even more: and without being able to impute to ourselves a reason, a motive . . . I always say it, dear commissioner, always: the motive is what must be found, the motive . . . [16]

As suggested by the three ellipsis points suspending his discourse, Scalambri's words linger ominously. In fact suspense remains, as the next paragraph concluding the novel is a long quotation from André Gide's *Les caves du Vatican,* which is, at first sight, far from giving any solution.

As we will see also for *The Crying of Lot 49,* any deconstructive anti-detective novel's open-ended nonsolution, if well worked out, leaves the reader with a proliferation of clues, allowing him to fabricate one or more possible denouements. This is a way to leave the novel "alive" (nonconsumed), an object of curiousity even after the end, since a plausible solution imposed by the reader implies a rereading or rethinking, in which the artistic qualities of the novel finally stand out. Thus open-endedness proves to be a means of planting the anti-detective novel's message more firmly in the mind of the reader than a conventional detective novel would. After the first moment of frustration, it is enjoyable to find a way through the proliferation of clues by tracing a possible solution. In my case, I do it because it fits with some ideas about the detective-criminal duality and with symbols in anti-detective fiction that I previously mentioned.

When the district attorney decided to close the hotel, he says he does it because "if we all go on staying here . . . we would end up as in that novel by Agatha Christie [*And Then There Were None*]:[17] all dead, one after the other. And we should resurrect one to find the culprit."[18] This is indeed an interesting clue, which dumb Scalambri gives without knowing it himself, or the sly I-narrator puts in his mouth. In fact I do think that the culprit (or, better, one of the two culprits) is dead by the end of *Todo modo.* The painter also mentions another significant detective story: "The Purloined Letter" by Poe.[19] An Agatha Christie novel that would also be worth mentioning is *The Murder of Roger Ackroyd.*[20] In fact many clues lead to the possibility of the I-narrator as murderer, as I may have already implied through my use of quotations from the novel. The reference to "The Purloined Letter" is an important lead. The final solution is "too obvious to be seen" as in Poe's story; the assassin of don Gaetano is in fact the narrator.

In *Todo modo,* as in *The Crying of Lot 49,* there is a proliferation of clues that also may be used to prove different solutions (or to confuse the reader totally). The following reconstruction more than others, however, fulfills patterns I am concerned with (the duality of detective and murderer; the mirror and the map patterns) and seems to fit with most of the otherwise obscure hints given by the I-narrator (e.g., the final quotation from *Les caves du Vatican*).

I can now try to explain the facts by piecing together the information I have. When the painter draws at night, he has an "epiphany" concerning the gun don Gaetano used to kill Michelozzi and which, of course, had not yet been found. As he is drawing and mentally exploring the ground in front of the hotel,[21] the narrator understands that the gun had been hidden by don Gaetano close to a stone belonging to a ruined old mill. In fact, on the day after the first murder, he had run into don Gaetano in the woods in front of the hotel, and the priest was sitting just over the old mill stone. The next morning the painter goes "to do the research which I had designed, so to speak, the day before,"[22] that is, he goes to retrieve the revolver. He then has lunch with Scalambri, the commissioner, don Gaetano, the state secretary, and the bank president.

[The state secretary and the bank president] laughed. They were still laughing when we [don Gaetano and I?] left the table. I went back to the hotel in *the late afternoon;* and proceeded directly to my room, because I had an idea about the Christ [the drawing] I had promised to don Gaetano. Not exactly promised; but *by now* I could consider it a promise to keep.[23]

What is peculiar in this passage is that the painter-narrator fails to tell the reader what he (and don Gaetano, if they leave the table together) did from lunch time to "the late afternoon." I could assume that the painter still carried the gun he had retrieved in the morning. Perhaps he took a walk with don Gaetano (who, along with the painter, Scalambri, and the commissioner was one of the four persons who could go freely out of the hotel watched by the police) and went "casually" just where he had found the pistol, to the old mill stone. There he killed don Gaetano and left the revolver next to him.[24] His "obsession for trinities" was finally fulfilled since three persons had by now been killed, and he could even playfully "confess" don Gaetano's murder to the dumb district attorney when the occasion presented itself. One clue is that, after killing don Gaetano, the I-narrator draws a crucifix "because I had an idea about the Christ I had promised to don Gaetano. Not exactly promised; but *by now* I could consider it a promise to keep."[25] The "by now" may be a macabre joke, which implies that don Gaetano "by now" is dead; the idea for the crucifix the painter wants to draw concerns of course a dead man, don Gaetano himself. The promise is kept *ad memoriam*. This interpretation is supported by the fact that the narrator's language goes on being ambiguous afterwards: "It did not greatly impress me to see him *again* dead."[26] This may mean two things: either, quite innocently, "to see him again and to see him dead," or "to see him dead for the second time (again, since I am the one who killed him)."

At the beginning of the novel the painter describes his wanderings by car as waiting for the moment in which to fulfill "an act of freedom,"[27] which the murder of don Gaetano may very well be. In this light, the final quotation from *Les caves du Vatican* (1914) could in fact emphasize the painter's murder of don Gaetano as an act of nihilistic freedom from the establishment, just as is the case with Lafcadio's gratuitous murder in Gide's *Les caves du Vatican*. However, I can also find psychological reasons for the killing: it would ideally be the murder of a "double," of someone who "[splits] visually, physically, in two halves,"[28] and has basically the same persona as the painter. In fact they are both cynical aliens, and also the painter is a "duality," if not at a visual, certainly at a mental level. He figures out the first murder (where the pistol is hidden and who used it) "by drawing the nude for Scalambri,"[29] and thus he is "creative" ("while my hand and my eyes wandered on the sheet")[30] and "resolvent" ("my mind wandered on the ground in front of the hotel")[31] like Dupin. It is worth noticing that the "mapping" of a solution (we saw how solution is equal to "map" in some anti-detective novels) actually occurs during the drawing of a design and that, at the beginning of the novel, the painter mentions his "act of freedom" as "inside a game of mirrors."[32] In this case the mirror foreshadows the double of the painter, don Gaetano, whose eyeglasses are symbolic of distortion and are an exact replica of those of the devil. Thus don Gaetano's eyeglasses link him to the devil and "justify" the mortal conclusion of the conflict always latent between the two doubles who attract and repel each other (think also of Poe's "William Wilson"). The murder is an "act of freedom . . . inside a game of mirrors [doubles],"[33] that is, freedom from the "devil," don Gaetano, who is a murderer himself, and from a disturbing double. Don Gaetano could have easily killed Michelozzi, who was on his left during the rosary, because of some money matters, and subsequently hid the revolver in the woods. Voltrano, who was on the left of Michelozzi, could have seen the fact and baited don Gaetano by saying publicly to the district attorney that he had had "the impression that he didn't always have him [Michelozzi] at his side."[34] Significantly, the day after the first murder, the painter and don Gaetano run into each other near the old mill stone (where perhaps don Gaetano had just hidden the gun) and don Gaetano, talking with the painter, uncannily foreshadows the second murder:

> "Here you [the painter] go again, coming back to the words which decide, to the words which divide: best, worst; right, wrong; white, black. And everything instead is only a *fall,* a long *fall:* as in dreams. . . ."—The last word lingered, as if absorbed by the air, by the trees, by myself: thus when I found myself alone, stunned, sitting on that round stone, it seemed to me I had been surprised for a moment by sleep and that I had dreamed; and perhaps for more than one moment.[35]

We saw before how don Gaetano's eyes have a strange hypnotizing power,[36] such as to leave a person stunned and dreamy for a while. When the painter "wakes up" and goes back, the fall don Gaetano was talking about has already occurred. During their meeting to set the price of the blackmailing, Voltrano has been pushed by don Gaetano off the terrace.

The painter is well aware of writing a manuscript that one day may be read and used for or against him: "Whoever reads this manuscript or, if it is ever published, this book, will ask himself at this point why I have mentioned don Gaetano's eyeglasses no more."[37] The painter is a typical "unreliable narrator" and, as such, stresses something and hides something else. That he does not tell us his name in the story possibly implies that he does not want us to know his identity since he is aware we may understand he is the killer of don Gaetano and that he is considering publishing the manuscript as an unusual detective novel under his pen name. At any rate, the painter is an ambiguous, mysterious character who has no name and all names, as does the devil, as we will see in *The Crying of Lot 49* (Tristero) and in *Falling Angel* (Cyphre).

It is no accident that the reader of *Todo modo* finds it difficult to sympathize with the narrator. In fact, the painter is more an anti-detective than a detective as he hides too much (his name, the solution) from the reader, so that one naturally suspects him and sees him as a wicked presence. For example, the eyeglasses as don Gaetano's connection with the devil provide a tantalizing "clue" throughout the fiction. They are mentioned even in the scene describing don Gaetano's corpse,[38] but they do not really seem to lead anywhere, unless we accept the fantastic connection and thus believe that don Gaetano is really the devil, as the narrator subtly implies, probably to justify his murder. Glasses play a role also in the innovative anti-detective novel *Il nome della rosa,* in which William of Baskerville is the owner of one of the first pairs of glasses. A monk wonders if they are a "diabolical machination,"[39] and William explains that there is diabolical magic and divine magic, and glasses belong to the latter. Still, glasses, the new invention, are even here associated, although by contrast, with the devil. In *Il nome della rosa,* however, the symbolical role of glasses is more clear-cut and less tantalizing than in *Todo modo*: William loses them during one of his secret visits in the library at night (that is, when he fumbles through the mystery) and finds them at the end, when he finds the solution. In *Il nome della rosa* glasses are a form of "mirror," a "reflection" of the solution, while in *Todo modo* they only reflect the duality of their owner.

We saw that an unfulfilled suspense-building process was typical also of *The Sunlight Dialogues,* whose main character, the Sunlight Man, shares some affinity with don Gaetano and the painter in *Todo modo.* The Sunlight Man appears and disappears "magically" as don Gaetano does; he is a murderer as (perhaps) the painter is and a well-read alien who loves paradoxes as both of them do. But, while the Sunlight Man wants justice, neither don Gaetano nor the painter (nor Laurana in *A ciascuno il suo*) are interested in justice at all; they are aliens far beyond any civil commitment. Indeed, no one better questions conventional detective novels and the society they represent than the alien. In fact, the alien is a misfit who fights society's rules, the ideal focus of that process of innovation or subversion typical of anti-detective novels.

In this light, the ending of *Todo modo,* in which the district attorney stresses the necessity of a motive in order to find the murderer, is particularly ironical. It is impossible to find a conventional solution because there is no conventional motive behind the third murder, since it has been committed by an alien, the painter, as an act of nihilistic freedom from the establishment. Even in this case, however, the murder of don Gaetano could be considered an affirmation, a positive act against the ambiguity of compromise with power epitomized by the priest and his "hermitage." Quite significantly, the novel ends as the monastery is closed and the corrupted representatives of power it contained are at least dispersed, if not defeated. In *Il nome della rosa* the monastery burns down when, at the end of the novel, William and Adso discover that Jorge is the culprit. Solution (disclosure) and destruction in that novel contrast with what is here nonsolution and "closure" (of the solution, of the monastery). In both novels the monastery settings also emphasize by contrast the unexpected corruption they contain, while the correspondence between days and murders stresses a playfully logical detective novel structure (seven-day-long action and seven murders in *Il nome della rosa;* three-day-long action and three murders in *Todo modo,* in which the painter, also, has "a neurosis of trinities"),[40] which is respectively undermined or deconstructed by the partial or total suspension of the solution.

Todo modo's peculiar structure becomes an implicit cry for what is conspicuously missing in its plot: justice. In fact, while in the conventional detective novel "justice" was implied in the solution and never stood out in the fiction, here the suspension of the solution leaves the lack of justice and the related mechanisms of power and corruption standing bare and unpunished in a "decapitated structure," so that they become the real theme and purpose of the fiction.

Thomas Pynchon's *The Crying of Lot 49*

Strangely, none of the many essays devoted to *The Crying of Lot 49* (1966) addresses one of its more strikingly obvious characteristics, its being a detective or, more widely, a mystery novel. I say mystery novel because the main point of the novel is the attempt at unraveling a mystery (what is the Tristero, or even is there a Tristero?) rather than the solving of a murder. It also can be considered a detective novel, however, since death is quite present in the fiction (the plot of the novel is "started" by an unexpected death—Inverarity's—and an unclear suicide—Driblette's—is part of it) and an amateur detective is its main character, as in *A ciascuno il suo* and in *Todo modo.*

Oedipa Maas, the protagonist of *The Crying of Lot 49,* is not the usual detective, but simply a California housewife. Like Laurana, she finds herself involved and caught rather unwillingly in a detecting process. Signs (the *unicuique suum* for Laurana, Tristero's silent horn for Oedipa) "attack" the detective's eye, demand to be deciphered, to be given life through connection (detection), so the detective becomes a "reluctant artist." She, in this case, knows in advance that knowledge will give her only trouble but nevertheless performs the investigation. As in Laurana's case, Oedipa's detection becomes compulsive and dangerous, yet, unlike Laurana's, it is linked to her need to create. She cannot help seeing Tristero's horns everywhere and making the relative connections ("I want to see if there is a connection. I'm curious.");[41] perhaps she cannot help seeing everything in terms of Tristero's clues, even when the clues are not there because, once the chain of detection has been started, she cannot abandon the quest for harmony and coherence. Mystery expects to be solved. It is linked with the detective's unconscious and with his (or her) longing, repressed and battered in everyday life, for creativity.

Tristero is Oedipa's "monstrous baby"; she does not want it, although its existence grows into her as she goes on collecting new information by talking to men connected with it. But the men disappear one by one, "take a Brody" walk into the Ocean (Randolph Driblette—but is it really a suicide?), fade and die off in a nursing home (Mr. Thoth), hang up on her (the Inamoratus Anonymous), and she feels so nauseated and yet tied to "her creature" that she thinks she is actually pregnant.[42] However, her pregnancy is not a real one, not the result of fertility, but rather the effect, first, of her rejecting a sterile housewife routine and second, of the sense of void and desperation she experiences when she realizes there is no way to solve the mystery of Tristero: "That night she sat for hours, too numb even to drink, teaching herself to breathe in a vacuum. For this, oh God, was the void. There was nobody who could help her. Nobody in the world."[43]

When the novel opens, she is "pregnant" with emptiness and lack of communication, ripe for attempting a change. Thus it is inevitable that her detective quest is going to be for communication. The quest for Tristero becomes "her creature" in a positive way when she hugs the old sailor with dt's.[44] Communication is, however, a very ambiguous business, and Tristero's ambiguous communication is projected even in the two lections of its name (Tristero and Trystero) recurring throughout the fiction. At first sight simply an alternative mailing system, Tristero turns out to be an indefinable and omnipresent entity. Sometimes it seems a bond of brotherhood among outcasts, aliens, desperate people, some sort of Salvation Army for the ones beyond hope; at other times it seems definitely diabolical, a murderous "octopus" that controls everything even more ruthlessly than the corporations of the establishment (e.g., Yoyodyne). The children chanting at night in Golden Gate Park "Tristoe, Tristoe, one, two, three, Turning taxi from across the sea . . ."[45] have something more ominous and devil-ridden in the perverted innocence of the tantalizing clue they offer than the swift and silent killers in "The Courier's Tragedy." If W.A.S.T.E. means "we await silent Tristero's empire," the question is what kind of communication that "silent" implies. Nothing appealing: perhaps annihilation, domination (empire), regression into darkness. A collusion with the Mafia is hinted in the GI men's bones transaction between Tony Jaguar (belonging to Cosa Nostra) and a firm connected with Pierce Inverarity, whose properties are all linked with Oedipa's discovery of the Tristero. As an alternative mailing system probably related to the financial empire of a deceased tycoon, Tristero constitutes along with a "state within the state," a conspiracy slowly taking over both the offical mailing system and America itself. In fact, Inverarity, by his real estate speculations, amassed so much property that to Oedipa he seems to have planned to take over the whole country. In Sciascia's *A ciascuno il suo* this silent and progressive takeover of the state was the typical Mafia method, thus it is no accident that in *The Crying of Lot 49* a connection between Tristero and Cosa Nostra is suggested.

While in *A ciascuno il suo* Laurana's investigation starts with a clue from the communication industry, Oedipa has communication itself, usually the medium of detection, as the object of her detection. Besides, like *A ciascuno il suo* (the minatory letter), *The Crying of Lot 49* opens with the arrival of a letter naming Oedipa executrix of the Inverarity estate. She receives the news in her living room, "stared at by the greenish dead eye of the TV tube,"[46] an unreliable means of communication. Normally the detective finds out the truth through communication, by talking with suspects and witnesses, but here communication is the center of mystification. In her conversations with Fallopian, Driblette, Koteks, Nefastis, Thoth, Cohen, the Inamoratus Anonymous, Oedipa is perhaps hallucinating, trying to see something that is not there, as "coincidences [were] blossoming these days wherever she looked."[47] She may be the victim of her attempt at creation, of her "growing obsession with 'bringing something of herself' . . . to the scatter of business interests that has survived Inverarity."[48]

Certainly there is a connection between Oedipa's detecting effort and her possible pregnancy ("waves of nausea . . . would strike her at random . . . she thought she was pregnant")[49] as well as between her need to create and her involvement with the Inverarity estate. Ultimately, Oedipa is "pregnant" with Inverarity. In fact, by dying and by nominating her as his executrix (out of a whim or a plot) he asked her to "recreate" him, to make him live again in her necessary detection. He passed on to her a legacy and compelled her to look into something, his assets, inextricably tangled with America and with the Tristero. Everything used "against" Oedipa to make her believe in the Tristero is owned by Inverarity; this everything is the American life-style (colleges, skycrapers, freeways, land, residential complexes), but reshaped and recreated according to the will of a man. By his legacy Inverarity passes on to Oedipa a painful knowledge; he hurts her, but makes of her an artist and a detective at the same time. In fact, she has to be "creative" and "resolvent," that is, to inject into the legacy her longing for communication (harmony) and to reconstruct its tangled assets as well. She is a particular kind of artist (*"Shall I project a world?"*[50] she wonders) since she works on the material of another dead "artist," Inverarity, who tries to create through possession, while she tries to create through understanding. As Inverarity's creation is all external (owning and transforming what he owns), Oedipa's is all internal. She struggles to create harmony through mental connections, cunning, gut feelings.

Oedipa tries to make things true by seeing through them, as

Pierce Inverarity's name explains and "compels" her to do (to pierce=to pass through; *inverare* in Italian=to make true). From Everywoman laying her lasagna, she fulfills her existential quest and finally becomes Oedipa in a chronological inversion of the myth. She is first blind and then she "sees through"; she first gets her "father" 's legacy and then "kills" him by achieving an awareness and a human compassion (the sailor's episode) that very likely Inverarity had not planned for her, if anything had actually been planned. Oedipa's compassion and potential for creation grow along with her new knowledge of the world. Her journey is from the N.A.D.A. of the car lots to the W.A.S.T.E. of the silent horn in the attempt to reach another lot, lot 49. During the journey, meanings and communication get more and more ambiguous. While we easily know that N.A.D.A. (National Automobile Dealer's Association) is ultimately "nothingness," annihilation by consumerism and mechanical routine, we are in doubt about W.A.S.T.E., which is threatening and mystical at the same time. When we get to lot 49, the possibilities are even wider; they range from the gold rush prosperity of California's forty-niners to a lot with a number evocative of prison camps or of those car lots haunting Oedipa's husband, Mucho, which we thought we left behind forever. The result is open-endedness, suspension of the solution; Oedipa the artist and the postmodern detective quits sizing up clues and accepts mystery as her story "ends" as it started, with five words that are also the title. Circularity emphasizes the fact that suspense remains; our only progress is that we finally know what the five words superficially mean, what the title means. Yet, we do not know what is (or if there is) the Tristero behind the crying of lot 49.

In *The Crying of Lot 49* there is a structural nonsolution (the open-endedness) and an emotional solution (Oedipa's growth to maturity and compassion). From a structural point of view the novel, at the end, leaves quite a few possibilities open. Actually, like in Sciascia's *Todo modo*, in *The Crying of Lot 49* the reader is tantalized by a proliferation of clues that lead nowhere. The novel disappoints the reader's expectations and deconstructs conventional detective fiction by denying its main characteristics: the denouement, the consequent triumph of justice, the detective's detachment (Oedipa goes as far as questioning her own sanity). The tension between the reader and the novel—namely, the tension from detection to solution—is increased in comparison with traditional detective fiction, since inconsequential clues are often much more tantalizing than the ones that eventually fall neatly into place. John Gardner's technique in *The Sunlight Dialogues* was to create "islands" of unfulfilled suspense, but to supply a logical denouement at the end in which, however, justice did not triumph.

In *The Crying of Lot 49,* suspense is obtained not by aborted thriller-like episodes, but rather by an overrichness of clues leading nowhere and by an interplay between the novel and the Jacobean revenge play in the novel. In fact *The Courier's Tragedy* sometimes "mirrors" episodes in the novel (the GI men's slaughter at Lago di Pietà corresponds to the slaughter of Faggio's Lost Guard in the play) and supplies Oedipa a first historical evidence of Tristero's existence. The reader may even hopefully think that *The Courier's Tragedy* is the key to a solution. (At least I got that far.) Rather, the play as a fiction within the fiction whose text Oedipa hunts throughout the novel supplies also a metafictional dimension to the primary deconstructive focus of *The Crying of Lot 49.* The novel concerns a system (Tristero) within a system (US mail) as well, and emphasizes repetition through "superimposition." For example, Lago di Pietà is the setting of two massacres: the GI men in World War II and the Torre and Tassis' coachmen in the sixteenth century. Thus the same thing (a massacre) happens in the same place (Lago di Pietà) or in similar settings such as lakes. In the fiction a slaughter occurred near the lake (now the Fangoso Lagoon) where the Wells Fargo men were killed by Tristero in 1853 and another one near the lake in which the corpses of Faggio's Lost Guard were then dumped by Angelo in *The Courier's Tragedy.*

Superimposition is a matter of communication as well: the GI men got killed because they could not communicate with the rest of the US troops; Tristero kills the Torre and Tassis' couriers and the Wells Fargo men to gain the monopoly on communication. In turn, communication is linked with a system (the US mail system, the Tristero system, Yoyodyne) which is the victim (US mail) or the organizer of a conspiracy (Tristero), or both (Yoyodyne). In fact Yoyodyne workers run both the corporation's space communication project and an illicit postal microsystem that takes advantage of a corporational facility, the Yoyodyne internal mail service, by using it for private communication at The Scope bar after working hours.

The ambiguous relationship between systems and conspiracy is mirrored in the private relationship between the detective as a "system" and the outside world, which "conspires" against Oedipa through the proliferation of clues and indecipherable signs. In fact, Oedipa herself is a "system," a human system striving for mental harmony and understanding, which are inherent and irrepressible human needs. Like the actual systems (US mail, Yoyodyne, Tristero), she may be either the victim or the (unaware) organizer of her private conspiracy, or both, as we do not discover whether she is "fantasizing." Thus *The Crying of Lot 49* remains in the realm of total illusion, open-endedness in strict terms even more than "nonsolution." On the contrary, *Todo modo* gives clues for a reconstruction which explains the mystery of the three murders. I could say that, proceeding from *The Crying of Lot 49* to *Todo modo* and then to *Falling Angel,* there is a progression from total ambiguity to explainable ambiguity and, finally, in *Falling Angel,* to no ambiguity at all, just plain irrationality. In fact *Falling Angel* is ultimately a "marvelous" novel, as it presupposes the acceptance of supernatural intervention (the devil); instead, *The Crying of Lot 49* leaves all the ways open. Any of the four possibilities Oedipa contemplates (the Tristero is real; she is hallucinating; the Tristero is only a plot mounted against her; she is fantasizing such a plot out of persecution mania)[51] may be true, and none of them is "marvelous," that is, none of them implies the intervention of supernatural elements.[52] Of course, I could call into question also an element hardly considered

before for *The Crying of Lot 49*—the omniscient third-person
narrator. "Thomas Pynchon," the reader would reply. But if,
instead of considering the narrator as outside the novel, I
consider him as part of the novel, one would spontaneously
think of Tristero as the narrator. Who else could know everything about Oedipa's actions if not he who set up the plot to
drive her crazy? All the tantalizing coincidences of *The Crying of Lot 49* in this way finally would be explained and even
the nonsolution would become the preliminary to an execu-
tion ("The men inside the auction room wore black mohair
and had pale, cruel faces. . . . Loren Passerine, on his po-
dium, hovered like a puppet-master, his eyes bright, his smile
practiced and relentless. . . . Passerine spread his arms in a
gesture that seemed to belong to the priesthood of some
remote culture")[53]—Oedipa's. To accept this possibility would
clarify and include within the fiction the role of an apparently
outside element, the omniscient narrator. Were Tristero to be
considered the narrator, he would be, like the author Thomas
Pynchon, omniscient in the sense that he created the situation, the developments of the basic plot; he put Oedipa
through a trial to test her and he spied her reactions. In this
sense Thomas Pynchon (the real, mysterious author) and
Tristero (the fictional, mysterious "author") are almost the
same person, and it is that tantalizing "almost" between them
that makes Pynchon's authorship a masterpiece. But even in
this case I have no foolproof evidence; rather, I develop a
combination of two out of the four possibilities offered
throughout the fiction (Tristero is real and he mounted a plot
against Oedipa).

Actually, Oedipa strives to reach a middle choice, to break
down these binary either/or, saved/damned alternatives that the
four possibilities give her, but, ultimately, she grows to maturity
because she cannot reach a middle choice. She learns to accept
nonchoice, the mystery, and to live with it: "Next day, with the
courage you find you have when there is nothing more to lose,
she [decided to attend the auction]."[54]

Thus Oedipa affirms herself as a human detective when she

goes to the auction and faces a mystery that ranges from total mistake and defeat (hallucination, fantasy) to total truth and victory (the Tristero is real, or is a plot mounted against her), and the final destiny of her system (her life, her search for harmony) remains as suspended and "eternal" as the open-endedness of her fiction and of the human condition.

William Hjortsberg's
Falling Angel

William Hjortsberg's [55] *Falling Angel* (1978) adds a fantastic dimension to deconstructive anti-detective fiction by developing characteristics that exist subtly in *The Crying of Lot 49* (1966) and in *Todo modo* (1974), such as a demonic presence in the novel (don Gaetano in *Todo modo;* Tristero in *The Crying of Lot 49*) and a conspiracy possibly organized against the detective (*The Crying of Lot 49*). Voodoo, black magic, inexplicable murders, and an interesting elaboration of the Oedipus myth and of the detective-criminal duality make this novel particularly entertaining and rich in surprises.

Hjortsberg attempts successfully to fuse two genres, the hard-boiled detective novel and the contemporary horror novel, which often deals with satanic cults and black magic (e.g., William Peter Blatty's *The Exorcist,* 1971: Stephen King's *Carrie,* 1974). In my first chapter I placed the hard-boiled detective novel on the "irrational" (popular and adventurous) side of detective fiction, since I saw it as opposed to the intellectual and static British "rational" detective novel. Since hard-boiled detective fiction provides a detection and a solution, however, it should be considered partly "rational," because it is counterposed to the irrationality of the underworld of magic, the modern version of Gothicism. The rational and the irrational clash and merge in *Falling Angel,* and the solution makes sense only if we accept an irrational premise: the devil exists and operates among us.

New York City provides a realistic and credible setting for

both the hard-boiled detection and the black magic in which private eye Harry Angel finds himself involved as he tries to trace Johnny Favorite, a crooner who vanished during World War II. Significantly, the action ominously unfolds from Friday, March 13th, 1959, to Palm Sunday, the 22nd: for Harry Angel it is not Christ who triumphantly enters Jerusalem on Palm Sunday but, rather, the devil.

The man who wants Angel to find Favorite is the elegant Louis Cyphre, who stipulated a contract with the singer back in the early forties: "I [Louis Cyphre] hope you won't consider me entirely mercenary when I tell you that my continuing interest in Jonathan Liebling [the real name of the singer which, translated from the German, is just Johnny Favorite] concerns only our contractual arrangement . . . All that mattered was whether he was alive or dead."[56] It is easy to recognize even in the physical description of Louis Cyphre a modern version of the devil:

> His hair was black and full, combed straight back on his high fore-
> head, yet his square-cut goatee and pointed moustache were white
> as ermine. He was tanned and elegant; his eyes a distant, ethereal
> blue. . . . Cyphre tapped his glass with a manicured finger. . . . It
> was easy to imagine those pampered hands gripping a whip. Nero
> must have had such hands. And Jack the Ripper. It was the hand of
> emperors and assassins. Languid, yet lethal, the cruel, tapered
> fingers perfect instruments of evil.[57]

Angel's nightmares and some clues cleverly planted through the novel prepare for the double revelation: the elusive Louis Cyphre is the devil, and Harry Angel is, quite unawares, the new identity of the idol of the early forties, Johnny Favorite. In a very Faustian way, the "contractual arrangement" concerns Favorite's soul, which the singer sold to the devil for stardom, and, of course, the many murders in the novel are the devil's job.

Newsweek's and *The New York Times*' reviews devoted to *Falling Angel* seemed to emphasize that "the ending, with its transformation of identities and its occult implications, is unexpected."[58] Rather, it seems to me that Hjortsberg gives the game away much before the end through Angel's nightmares.

The first is about a menacing double;[59] in the second Angel is executed in a French revolution setting (Cyphre seems to betray a French origin) by a phonily smiling Johnny Favorite, and Cyphre is part of the "audience";[60] in the third Cyphre mauls and makes love to Angel's new girl friend, Epiphany Proudfoot.[61] In the fourth, "Louis Cyphre laughed and hurled the dripping heart of his victim high into the air. The victim was me."[62] Angel suffers his last nightmare the night after having discovered Margaret Krusemark, Favorite's longtime fiancée, murdered in her apartment, her chest slashed and her heart "resting in the basin of a tall bronze Hellenic tripod."[63] Other significant hints are that Angel remembers "only blurred snapshots from the past,"[64] namely, that he was an adopted child (like Favorite), was wounded as a soldier in World War II in Algeria, went through shell shock and amnesia, was hospitalized and subjected to intensive plastic surgery (like Favorite). On New Year's Eve of 1942 he was in Times Square, just after he had been released from the army hospital.

In the last pages of the novel, we learn what happened that night in Times Square. Favorite picked up Angel, drugged him in a bar, killed him, and, after a black magic ritual, fed the corpse to the dogs and himself ate Angel's heart, thereby gaining possession of Angel's soul. Through a new soul, Favorite thought to get out of his deal with the devil, "drop out of sight when he had a chance and resurface as the soldier."[65] This seems to be a flaw in the plot or a remarkable lacuna in Favorite's knowledge of satanism, since it is commonly known that the devil is omniscient and omnipresent, and cannot be tricked like a normal human being. Luck (the devil?), however, did not assist Favorite. Sent to World War II as a soldier, he was wounded and went through shell shock and plastic surgery just as the dead Harry Angel did; amnesia made him forget his identity and his new soul. His fiancée Margaret Krusemark and her father Ethan, a wealthy shipowner who practiced black magic, took him out of the hospital where he was, at least physically, recovering, and on New Year's Eve of 1943 dropped him in Times Square, where he had picked up the soldier Harry

Angel exactly one year before. "It was the starting point, the last place the soldier remembered before Johnny drugged him,"[66] explains Ethan Krusemark at the end of the novel to an aghast Harry Angel. It was also the last place Johnny himself remembered since, being under shock and having the soldier's soul, at that point he was also the soldier, Harry Angel. Margaret and her father left him there, deeming it the best way to have the transmutation of souls fulfilled in a total switching of identities, and naïvely hoping that the devil would not recognize Favorite, who had at that moment both a new soul and a brand-new face. The contrived corresponding memories of Times Square (even the name of the place is symbolic) and of their actually similar pasts blurred in the confused mind of Johnny Favorite-Harry Angel, who on New Year's Eve of 1943 saw the lights on in the Crossroads Detective Agency office and "played a hunch which led [him] to . . . a job which [he] never left."[67]

The fact that the reader can guess relatively easily, through the nightmares and other hints, that Angel and Favorite are the same person and Cyphre is the devil tells us that an opaque detective plot was not Hjortsberg's main preoccupation in writing the novel. One could even consider *Falling Angel* a spoof, a crafty parody of hard-boiled and horror novels and nothing more. I would say, rather, that Hjortsberg uses a detective plot to bring out some elements implicit in conventional detective fiction and, even more, in anti-detective fiction: the existential quest, the duality of detective and criminal, the concept of time, the Oedipus myth, and the latent irrationality of the genre. He enforces these characteristics by playing them against a "satanic" metropolitan environment, which supplies the detective quest with an unsettling dimension absent in the metropolitan environment *tout court* typical of the conventional hard-boiled detective novel.

Hjortsberg innovates the hard-boiled tradition by energizing it with magic. The existential quest typical, for example, of Philip Marlowe's investigations becomes here quite a literal and original one: Harry Angel looks for someone who assumed his existence—his identity and his soul—by eating his heart; he must solve the crime of his own existence. In *Todo modo* the detective (the painter) and the criminal may be the same person; in *Falling Angel* they are indeed the same person. Pursuing the typical Poesque duality, I could even say that Favorite is the darkly "creative" (black magician, singer) side of the "resolvent" Angel (the detective). This discovery corresponds to another disturbing duality: Cyphre *is* Lucifer as don Gaetano may be the devil in *Todo modo*. *Falling Angel* affirms what *Todo modo* hints at. The Jekyll-Hyde double is here composed in the same person, but not in the same time. In fact this is a doomed chase because both the pursuer and the pursued never exist at the same time: when Favorite was a famous singer, Harry Angel as we know him now (the soul of Angel and the "brand-new face" of Favorite) could not possibly exist; and when the Harry Angel we know is looking for Favorite, the singer no longer exists: his face has been disfigured by war and reshaped by plastic surgery, and his soul is the one of Harry Angel. In his investigation, Angel goes back in time, in the attempt to find his quarry, from 1959 to the early forties, but time and magic have ironically changed the man he is looking for into himself. In *Falling Angel* there is no free time; all Angel's actions are doomed by what has already happened (the transmutation of souls) and by the fatal joke the devil is playing on him (at the end of the novel Angel is accused of the devil's— Cyphre's—four murders). Besides, the action in *Falling Angel* has already happened; it is all a first-person narration (Angel's) written in the past tense; and according to what we can infer from the ending of the book, it may very well have been written by Angel during his time in an upstate prison for the devil's four murders. Angel is doomed as his story opens, in its two very first lines: "It *was Friday the thirteenth* and yesterday's snowstorn lingered in the streets *like a leftover curse.*"[68]

The sense of an irremediable past, whose sins are dooming the present, and the problem of duality are both connected with the use of the Oedipus' myth in the novel. In the early forties Favorite's mistress, Evangeline Proudfoot, a black sorceress from Harlem, bore Favorite a daughter he never knew about,

Epiphany, who became herself a voodoo priestess. Wickedly enough, chance (or devil's plans) leads Angel to contact Epiphany and fall in love with her. Oedipus killed his father and committed incest with his mother; here Favorite killed Angel, assumed his identity and soul, and through them came to make love to his own daughter. In the last page of the novel, Angel rushes home to find out that Epiphany has already been murdered by Cyphre and, of course, he is framed for the devil's killing:

> "Who is she?" Sterne [a cop] jerked his thumb at Epiphany's body.
> "My daughter."
> "Bullshit!"
>   . . . .
> "Give it to me again, Angel. Who's the girl?"
> "Epiphany Proudfoot. She runs an herb shop on 123rd and Lenox."
>   . . . .
> "You'll burn for this, Angel."
> "I'll burn in hell."
> "Maybe. We'll be sure and give you a head start upstate." Sterne's shark-slit mouth widened into an evil smile. . . . There was only one other smile like it: the evil leer of Lucifer. I could almost hear His laughter fill the room. This time, the joke was on me.[69]

Angel-Favorite has by now reconstructed his story. After a dramatic revelation by Ethan Krusemark, he is aware of the incest and of the fact that the devil has quite effectively reciprocated his attempt at deceiving him. Angel will burn in hell, after spending the rest of his life in prison. Sterne, who has been harassing him relentlessly throughout the novel, is not the usual cop who hates private eyes, but, like Cyphre, another incarnation of the Big Trickster, the devil. The joke, this time, is definitely on Angel.

In *Falling Angel* the satanic plot allows something that would not otherwise be possible: a transmutation of souls, which is the source of the existential quest, of the game of doubles, of the concept of time in the novel, of the adaptation of the Oedipus myth. These themes, usually latent in detective and anti-detective fiction, are made explicit and crucial thanks to the "satanic spring" of the plot, which ultimately produces an original version of the by now conventional hard-boiled detective novel. Even the hectic and shabby metropolitan setting typical of the hard-boiled school acquires in *Falling Angel* new and unsettling connotations, thanks to the satanic atmosphere: a voodoo ceremony in Central Park at night, a black mass in an abandoned subway station, sadistic murders. New York City certainly has potential for all this, and Hjortsberg plants satanism quite craftily in an environment that responds very well to it. Also the calculated vulgarity of some lines in the novel helps to reproduce the squalid and brutal New York setting, in which Angel must operate, and goes along with violence and satanism in the plot.

As in *The Crying of Lot 49,* names have in *Falling Angel* self-mocking and symbolic meanings: Angel is no angel, but the combination of tough private eye and black magic priest (Favorite); the name also ironically implies that his identity is related to his soul. Johnny Favorite, alias Jonathan Liebling, is a favorite, a pet of his audience, a phony public image with an ugly personality behind the facade. Lucifer himself was God's *favorite,* the *angel* he loved the most before his fall from Grace. The Crossroads Detective Agency implies that the life-roads of Angel and Favorite intersect and become one. On New Year's Eve 1943 the first act of the doubled Favorite-Angel is in fact to ask Ernie Cavalero, the agency owner, for a job. Perhaps we could say that name symbolism is too obvious in *Falling Angel,* although always wryly amusing. Epiphany Proudfoot, the voodoo priestess, does indeed provide an epiphany, a painful revelation in Angel's life: he is in love, and in love with his daughter, who reveals to him lots of things about the underworld of magic and pagan rites in New York City. Louis Cyphre (whose last name in the novel is spelled in different ways—Cypher, Cipher, Cyphre—like Tristero in *The Crying of Lot 49*) has a very significant name as well, since cypher means zero and, as Cyphre himself says, "*zero* [is] *the point intermediate between positive and negative, is a portal through which every man must eventually pass.*"[70] Cyphre is Angel's "portal" from "neutrality" (zero) to damnation, while the many lections of the devil's name emphasize his trickster's ambiguity, his many possible disguises, and the confusion he provokes in his victims.

What remains in doubt for Oedipa in *The Crying of Lot 49* is certainty for Angel: he is indeed the victim of a complex and sophisticated setup fabricated just for him. Like Oedipa, Angel has hunches about his case being a setup ("Or else it was a setup. An act meant for me to catch.")[71] but he finds it hard to explain how such an effort can be meant only for one person. But a promised soul is to the devil what a Thurn and Taxis courier is to Tristero: something on which he has a claim. Angel-Favorite's soul belongs to the devil by a stipulated pact, the postal monopoly belongs to Tristero "by right of blood":[72] any single effort, no matter how disproportionate, is symbolic of the eventual takeover of the whole.

In *Falling Angel* Cyphre, as a client paying Angel to trace Favorite, seems to have the same "starting role" that Pierce Inverarity has in *The Crying of Lot 49*, as he nominates Oedipa his executrix and thus compels her to disentangle his assets and to run into the Tristero. Cyphre is one of the incarnations of the devil, as perhaps Pierce is one of the "incarnations" of the Tristero, which certainly has a satanic connotation, as don Gaetano has in *Todo modo*.

Both Harry Angel and Oedipa Maas experience the same bewilderment in the face of a "puzzle" they optimistically thought solvable by logic and cunning, by the rules of classical detection, but which instead reveals itself as a "conspiracy" going far beyond the rational reach of a single human being. Tristero and Cyphre play cat and mouse with the two detectives. After her nightmarish night in San Francisco, Oedipa must admit that she was an "optimistic baby [who] had come on so like the private eye in any long-ago radio drama, believing all you needed was grit, resourcefulness, exemption from hidebound cops' rules, to solve any great mystery."[73] Tristero is indeed everywhere: "Last night, she might have wondered what undergrounds apart from the couple she knew of communicated by WASTE system. By sunrise she could legitimately ask what undergrounds didn't."[74] And private eye Angel, who eventually decides to kill his client and ambushes him at the exit of the elevator where he had seen him entering, finds the car empty. The rationality of the detective method proves inadequate as it confronts conspiracy and satanism:

> Posing as the devil might con voodoo piano players and middle-aged lady astrologers, but it didn't wash with me. He picked the wrong man to play the patsy. . . . Louis Cyphre's satanic charade had come to an end. The red metal door [of the elevator] slid open. The car was empty. I staggered forward like a sleepwalker, not believing what I saw. He couldn't be gone. There was no way. I had watched the indicator above the door and seen the numbers light up as the car descended without stopping. He couldn't get off if the car didn't stop. . . . I tried to combat my confusion with logic. . . . I returned to my office feeling lost. It didn't make sense. None of it made sense. No one can vanish into thin air.[75]

Oedipa must reluctantly believe in the underground world of the Tristero system, as Angel must accept the existence of the devil; yet the symbolic ranges of their acceptances and what they derive from them are quite different. Oedipa learns about communication and human compassion, grows to self-awareness, ultimately learns about America; Angel's knowledge of the devil is instead completely private and destructive. It is no accident that the novel's epigraph is from Sophocles' *Oedipus the King* and reads: "Alas, how terrible is wisdom when it brings no profit to the man that's wise!" In comparison, the scope of *The Crying of Lot 49* seems wider than that of *Falling Angel,* whose final and direct satanism is necessary to prop up (although in an irrational way) the whole plot of the novel. *Falling Angel*'s irrational ending does not seem to achieve that ambiguous symbolic spectrum present in the suspenseful last page of *The Crying of Lot 49,* in which everything can still happen. Suspense does not come in *Falling Angel* from a "proliferation of clues" as in *The Crying of Lot 49;* rather, it is of the conventional kind, and follows the hard-boiled fiction's traditions, as does the "doomed" sense of time present in the novel. What is not conventional is the satanic "explanation" at the end of the novel, because it is rationally unacceptable. Although until the end Oedipa thinks that perhaps she is "out of her skull"[76] and has been fantasizing about the Tristero, Harry Angel does not question his sanity; the devil exists. He passes from disbelief to belief after the elevator episode and Epiphany's murder. We may question his sanity ourselves or think he overlooked something, yet the elements that he gives to the reader do not allow any possible alternative. In fact, he tries everything to find a logical explanation for Cyphre's disappearance from the elevator; he even searches the cables up on the roof of the car and throughout the whole building; Cyphre had simply vanished.

The final message of *Falling Angel* remains one of innovation of the hard-boiled conventions through a satanism in which we can believe only in strictly fictional terms. But satanism, just because we do not believe in it per se, also subverts, by the irrational solution it proposes (which is ultimately a nonsolution), the rationality we expect in a novel that until the end "follows the rules," that is, has a disturbing but logical plot. In other words, *Falling Angel* is a deconstructive anti-detective novel, as it "pulls apart" the reader's expectation by proposing a solution he cannot rationally accept. In his study on the fantastic as a genre, Todorov makes a distinction between the "uncanny" (the apparently unexplainable phenomenon that is explained at the end of the fiction in rational terms) and the "marvelous" (the unexplainable phenomenon that can be explained only by supernatural intervention).[77] *Falling Angel* falls in the second category and is especially mocking because, in sensing the "solution" in advance (Favorite is Angel, Cyphre is the devil), I thought it was too easy, and I expected in vain a final "turn of the screw" which would not rely on a supernatural explanation and thus would not break the old British rule: "No Chinaman [magic] is allowed."

However, the plot has no flaw but its conclusion, that, in the case of a second reading, must become its premise if the reader wants to enjoy the novel. In fact *Falling Angel*, to be really appreciated, requires that "leap of faith" Kafka asks from us at the beginning of his metaphorical stories. After that, everything runs smoothly. Just believe that Gregor

Samsa in "Die Verwandlung" ("The Metamorphosis") one day woke up and discovered he had turned into a man-size insect during the night and, after that, you will have no trouble; everything will be *real* and *logical.* Just believe in the devil, and *Falling Angel* will be a perfect novel. But, if I want to use further Todorov's ideas on the fantastic, there is a noticeable difference between the two fictions. The supernatural in "The Metamorphosis" is characterized by a total lack of surprise in Gregor's relatives as they discover that he has turned into an insect. In Kafka's fiction this absence of amazement turns the supernatural normally considered as an exception into the supernatural as a rule.[78] In *Falling Angel* Angel is indeed suprised by Cyphre's disappearance from the elevator; thus the supernatural is there still an exception, not the rule. This also happens because, in *Falling Angel,* the supernatural episode is supposed to have a climactic ("exceptional") function, as it is at the end and not at the beginning of the fiction as in "The Metamorphosis."

As we have seen, in deconstructive anti-detective fiction mystery is the issue. The mystery can be the devil's ambiguous relationship with power and religion (*Todo modo*), or the devil's conspiracy to snatch the soul of the detective (*Falling Angel*), or a larger conspiracy, involving all the outcasts of society and still, perhaps, run by the devil (*The Crying of Lot 49*). The detective's sanity is tested in all these cases; he may be himself a crazy assassin gifted with a wry and nihilistic logic (the painter in *Todo modo*); or the detective may be a housewife bound in routine, mental sterility, who, in a very Poesque way, tries desperately to "project (imagine?) a world" in order not to go crazy; or he may be a tough city sleuth who, because of some disconnection in his logical process and some "drowning in atmospheres," ends up believing in the devil.

Why are writers led to "deconstructive" forms of anti-detective fiction? In this century man has passed from the assumption that the mystery of the universe is explainable through science to the acceptance of the mystery, as the progress of science automatically raises further mysteries and the gap between the known and the unknown increases. Yet as the detective in anti-detective fiction goes from the attempt to solve the mystery to the hope to accept and endure it, she or he always discovers something (pleasant or unpleasant) about herself or himself (Oedipa, Angel), because the mystery begins inside the detective and the solution of the private mystery is the first step toward a solution (a nondistortion) of the mystery outside, reality.

We can notice a progressive difference in the ways Italian and American writers approach the anti-detective novel in its innovative and deconstructive forms. So far as the innovative category goes, Sciascia and Eco (here especially Sciascia, but I could say the same for Gadda's *Quer pasticciaccio brutto de via Merulana*)[79] seem to have a more pessimistic outlook. In fact, while Gardner's message in *The Sunlight Dialogues* is that the answer to mystery is human compassion and that a solution can still be found although justice does not triumph, Sciascia says that human feelings undo the detective, who is unable to find any social commitment in his society (*A ciascuno il suo*). Eco points out the limits of rationality, as the detective can make up a solution by following the wrong clues, or by interpreting clues that are only casual (*Il nome della rosa*).

While in this first category the narrative moves between the two poles of justice and solution, in the deconstructive category the story circles in reality as mystery, and even here Sciascia seems to be far more nihilistic than Pynchon and Hjortsberg. Oedipa is saved by compassion and by the acceptance of mystery, eventually finding at least her own identity; Angel is doomed, but saves his humanity as he cares for Epiphany; instead the painter in *Todo modo* may kill the "devil," but his cold logic and cynicism do not allow us to sympathize with him. As he withholds the solution, we are allowed to think that he is the murderer; thus he epitomizes mystery and, by his possible murder, the connection of the mystery with the "devil," don Gaetano, who is in any case his double. It is striking that all these three writers allude to the devil, but what is even more interesting is that belief in the devil and damnation (Angel) are altogether less dooming than "killing the devil" (the painter perhaps kills don Gaetano). This is perhaps because, according to an old Poesque "rule" ("William Wilson"), to kill the double is to accept his reality and, even more, to become the double that, in this case, is the devil.

It seems that the Italian outlook in anti-detective fiction does not share that inherent American optimism present even in the innately disruptive deconstructive form. It is hard to say why this happens, to give a complete and satisfactory answer to this polarization. Ultimately, it is one view of the world against another, an updated version of the Jamesian "corrupted European" versus the "innocent American." On the one hand we have the composite, politically and economically shaky Italian society, whose wisdom is the acceptance of compromise and of day by day "survival," a mixture of progressivism and disbelief, controlled cynicism with a self-destructive streak. The devil may be killed, but would it really make any difference? Innocence is lost anyway. On the other hand there is America and its myths of freedom, new frontiers and opportunities, which die hard and which are actually revived every time things get particularly bad. It is a conservative myth (like all myths), an optimistic "regression in the future" which conservative political forces know how to take advantage of especially well. The base of the myth is rooted in the American self-conception: individualism, self-reliance, fairness, intelligence (that is, the detective) may not kill the devil but will eventually lead to growth and self-discovery, to initiation, since innocence must be lost, but only in order to achieve maturity (Oedipa), which is another basic American myth.

In the case of Angel, the loss of innocence is, quite literally, the loss of his soul. His own story is more exasperated (and less sophisticated) than Oedipa's. Even in his case, however, a degree of "innocence" (his love for Epiphany; how he suffers the revelation about his soul and Favorite) is still present. In Hjortsberg's case, the American optimism could be linked to the conception of a clearcut (almost moral) mystery in which the Devil and the "Angel of God" (man) face each other. The outcome of the confrontation is obvious. But would the devil have a role and a moral meaning if he could be defeated? He "exists" because he has never been defeated. The fact that Angel understands the devil's trick and fights him is a sign of moral sanity by far more hopeful than the collusion between don Gaetano and the jaded painter in *Todo modo*. It is a degree of innocence (or cynicism) that still separates the fiction of the Jamesian American and the disillusioned European.

5
The Metafictional Anti-Detective Novel

Metafictional anti-detective novels belong only in a general way to anti-detective fiction. In innovative anti-detective fiction the stress was on social criticism and on a solution without justice; in the deconstructive category I emphasized the nonsolution, the ambiguous perception of reality from the point of view of the detective, the sense of conspiracy and satanism. The characteristics of the second kind are, in comparison with the first, more subjective, bordering on the irrational. The anti-detective game gets more sophisticated and less preoccupied with reality (justice, social criticism) and objectivity (solution) as we proceed from one category to the next. Thus, when we get to metafictional anti-detective novels, the conventional elements of detective fiction (the detective, the criminal, the corpse) are hardly there. By now the detective is the reader who has to make sense out of an unfinished fiction that has been distorted or cut short by a playful and perverse "criminal," the writer. Thus detective, criminal, and detection are no longer within the fiction, but outside it. The detective is no longer a character but a function assigned to the reader as the criminal is no longer a murderer but the writer himself who "kills" (distorts and cuts) the text and thus compels the reader to become a "detective." The fiction becomes an excuse for a "literary detection," and if there is a killer in the fiction, he is a "literary killer," a killer of texts (Kinbote, the commentator in *Pale Fire*, distorts the meaning of the poem "Pale Fire"; Marana, the translator in *Se una notte d'inverno un viaggiatore*, cuts and forges the texts of the novels in the novel), not of human beings, and this killer represents within the fiction the operation that the writer (Nabokov, Calvino) performed on it.

Some of the elements in metafictional anti-detective fiction, however, are similar to those in innovative and deconstructive anti-detective novels. Hence we find games of doubles, conspiracy, unfulfilled suspense, and unfinished novels in *Se una notte d'inverno un viaggiatore* by Italo Calvino, and a conspiracy, an unfinished poem, a murder, and a disappointing "legacy" in *Pale Fire* by Vladimir Nabokov. But if some of the previous elements remain, what is different is the atmosphere and the relationship between reader and writer. In metafictional anti-detective fiction the writer is no longer an "absent" third-person narrator but part of his text, which he enters and leaves continuously (Calvino in *Se una notte d'inverno un viaggiatore*) or playfully and misleadingly "explains" through a fictional persona (Kinbote in *Pale Fire*). He keeps reminding us that what we are reading is only fiction and that he is the conjuror in this magic game, which has no reality but its own.

Italo Calvino's *Se una notte d'inverno un viaggiatore*

Italo Calvino's most recent novel, *Se una notte d'inverno un viaggiatore* (1979), is about writing and, more than that, about the act of reading. It is actually questionable whether we should term *Se una notte d'inverno un viaggiatore* a single novel. Rather, it is an assemblage of beginnings of novels which, for some reason (wrongly bound, wrongly printed, forged, censored, etc.) cannot be finished, and leave the reader—both the fictional one in the novel and the real reader—tantalized and frustrated at the same time. *Se una notte d'inverno un viaggiatore* is composed of the first chapters of ten "interrupted" novels,[1] each preceded by an "introduction" concerning a He-Reader and a She-Reader (*il lettore* and *la lettrice* in Italian)[2] who get to know each other because of the mystery of the unfinished books.

The He-Reader is presented as an Everyman who considers reading one of the most enjoyable activities in life. As he finds out that the copy of the book he bought (which is, of course, *Se una notte d'inverno un viaggiatore*) has been badly bound and that the novel is an assemblage of the same first chapter, he is outraged and hurls the book on the floor:

> The thing that most exasperates you [the He-Reader] is to find your-self at the mercy of the fortuitous, the aleatory, the random. . . . In such instances your dominant passion is the impatience to erase the disturbing effects . . . to re-establish the normal course of events. You can't wait to get your hands on a nondefective copy of the book you've begun. You would rush to the bookshop at once if shops were not closed at this hour. You have to wait until tomorrow.[3]

The He-Reader is a man who looks in books for an order he cannot find any more in life. He is a disillusioned, disappointed person who knows that "the best [one] can expect is to avoid the worst. This is the conclusion you have reached, in your personal life and also in general matters, even international affairs."[4] Books are the only exception to this conclusion:

> What about books? Well, precisely because you have denied it in every other field, you believe you may still grant yourself legiti-mately this youthful pleasure of expectation in a carefully circum-scribed area like the field of books, where you can be lucky or unlucky, but the risk of disappointment isn't serious.[5]

The He-Reader is the perfect reader of novels in general, and of detective novels in particular. In fact he projects himself men-tally, almost physically, into the world of books and finds in reading a vicarious and appealing alternative life in which he can release those anxieties and expectations that are much harder to get rid of in the real world. We know by now that a detective novel's reader is mainly a reader who has expectations for order, who looks forward to a neat, well-made solution, just like the He-Reader in Calvino's book.

The He-Reader meets the She-Reader in the bookstore where he goes to return the defective copy. There the clerk tells him that the book, besides being badly bound, also has the wrong cover; what he has been reading was not by Calvino but a novel by a Polish author, Tazio Bazakbal's *Fuori dell'abitato di Malbork* (*Outside the town of Malbork*). Now the compulsive

He-Reader (perhaps also out of unconscious retaliation) wants to go on with that novel and exchanges the "false" Calvino's with a mint copy of Bazakbal's book, just as the She-Reader had done a minute before. Coincidence makes them meet and, as they talk, we learn that the She-Reader's tastes are similar to the ones of the He-Reader:

> I prefer novels . . . that bring me immediately into a world where everything is precise, concrete, specific. I feel a special satisfaction in knowing that things are made in a certain fashion and not otherwise.[6]

Again, reading means entering a well-ordered alternative world that gives satisfactions which the real one gives no longer. The encounter with the She-Reader means to the He-Reader the possibility of romance, the intrusion of the "fortuitous" into the order he is striving to achieve at least in reading. But this is a pleasant "fortuitous," and "the novel to be read is superimposed by a possible novel to be lived. . . . Does this mean that the book has become an instrument, a channel of communication, a rendezvous? This does not mean its reading will grip you less: on the contrary, something has been added to its powers."[7]

In the novel, the act of reading is continuously described as a mental but at the same time physical experience (think of Roland Barthes' *Le plaisir du texte*). The book-object is viewed almost as a "woman-object"; the expectation and the pleasure derived from cutting open the new pages and from being almost physically absorbed into the plot is a metaphor for lovemaking. Calvino, quite ironically, proposes an eroticism of reading that goes hand in hand with the actual romance developing between the He-Reader and the She-Reader.

While we never know the name of the He-Reader, we finally find out the She-Reader's: Ludmilla Vipiteno. She is the ideal "she-reader" and has been loved by two men of letters (a translator and a thriller-writer) just for this reason.

The translator, Ermes Marana, is directly or indirectly responsible for all the problems and book-hunts the He-Reader and Ludmilla go through. He used to be in love with Ludmilla; he was fascinated and obsessed by the way she could abandon herself to the act of reading, by her almost physical and sensual involvement with it. Eventually Marana saw in the books a rival to which Ludmilla gave much more attention than to him and, as his affair with her was dying, plotted a complex, gigantic revenge against her and the books. Its purpose was to deprive Ludmilla of the pleasure of reading by translating novels and then by interpolating or counterfeiting different texts and authors:

> Always, since his taste and talent impelled him in that direction, but more than ever since his relationship with Ludmilla became critical, Ermes Marana dreamed of a literature made entirely of apocrypha, of false attributions, of imitations and counterfeits and pastiches. . . . [If he had succeeded, he] would no longer have felt himself abandoned by Ludmilla absorbed in her reading: between the book and her there would always be insinuated the shadow of mystification, and he, identifying himself with every mystification, would have affirmed his presence.[8]

Eventually Marana loses control of his organization, the OAP (Organization of Apocryphal Power), which splits into two factions: the Wing of Light and the Wing of Shadow. The followers of the Wing of Light try to find among the flood of trash-books produced daily in our society the few books containing some essential and transcendental truth. The followers of the Wing of Shadow believe that only a further mystification of a novel, which is per se a mystifying representation of reality, can lead to an absolute truth intended as the mystification of the mystification; just as a negative number (a "lie"), once squared, gives a positive one (the "truth"). Marana offers his services to the censors of Latin American dictatorships and cooperates in cutting, disfiguring and falsifying as many books as he can and all the books we run into in *Se una notte d'inverno un viaggiatore.* Thus the He-Reader soon discovers that even *Fuori dell'abitato di Malbork,* supposedly by the Polish author Tazio Bazakbal, is actually the victim of a false attribution, Marana's translation into Italian of someone else's novel, and, besides, after the first chapter, the pages are blank.

Silas Flannery,[9] an Irish thriller-writer whom Ludmilla considers the perfect, elemental author (he writes books as "a pumpkin vine produces pumpkins"[10]) becomes of course one of Marana's favorite victims. His books are counterfeited by the forger just as he is going through a writing crisis and is no longer able to produce books like "a pumpkin vine." After having written so much commercial trash (thrillers!), Flannery wants to write a "true book" and is thus spied upon by both the Wing of Light (which expects that the repentance of one of the greatest writers of lies should give birth to the perfect truth) and the Wing of Shadow (which expects that a liar like Flannery, just by trying to write the truth, will end up writing the ultimate lie) and of course by Marana himself. As Silas Flannery tries in vain to write the "true book" in his residence in Switzerland, he happens to observe with his binoculars a young woman on the other side of the valley sitting in a deck chair and reading a book which, he painfully feels, is not one of his own. He sees her as the ideal "she-reader," someone who can still read naturally, while he, on the other hand, has lost the taste for that pleasure because of the nausea of hack-writing. The woman is Ludmilla, the "She-Reader" for whom every writer wishes he would or could write.

> Since I [Silas Flannery] have become a slave laborer of writing, the pleasure of reading has finished for me. What I do has as its aim the spiritual state of this woman in the deck chair framed by the lens of my spyglass, and it is a condition forbidden me. . . . At times I convince myself that the woman is reading my *true* book, the one I should have written long ago, but will never succeed in writing . . .
> Perhaps the woman I observe with the spyglass *knows* what I should write; or, rather, *she does not know it,* because she is in fact waiting for me to write what she *does not know;* but what she knows for certain is her waiting, the void that my words should fill.[11]

Thus the She-Reader becomes a "passion terminal"; her sensual abandonment to reading is viewed and "translated" in different ways by the translator (jealousy and conspiracy), the writer (quest for artistic truth), and the He-Reader (the possibility for order and love).

In contrast, her sister Lotaria proposes a hyperintellectual and dehumanized form of reading, overburdened by all the possible fad forms of interpretation (Freudian interpretation, feminist interpretation, Marxist interpretation) and claims that the "reading" by computer, which deconstructs the text into a list of word-frequencies, is the best (and certainly the quickest) possible.

Doctor Cavedagna, the sad factotum of the publishing house where the He-Reader goes to complain about the interrupted books, still believes in a natural way of reading. Such a belief, however, implies ignorance of the commercial side of book making, an "original innocence" he lost by working in a publishing house. Thus he loves and idealizes the books of his youth, the ones he read before the sin of knowledge, his present work.

Irnerio, a conceptual artist and a friend (what kind of a friend? broods the jealous He-Reader) of Ludmilla, maintains a nonchalantly and almost surrealistically iconoclastic attitude toward books. He does not read books, but uses them as objects to make his paintings and sculptures.

Opposite attitudes toward reading are finally reconciled by Arkadian Porphyritch, Director General of the State Police Archives in a fictional Latin American country named Ircania. In fact he leads a schizophrenic double life: during the day, with the merciless efficiency required by his position, he censors the books that may harm the regime; at night he lies in the comfortable couch of his office to become again only a reader, and treats himself with the unabridged versions of the very same works he expurgated during the day.

Ultimately, I could say that the real protagonist of *Se una notte d'inverno un viaggiatore* is neither the He-Reader nor Ludmilla, but the act and process of reading, around which the actions and thoughts of all the main characters obsessively revolve. Calvino's microcosm deals with a wide spectrum of attitudes toward reading and is eventually split among the persons who still read (the He-Reader, Ludmilla, the "night-side" of Porphyritch) and the ones who do not read anymore (Marana, Irnerio), or cannot read anymore (Dr. Cavedagna, Silas Flannery), or read in a dehumanized way (Lotaria, the "day-side" of Porphyritch).

Readers and the act of reading actually have quite a lot to do with detectives and detection. In fact a good reader is always a "detective," since he consciously or unconsciously strives for "what is next" as well as for what is left unsaid and ultimately for the end (the denouement, the "composition" of the plot) when he reads a fiction, no matter whether it is a detective novel or not. The reader's often compulsive "detection" is proportional to his involvement with plot and characters, to the fascination that the text exercises on him through the act of reading. The fascination of reading has at least two variables outside the text: the personality of the reader and the contingent situation in which the reading is done. These are variables valid for any of us "outside readers." Concerning the readers inside the fiction, the He-Reader is annoyed by the interruption in the first book, but gets more and more involved in his quest for an entire, complete novel because he is going through this quest with Ludmilla. Thanks to the sensual abandon she experiences and "radiates" in her way of reading, the He-Reader feels he has at least a "mental love affair" with her, as he is reading the same interrupted books she is reading and goes through the same quest for a complete one. Arkadian Porphyritch's "night side" reacts in a similar way; he candidly confesses to the jealous He-Reader:

> "[A]s long as I know there is a woman [Ludmilla]who loves reading for reading's sake, I can convince myself that the world continues . . . And every evening I, too, abandon myself to reading, like that distant unknown woman . . ."
> Rapidly you [the He-Reader] wrest from your mind the inappropriate superimposition of the images of the Director General and Ludmilla, to enjoy the *apotheosis* of the Other Reader . . . and you savor the certainty . . . that between her and you there no longer exist obstacles or mysteries, whereas of the Cagliostro [Marana], your rival, only a pathetic shadow remains, more and more distant . . .[12]

Ludmilla is the "contingency" that makes reading a fascinating experience and makes the detection of the He-Reader not only the mental one typical of any reader but an actual, physical detection, since the He-Reader soon begins to use his pursuit of a complete text as an excuse to keep in touch with Ludmilla and to see her. Furthermore, since the He-Reader is a person who compulsively strives for order, he must unravel the mystery of the interrupted books, which jeopardizes his attitude toward reading. In fact reading is for him a vital "safety blanket," the kingdom of order from which the "fortuitous" is banished, and where expectations are mostly rewarded. To solve the mystery is to reestablish order in reading, which otherwise is corrupted by disorder and, as is the case for Ludmilla, by the fear that anything he reads is going to be interrupted or distorted by the false "narrative voice" of the forger Marana.

Ironically, Ludmilla becomes some sort of "Dante's Beatrice." In a sick world that makes reading (withdrawal and vicarious existence) the only possibility for "safe" expectations and enjoyment, she is the model for readers and nonreaders, the "passion-terminal" that changes their lives. Without Ludmilla they would not act as they do, and somehow their more or less successful real or mental relationships with her prompt each of them to go either deeper into the "Paradise" of the readers (the "night-side" of Porphyritch, the He-Reader) or into the "Hell" of the nonreaders (Marana, Lotaria), or even through that "Purgatory," which is a troubled but redeeming crisis (Silas Flannery). Hence the He-Reader is right when he thinks of her success as an "apotheosis."

Se una notte d'inverno un viaggiatore's emphasis on reading is both a metaphor for the detection performed by any reader of any novel and simultaneously an account of literal detection. The He-Reader and Ludmilla read avidly only to find first chapters repeated—or blank, stolen, or apocryphal—and in their search for a solution come upon other tales yet more in need of a second chapter, always to be interrupted by some accident or printing problem.

As I mentioned in the overview of the metafictional anti-detective novel in chapter 2, the "hide-and-seek" relation between writer and reader occurs outside and within the fiction: 1) Writer (Calvino) deviously writing (hiding the solution of) the text and real reader trying to make sense out of it (seeking the solution—the reader as a detective). 2) Fictional "writer" (Marana, the translator-forger) forging and interrupting the texts within the text (hiding their conclusions) and fictional readers (the He-Reader and the She-Reader) trying to make sense out of them (seeking their conclusions).

What makes Calvino's book particularly sophisticated and dynamic is that these relationships outside and within the fiction overlap and interact continuously. Calvino achieves the effect of simultaneity through a game of personal pronouns. In fact the protagonist of every first chapter the He-Reader gets to read always addresses himself to a hypothetical reader and very rationally explains his emotions and describes the environment in which he acts. He is a first-person narrator very well aware of telling a tale, of being the main character of the novel he is narrating. He continuously conveys to the outside reader the feeling that the "book" he is narrating is perfectly conscious of its "bookness" and yet he undermines this abstractness by the physicality of the emotions and descriptions in the story he is narrating. Fiction (like *finzione,* pretense) and "reality" (the fascination, the involvement in the narration experienced by the reader because of the story-telling power of the narrator) swing back and forth in front of the outside reader. He is compelled to believe in the fiction as a "real world" and to disbelieve it, to discard its pretense a moment later when the protagonist again reminds him of the fictional mechanisms. It is like being in front of a conjuror who continuously turns the palm of his hand and sometimes there is a card and other times nothing.

As an example, we can consider the opening of the first interrupted novel, whose title, *Se una notte d'inverno un viaggiatore,* is also the title of the whole book.

> The novel begins in a railway station, a locomotive huffs, steam from a piston covers the opening of the chapter, a cloud of smoke hides part of the first paragraph. In the odor of the station there is a passing whiff of station café odor. . . . The pages of the book are clouded like the windows of an old train, the cloud of smoke rests on the sentences. . . . All these signs converge to inform us that this is a little provincial station, where anyone is immediately noticed. . . .

I am the man who comes and goes between the bar and the telephone booth. Or, rather: that man is called "I" and you [reader] know nothing else about him, just as this station is called only "station" and beyond it there exists nothing except the unanswered signal of a telephone ringing in a dark room of a distant city. . . . For a couple of pages now you have been reading on, and this would be the time to tell you clearly whether this station where I have got off is a station of the past or a station of today. . . . Watch out: it is surely a method of involving you gradually, capturing you in the story before you realize it—a trap. Or perhaps the author still has not made up his mind.[13]

The railway-station opening is very much evocative of the opening of *L'emploi du temps* (1956, *Passing Time*) by Michel Butor, and certainly Calvino's technique in *Se una notte d'inverno un viaggiatore* owes something to the *nouveau roman*. This influence is present not in the relation among the "I" (narrator), the "You" (reader), and the "He" (writer), which is uncommon in the French literary movement, but rather in the sense of detachment and objectivity Calvino's writing conveys and in the precise description of things and sensations following each other in a consequential and almost automatic way. "The text writes itself" is one of the *nouveau roman*'s major theoretical assumptions, but here Calvino enlivens the *nouveau roman*'s descriptive and static "automatic self-writing" by the continuous shifts in the narrative voice caused by the "I-You-He" technique. The fictional game is shown off and withdrawn continuously, thanks to Calvino's ability as a conjuror of language. This technique is designed to remind the reader that he is dealing with a fictional world and to unsettle his desire to identify himself with the characters. The protagonist of the narration is an "I" who is telling a story, and thus he must address it to a hypothetical second person, a "You," the reader. As the first-person narrator refers to the author, he must hence use the third-person singular. The "He" is an "antagonistic" personal pronoun (I and he), and this "grammatical opposition" indeed forbids any possible "complicity" between "creator" (as "He") and "creature" (as "I")—a complicity that the I-narrator rather tries to establish with the You-reader against "He," the author ("Watch out: it is surely a method of involving you gradually . . . a trap. Or perhaps the author still has not made up his mind"). This could become in the long run a tiresome, confusing, hyperintellectual game, but Calvino uses it judiciously, with the lightness and the playfulness he perhaps derives from his experience with fairy tales. He seems always to know when to "poke" the reader's attention by the I-You-He game, that is, every time the narration rests too long on conventional techniques.

The metafictional aspect of the "interrupted novels" in the book corresponds to a similar rapport between the writer (Calvino, the "I") and the He-Reader (the "You") in the introductions to the "interrupted novels" themselves. These introductions describe the vicissitudes the He-Reader and Ludmilla undergo while attempting to get a mint copy of what they think is the previous interrupted novel but which always turns out instead to be another book—which is, however, even more fascinating than the one they were looking for, so that they give up the previous and try to find the rest of the new one. Thus in *Se una notte d'inverno un viaggiatore* there are two parallel pronoun-chains, which differ slightly depending on who is narrating,[14] the protagonist of the interrupted novel within the novel or the writer-Calvino in the introduction to the interrupted novels:

1) I   (the narrator of the novel)
    YOU (reader, both real reader and He-Reader)
    HE   (the writer, Calvino)
    IT   (the narrated novel)

2) I   (the writer, Calvino)
    YOU (He-Reader)
    SHE (Ludmilla)
    IT   (the interrupted novel, its characters)

The second chain changes at a crucial point in one of the introductions, that is, when Ludmilla gives the He-Reader the keys to her apartment so that he can go there and wait for her. He takes advantage of the keys to undertake "a detective investigation"[15] of her place and discover something more about her and her tastes. At this point Ludmilla, the She-Reader, is addressed by the I-Calvino not as a "She," but as a "You":

> What are you like, Other Reader? It is time for this book in the second person to address itself no longer to a general male you [the He-Reader], perhaps brother and double of a hypocrite I [Calvino, the writer, who identifies himself also with the He-Reader], but directly to you who appeared already in the second chapter as the Third Person necessary for the novel to be a novel, for something to happen between that male Second Person and the female Third, for something to take form, develop, or deteriorate according to the phases of human events.[16]

When soon afterwards the He-Reader and the She-Reader at last make love, they "read each other" ("Ludmilla, now you are being read. . . . And you, too, O Reader, are meanwhile an object of reading")[17] and from the point of view of the I-Calvino they become a you (in Italian: *tu*) plus a you, that is, a *voi*, a you second person plural,[18] which makes a lot of difference, especially for the He-Reader, who is in love with Ludmilla.

As suggested since the beginning of the novel by Ludmilla's abandon to fiction reading, to read is an "erotic act," something like "to know" in the Biblical sense. The consequence of such a view is that, ironically, fiction is as true (and erotic, corporeal, existent, alive) as lovemaking; actually, lovemaking and fiction-reading are in some ways the same thing. They are both an extension of the self toward an "object" (the text, the lover) with whom the self gets very involved (fascinated) if the object can hold his attention.

We must not forget, however, that Calvino's novel implies a division between a fiction proposed to us as "reality" (the outer story of the He-Reader and Ludmilla) and fictions proposed as such (the ten unfinished novels) in which the ultimate outcomes of the love stories narrated are never happy, as is instead the affair between the He-Reader and Ludmilla, who in the last page of *Se una notte d'inverno un viaggiatore* are husband and wife. This happens not only because the ten fictions are unfinished and so the love affairs they narrate are unsolved, "unconsummated," but also because through the ten interrupted fictions Calvino leads us in a cavalcade of the modes of the modern and contemporary novel, and recent world literature—Calvino says—seems to share a common pessimism about happy denouements. Calvino saves that kind of ending for fairy tale collections and, perhaps ironically, for "reality" (the outer story of Ludmilla and the He-Reader).

Calvino's overview of the novel genre through parodies of ten different styles and novelistic forms is a true *tour de force*. The ten interrupted fictions have in common a self-questioning, introspective, analytical narrator who is well aware of telling a story (e.g., "The first sensation this book should convey is what I feel."),[19] his story, and thus something that has already happened. In fact we do feel that the narrator is going in his tale toward a denouement even in the ten to fifteen pages of the interrupted first chapter, as he is telling us about something in the past that has by now been thoroughly lived and is going to be concluded through the ultimate filtration of writing and narrating it. However, we do not get to that ending that seems to exist (these are not open-ended novels, but interrupted novels) in the next chapters the He-Reader will never find. The narration is, perversely enough, interrupted in a moment of high suspense, just as it used to happen in the French feuilleton, and irrelevant and inconclusive clues are planted in the unfinished works. Names of characters (Jan, Zwida, Amaranta), of geographical places (Kudgiwa), of nightclubs (the "New Titania") recur from one fiction to the other, but are used in different ways and contexts (e.g., Kauderer is a rich farmer in the second novel, a meteorologist in the third, the name of an ammunition factory in the fourth; Kawasaki is, of course, a motorcycle in the seventh novel and a Japanese professor in the eighth), so that it is impossible to get anything out of them except for the impression of being teased throughout the fictions. This proliferation of inconclusive clues reminds me of *The Crying of Lot 49*, and of the "islands" of unfulfilled suspense in John Gardner's *The Sunlight Dialogues*.

The narrators of the aborted novels, although all hyper- and self-analytical, have different voices and ways to obtain the sympathy of the reader; these ways are related to the kind of story (the kind of imitation of a novel form) they tell. The first, *Se una notte d'inverno un viaggiatore,* is the imitation of a spy-novel and is set in the railway station of a provincial town. The reader participates little by little in the narrator's frustration over the missed appointment with another member of the organization with whom he was supposed to switch bags in the crowded station. Thanks to the "I-You-He" technique and the pull-and-push game now emphasizing fictional involvement (the sympathy that the narrator elicits from the reader), now fictional awareness (the defamiliarization from the narration), the reader's attention is stirred continuously; he can almost smell the odors of the shabby station and see the habitués lingering around the counter of the station buffet kidding each other with the same jokes every night. The description of the scene is as visually evocative as an Edward Hopper painting. All the fictions are "translated," filtered through the I-narrator's physical sensations in terms of smell, body contacts, weather-dictated moods, noises, lovemaking, in such a masterful way that it is really hard to resist a participation which is, however, continuously questioned by the "fictional awareness" of the narrator.

The second aborted novel is a "realistic" novel with a farm setting in Eastern Europe; the third is an existential novel, imitating the diary style of Sartre's *La nausée;* the fourth is the story of an uncanny ménage à trois occurring in the midst of the Russian (or of a Marxist) revolution; the fifth is a parody of the hard-boiled style set in France; the sixth is an obsessive thriller on a United States university campus; the seventh is a story of mirror games and deceitful reflections in the Borges style; the eighth is an erotic and titillating "Japanese novel"; the ninth imitates Marquez's *Cien años de soledad (One Hundred Years of Solitude)* in setting and narrative voice and is about "doubles" and repetition in time; the tenth is a "metaphysical novel" that seems to come out of a De Chirico painting. This is a simplification, however, because each aborted novel cannot be really pigeonholed but has an autonomous (although "aborted") artistic life.

Hence the forger of novels in the novel (Marana) corresponds to a masterful outside forger, Calvino, who lets himself be identified by the reader with three of the main characters: Marana, the He-Reader,[20] and Silas Flannery, the writer who can no longer read or write. Silas Flannery seems to be a self-parody, as is the He-Reader (who, more exactly, is a playful projection of the writer's self, the double of the writer, that is, the reader) but, further than that, Silas Flannery-Calvino supplies the key to the whole fiction:

> I [Silas Flannery] have pondered my last conversation with that Reader. [In his attempt to solve the mystery of the unfinished novels, the He-Reader went to visit Silas Flannery.] Perhaps his reading is so intense that it consumes all the substance of the novel at the start, so nothing remains for the rest. This happens to me in writing: for some time now, every novel I begin writing is exhausted shortly after the beginning, as if I had already said everything I have to say.
>
> I have had the idea of writing a novel composed only of beginnings of novels. The protagonist could be a Reader who is continually interrupted. The Reader buys the new novel A by the author Z. But it is a defective copy, he can't go beyond the beginning . . . He returns to the bookshop to have the volume exchanged . . .
>
> I could write it all in the second person: you, Reader . . . I could also introduce a young lady, the Other Reader, and a counterfeiter-translator, and an old writer who keeps a diary like this diary . . .[21]

Unexpectedly, the "book aware of its bookness" explains itself through the writer within the book who is a fictional reflection of the writer outside the book, Calvino himself. And, of course, the ten interrupted novels are all characterized by suspense because they have been "written" by a thriller-writer, Silas Flannery.

Calvino's magic hat always produces a new white rabbit for his amazed reader, who almost resents this "waste" of imagination, of beautiful but unfinished stories that an old writer in crisis (who is not in crisis at all) mockingly flashes at him behind a flight of mirrors. One might even say that Calvino is eventually undone by the height of his talent; toward the end of the book the reader is not yet bored but certainly stunned and a bit confused by the rarefied games the writer is playing on him (think of the just mentioned "turn of the screw" by which Flannery explains the whole book). An overlong exposure to thin mountain air does not help one to breathe, and when the reader gets off Calvino's merry-go-round on the top of the mountain he certainly enjoyed the trip, but he may have a slight headache and be especially glad to be back on solid ground.

At any rate, the ten aborted novels from around the world offer quite a mine of themes and deceitful clues that some re-thinking and a second reading (which seems to be an operation mandatory for most anti-detective novels) can partially sort out. For example, in the seventh novel, *In una rete di linee che si intersecano* (*In a network of lines that intersect*) there is again a mirror-map-labyrinth pattern. This is how the novel opens: "Speculate, reflect: every thinking activity implies mirrors for me. . . . I need mirrors to think: I cannot concentrate except in the presence of reflected images, as if my soul needed a model to imitate every time it wanted to employ its speculative capacity."[22] The narrator is a crooked financial genius; he "translates" the mirror's activity (to reflect = to think) into devious thinking to cheat his business enemies, and (to reflect = to reproduce illusorily) into creating an impression of power "[by] multiplying, as if in a play of mirrors, companies without capital, [by] enlarging credit, [by] making disastrous deficits vanish in the dead corners of illusory perspectives."[23] In his house he builds a "catoptric room," basically a labyrinth of mirrors, on the design of a seventeenth-century Jesuit, Atha-nasius Kircher. Since he is afraid of being kidnapped, he plans ahead on a mapboard of the city his route and then cancels or modifies it at the last minute in order to baffle possible spies and kidnappers. Hence this unfinished novel enhances the mir-ror-labyrinth-map pattern neither at a chronological level (e.g., the *nouveau roman*'s concept of time) nor at a literal level (e.g., the pattern in Eco's *Il nome della rosa*), but rather focuses on the deceitful aspect of mirrors and their consequent creation of labyrinths as an endless number of reflections. Even tracing a route on a map implies no "solution," no affirmation of a cer-tainty (while in *Il nome della rosa* drawing the map of the laby-rinth meant making sense out of it), but rather becomes a misleading bait against kidnappers. Of course, this is a very Borgesian vision of mirrors and their games; think, for example, of the story "El Aleph," in which the Aleph is a sphere where the whole world is mirrored, reflected.

Mirrors refract images that are specularly opposite to the "original." So Lotaria is the mirror image of Ludmilla,[24] the Wing of Shadow faction of the OAP is the mirror image of the Wing of Light, and Silas Flannery, the "impotent writer," is the mirror image of Calvino. Opposite dualities and mirror images go hand in hand. Even the He-Reader and the She-Reader are "opposite dualities" (at least in terms of sex) but they are even more than that: they are a *couple* of detectives looking for a book (just like William and Adso in *Il nome della rosa*) and going through elusive and intricate adventures—another version of the labyrinth pattern. The inner *duality* of the Poesque detective ("creative" and "resolvent") is here split, externally and more innocuously, into a *couple* in which we may glimpse traces of a "creative force" in Ludmilla (the passion-terminal) and more of the resolvent side in the especially persistent, clue-following He-Reader. Likewise, in *Il nome della rosa,* Adso ends up being the "creative" force behind the story: he evokes, "creates," the story by finally writing it down many years after the events occurred; William is, of course, mainly resolvent— just as it always happened with Watson and Holmes in Doyle's stories.

As in *Falling Angel* and in *The Crying of Lot 49,* in *Se una notte d'inverno un viaggiatore* a disproportionate conspiracy is set up against a "detective" (Ludmilla). The OAP wants now to destroy the relation of trust between the reader and the text, but the whole conspiracy had originally been mounted by Marana for the exclusive manipulation of one single person, Ludmilla Vipiteno, because she loved books more than she did him.

In *The Crying of Lot 49* the conspiracy was connected with the hunt for the corrupted version of a book, *The Courier's Tragedy,* which had been forged by the Scurvhamites, who wrote an apocryphal pornographic version of it (the one containing the line about Tristero Oedipa was looking for) "as a moral example,"[25] in order to celebrate purity through its opposite. Similarly, the Wing of Shadow wants to steal the "true book" Flannery tries to write during his crisis on the assumption that the "true book" of a great liar would represent the ultimate falsity. In *Il nome della rosa* by Eco the hunt for a book was also present, as William and Adso were looking for a mysterious codex, which turned out to be the lost second part of the *Poetics* by Aristotle. In this case the book was the solution to the mystery as it contained a truth (the saving grace of laughter) which prompted lugubrious Jorge to hide and poison it and thus to cause indirectly the deaths of the monks looking for it. The problem of the inadequate translation and of the consequent hunt for the original, which is so central to *Se una notte d'inverno un viaggiatore* (1979), is also present in *Il nome della rosa* (1980), albeit peripherally, since it appears only in the preface. In fact in the preface the "translator" Umberto Eco tells the reader that the text he is about to read is the Italian translation of a French translation of a book in Latin, and that, after a vain chase for the Latin original, he decided to print his translation from the French version. Also, in the account of his labyrinthine "search for the Latin original," Eco mentions—very slyly—the Jesuit Athanasius Kircher who is the seventeenth-century author of a book on mirrors mentioned by Calvino in the seventh interrupted novel of *Se una notte d'inverno un viaggiatore*. This is, indeed, metafiction.

Hunts for lost, corrupted, and complete texts play a main role in the mystery (*Il nome della rosa*) or the conspiracy (*The Crying of Lot 49, Se una notte d'inverno un viaggiatore*) against which the detective fights; they link together Eco's, Pynchon's and Calvino's novels. In *Se una notte d'inverno un viaggiatore*, however, the antibook conspiracy assumes paradoxical and ludicrous connotations extraneous to *The Crying of Lot 49, Todo modo,* and *Falling Angel*, the deconstructive anti-detective novels in which a conspiracy is present. For example, Arkadian Porphyritch, Director General of the Police Archives in Ircania, states wryly:

What statistic allows one to identify the nations where literature enjoys true consideration better than the sums appropriated for controlling it and suppressing it? . . . To be sure, repression must also allow an occasional breathing space, must close an eye every now and then, alternate indulgence with abuse, with a certain unpredictability in its caprices; otherwise, if nothing more remains to be repressed, the whole system rusts and wears down.[26]

In fact, in the metafictional anti-detective novel the relation between reader and writer gets more overt and teasing than in the other two categories. Somehow it also influences the general tone of the narration, which resorts more often to light humor and parody than do the other kinds of anti-detective novels. Anti-detective novels having a first-person narrator do not get "filtered" and de-dramatized by the playful relation among narrator, reader, and writer typical of metafictional anti-detective fiction, or by the critical authorial voice typical of third-person narrations. Compare, for example, the sometimes dramatic I-narration of Angel in *Falling Angel* with the humorous and diversified I-You-He technique in *Se una notte d'inverno un viaggiatore,* or even with the often ironical third-person narration of Sciascia in *A ciascuno il suo.*

Metafictionally, *Se una notte d'inverno un viaggiatore* proposes a playful "intertextual solution" to the mystery of the unfinished novels which is connected to a "circular ending" of the novel. In fact the He-Reader, who has been diligently jotting down all the titles of the aborted novels, discovers during a conversation with other readers in a library that all the titles connected together form a long complete sentence which makes sense, and that "[t]he ultimate meaning to which all stories refer has two faces: the continuity of life, the inevitability of death."[27] This last consideration (life is short) prompts the reader to marry Ludmilla, and the novel, which opened with the beginning of the reading ("You are about to begin reading Italo Calvino's new novel, *If on a winter's night a traveler*"),[28] concludes itself with the end of the reading:

Now you are man and wife, Reader and Reader. A great double bed receives your parallel readings.
Ludmilla closes her book, turns off her light, puts her head back

against the pillow, and says, "Turn off your light, too. Aren't you tired of reading?"
And you say, "Just a moment, I've almost finished *If on a winter's night a traveler* by Italo Calvino."[29]

Beginning and end close a circular structure; the novel finds a solution within itself by connecting its titles in a way which reminds me of John Barth's *Letters* which, by some very metafictional coincidence, was published at exactly the same time.

Letters and *Se una notte d'inverno un viaggiatore* seem to owe something in both technique and conception to the most recent fringes of the *nouveau roman*. Calvino, who had been living in Paris for a long time when he wrote *Se una notte d'inverno un viaggiatore,* is wryly aware of playing with a literary movement, for he opens the novel with "You are about to begin reading Italo Calvino's new novel [Italo Calvino's *nouveau roman!*], *If on a winter's night a traveler.*"[30]

From a more distanced perspective, in a very *nouveau roman* fashion, *Se una notte d'inverno un viaggiatore* designates no other reality but its own, and actually even finds a "solution" in its macro-structure (the ten titles composing a complete sentence). This connection among the titles and thus among the narrative voices (which deliberately stress the artificiality of the fictional mechanisms) emphasizes the autonomy of the novel, of the microcosms the novel "writes and reads about." While the *nouveau roman* writers and critics claim that the text writes itself, Calvino enlivens this assumption by the I-You-He game and shifts the emphasis to reading, since the text, no matter if it writes itself or not, does justify its existence because of the act of reading. No matter which emotion the text wants to convey, it exists because of the readers who read it, who in Calvino's novel become the detectives within and outside the text (the He-Reader and the She-Reader within; the real reader outside). The perfect reader, however, is neither the real reader nor the He-Reader, but Ludmilla; both reader and detective, but especially reader, she gives life to the text through her sensual reading, through her participation in it. Ultimately the text is only a means of communication and "detection" between two creators, the writer and the reader, a "pale fire" that is the result of the writer's filtration and personal "rearrangement" of reality, in turn filtered and rearranged by the reader's perceptions and personal response to the writer's creation.

Vladimir Nabokov's
Pale Fire

Pale Fire (1962) by Vladimir Nabokov anticipates in terms of anti-detective themes and techniques both *The Crying of Lot 49* (1966) and *Se una notte d'inverno un viaggiatore* (1979). As in the case of Pynchon's and Calvino's novels, *Pale Fire* includes the hunt for a text; however, while Oedipa and the He-Reader simply want to get the "right text" (Oedipa the Scurvhamite version of *The Courier's Tragedy;* the He-Reader the rest of the novels he tries to read), Kinbote goes to the roots of the problem. In fact he does not hunt an already written text, but a text that will be written, Shade's poem-to-be. This allows him to think he can influence the text, "make it right," that is, have it written according to his desires. Kinbote's quest for the text is not in the past (in the realm of the "already written"), but in the future, and his hopes of success ironically rise as the potential (the future) turns into actual (present). When he narrates to the reader of his pseudocommentary to "Pale Fire" that "finally, under the date of July 3 [he wrote in his journal]: 'poem begun!' "[31] he describes the crucial moment of the passage from potentiality to actuality. When Shade starts writing his poem, the victory Kinbote dreams now as certain becomes indeed defeat, since Shade is *not* writing about Zembla.

Kinbote's efforts to push Shade into writing his story are characterized by an obsession with time in general and with the past in particular. It is no accident that twice in his commentary Kinbote mentions Proust's *À la recherche du temps perdu.* Somehow Shade's writings about Zembla should give Kinbote's fantasy both reality and artistic eternity. He says to Shade: "Once transmuted by you into poetry, the stuff *will* be true, and the people *will* come alive . . . as soon as the glory of Zembla merges with the glory of your verse, I intend to divulge to you an ultimate truth."[32] Hence thanks to Shade's alleged epic of Zembla, Kinbote's "past with no past" would have the timeless reality of art. Kinbote attempts quite an original enterprise: he tries to impose on the future (what *will* be written by Shade) the poetry of a never existent past. Eventually both "tenses" (times) escape him: the future (Shade's text) disappoints him, the past was never real; however, Kinbote does have the present. While we are reading, he reminds us continuously that he is writing the commentary at that very moment, that there is an amusement park outside, quite a noisy one, and that he is typing and living in his mind, once again, the story of Zembla, the "distant northern land"[33] of which he dreams himself the exiled king, Charles the Beloved.

Kinbote is a harmless juggler of time; anybody can do what he wants with his past, even invent it, and an imaginary past is easily "evoked" in the present, actually exists only in the present. As he talks with a lady at a party, sympathetic Shade implicitly recognizes that Kinbote is, at least potentially, a brilliant artist: " 'That [mad] is the wrong word,' he [Shade] said. 'One should not apply it to a person who deliberately peels off a drab and unhappy past and replaces it with a brilliant invention. That's merely turning a new leaf with the left hand.' "[34] As the lady tells Kinbote about a railway-station man (she is actually talking about Kinbote) who "thought he was God and began redirecting the trains,"[35] he agrees with Shade: the man was not a loony but a poet. In fact Kinbote replies that "We are all, in a sense, poets, *Madam* [poets, that is, *madmen*]."[36] Kinbote, for once, rightly anticipates his future: by writing his distorting commentary he will prove to be a brilliant "poet."

Kinbote's juggling with time ultimately proves itself quite fortunate: while by a scholarly correct commentary he would at best explain "Pale Fire," by performing on the poem an "inverted detection" (that is, not explaining but hiding things in it), he creates another "poem," his own Zemblan epic, which "Pale Fire" was supposed to create and actually did not. In his foreword, Kinbote remembers that, as he was one day going to help the Shades who were "having trouble with their old Packard in the slippery driveway . . . [he] lost [his] footing and sat down on the surprisingly hard snow. [His] fall acted as a chemical reagent on the Shades' sedan, which forthwith budged and almost ran over [him] as it swung into the lane."[37] The "fall" of Kinbote's expectations about Shade's poem has a similar function: it is a "chemical reagent" that brings Kinbote's potential as an artist into actuality.

As he denies his work as a commentator and refuses to explain the poem (although he claims that he has "no desire to twist and batter an unambiguous *apparatus criticus* into the monstrous semblance of a novel"),[38] he does actually write a novel and gives to Shade's homey and Frostian "Pale Fire" a theatrical and Wagnerian antithetical dimension. As John Hagopian points out, "[u]nlike Shade, Kinbote does not observe, respond to, and draw from the real world; he makes of it a stage on which he enacts his own fantasies (Charles the Beloved fled from Zembla through a theater, and theatrical images abound in his account)."[39] The two men themselves are one the opposite of the other:

> Shade is heterosexual, married, family-oriented. Kinbote is a homosexual. . . . Shade is gregarious, friendly and at ease with others, kind and generous; Kinbote is a social pariah, demanding and tense. Shade has a sick body, but a healthy mind in tune with nature; Kinbote has a healthy athletic body, but a sick mind and fears nature.[40]

In a parallel way Shade's "Pale Fire" and Kinbote's commentary could not clash more; they are a thesis and its antithesis, something monstrous like a horse with wings. But the reader fulfills the synthesis, the horse miraculously flies and *Pale Fire* becomes a "Pegasus," a perfect creation, half poem and half prose, which merges the fascination of poetic magic in everyday life and of magic folly in a timeless dreamland. Actually it is Kinbote the scholarly hack who finds his wings. Like Oedipa, thanks to a "legacy" he becomes a "reluctant artist" since, realizing that Shade did not translate his fantasy into poetry, he is compelled to do it himself by his pseudocommentary. We know that Inverarity's testament came to Oedipa totally unexpectedly and chance (or Inverarity's devious scheme) had on her an effect perhaps different from the one anticipated by the California tycoon, if her running into the Tristero had really been planned. In fact by her discovery of the Tristero Oedipa risks indeed her mental sanity but, more than that, grows to maturity and compassion. As she tries to "project a world"[41] and to make sense out of Inverarity's entangled assets, she is creative and resolvent, an "artist" and a detective. Kinbote wants and actually snatches Shade's "legacy," "Pale Fire," but he finds an unexpected content ("I sped through it, snarling, as a furious young heir through an old deceiver's *testament*").[42] Quite ironically and consistently, Kinbote's madness and topsy-turvy vision of sexuality turn into an inverted detection. In fact he does not create and resolve as Oedipa does, but *first* refuses to resolve the text as a commentator would be expected to do, and *then*, out of rage, he creates his own text and fulfills his Zemblan dream. By refusing to be a commentator, a "scholarly detective," by inverting the Poesque classical sequence (first "creation" and then "resolution") into refusal of the resolution and thus only creation, Kinbote becomes an anti-detective secondarily and an artist primarily, while Oedipa is an "artist" secondarily and a detective primarily.

As in any detective novel, the murder (John Shade's death) "starts" the reader's detection but, since the murder is described at the end of Kinbote's pseudocommentary, the reader very likely has to reread it to discover clues related to the fact that the assassin is not Jakob Gradus sent by the Shadows but only crazy Jack Grey escaped from the asylum for the criminally insane. At the same time, the murdered man is not Judge Goldsworth—the assassin was misled by a physical resemblance—but proves to be the poet John Shade. Thus the murder at the end of *Pale Fire* (and not at the beginning as in a conventional detective novel) is explained through the reader's discovery of clues and slips concerning invented (Gradus-Grey) or mistaken (Goldsworth-Shade) identities in Kinbote's pseudocommentary.

The first hint concerning the fact that the imaginary Jakob Gradus (whom Kinbote names also Jacques d'Argus, Jack Degree, Vinogradus, etc.) is actually Jack Grey is given by Kinbote while he is describing an album in the house of Judge Goldsworth "in which the judge had lovingly pasted the life histories and pictures of people he had sent to prison or condemned to death: unforgettable faces of imbecile hoodlums, last smokes and last grins, a strangler's quite ordinary-looking hands, a self-made widow, the close-set merciless eyes of a homicidal maniac (somewhat resembling, I admit, the late Jacques d'Argus)."[43] The reader eventually becomes aware that Kinbote is crazy and that his fancied assassin from Zembla is indeed only a maniac Goldsworth had sent to prison and who had escaped to take revenge. It was by chance (perhaps) that Shade, who resembles Goldsworth, was in front of the judge's house with Kinbote, who had rented it while the judge was on sabbatical in England. Thus Shade is mistaken for the judge and shot by Jack Grey. The solution is almost given away when Kinbote tells the reader:

> [After Shade's murder] I did manage to obtain, soon after his [Jack Grey's] detention, an interview, perhaps even two interviews, with the prisoner. . . . By making him believe I could help him at his trial I forced him to confess his heinous crime—his deceiving the police and the nation by posing as Jack Grey, escapee from an asylum, who mistook Shade for the man who sent him there [the judge].[44]

It is hard to see how Kinbote could be allowed in a prison to talk with someone recently convicted of murder. His vagueness about the number of interviews he had with him arouses suspicion in the reader. The truth has been "inverted," is what Kinbote denies: Jakob Gradus is actually Jack Grey, escaped from the insane asylum. The connection between Goldsworth's and Shade's similar features is made in a more indirect way, by stressing the resemblance between the judge and a cafeteria maid who is also said to look like Shade.[45] Thus in *Pale Fire* there is no detective but the reader, who has to be continuously alert to pick up the clues that Kinbote, unawares, scatters around. The mad scholar is rather an anti-detective, as he hides evidence and tries to impose on the reader a hallucinated version of the facts.

Hence after solutions with no justice, solutions through wrong clues, nonsolutions, and satanic solutions, we arrive in *Pale Fire* at the "double solution" (Kinbote's version and the reader's version) concerning the mystery of Shade's murder. The double solution coincides with the rational and irrational currents typical of detective fiction. In fact the choice is between a rational and plausible solution (the one the reader detects thanks to Kinbote's slips, that is, Jack Grey meant to kill Goldsworth and mistook Shade for him) and an irrational and "artistic" one, made up by hallucinating Kinbote. Of course, the reader knows which is the right version of the facts, but art has its own truth, and "artifice . . . is the only thing that can make reality endurable."[46] Certainly John Shade's assassination seems less meaningless if performed by Jakob Gradus rather than by Jack Grey. In the first case an old poet stumbling "by chance into the line of fire"[47] saved the life of a young king in exile; in the second a madman clumsily and senselessly mistook a poet for a judge. "Poetic justice" resides in the first "solution" since it is the one through which Kinbote's commentary finds its reason to exist and to complete with fantastic wings the Frostian resonance of Shade's "Pale Fire."

Kinbote is an anti-detective, a distorter of the text and not a "maker of meaning." Thus he can be easily connected with Calvino's Marana, who, however, is not an editor, but a translator who forges and mangles texts not out of love for an imaginary past but out of love and hate for a real woman. The readers of *Pale Fire* and of *Se una notte d'inverno un viaggiatore* must go through a similar operation because of these two characters. In comparison with *Pale Fire*, Calvino's novel requires an additional metafictional transition, for the real reader's reaction to the ten interrupted novels are "mirrored" and anticipated by the He-Reader and the She-Reader within the fiction. In fact *Se una notte d'inverno un viaggiatore* presents one relation between writer and reader outside the fiction and one within: 1) Writer (Calvino) deviously writing (hiding the solution of) the text and real reader trying to make sense out of it (seeking the solution—the reader as a detective). 2) Fictional "writer" (Marana, the translator-forger) forging and interrupting the texts within the text (hiding their conclusions) and fictional readers (the He-Reader and the She-Reader) trying to make sense out of them (seeking their conclusions).

In *Pale Fire* the "hide-and-seek" relation between writer and reader is simplified by the fact that there is no reader within the fiction: 1) Writer (Nabokov) deviously writing (hiding the solution of) the text and real reader trying to make sense out of it (seeking the solution—the reader as a detective). 2) Fictional "writer" (Kinbote, the commentator-distorter) distorting the text within the text (the poem "Pale Fire") by his comment.

Like Calvino's ten novels, "Pale Fire" also is unfinished, for Shade has not yet added the 1,000th line when he is shot by Jack Grey. Of course, Kinbote is happy to complete it for him by using as last the first line of the poem ("I was the shadow of the waxwing slain")[48] which does rhyme with the 999th ("Trundling an empty barrow up the lane.")[49] and gives "Pale Fire" a sense of circularity. This urge for circularity comes from the same anxiety for artistic timelessness that drove Kinbote to impose his fantasy on Shade and finally to write it himself in the hope to exorcise (to "complete") his Zemblan obsession through art.

The fact that Kinbote is hardly aware of being an artist as good as Shade when he writes in fiction what he wanted Shade to write for him in poetry does not make any difference. As usual, Kinbote's perception is "inverted," and, as in a game of mirrors, it becomes true if refracted again. In fact he says in his foreword: "Let me state that without my notes Shade's text simply has no human reality at all . . . a reality that only my notes can provide."[50] Rather, it is just reality that Shade provides, while Kinbote takes care of its antithesis, theatrical fantasy, and the reader must provide at last a synthesizing appreciation.

The hunt for a text and the circular structure are not the only characteristics by which *Pale Fire* anticipates *Se una notte d'inverno un viaggiatore* and *The Crying of Lot 49*. In fact, another characteristic Nabokov's work shares with Calvino's and Pynchon's novels (and also with the other deconstructive anti-detective novels) is a sense of conspiracy. Actually, *Pale Fire* includes the "classic conspiracy," which degenerates into a revolution and forces Charles the Beloved to flee his country through a secret passage in the royal palace. The passage leads into a theatre and from there the king reaches the border in a romantic hike through the mountains of Zembla. As in *Falling Angel*, *The Crying of Lot 49*, and *Se una notte d'inverno un viaggiatore*, the conspiracy in *Pale Fire* is mounted (imagined) for the exclusive "benefit" of one person, John Shade, who should write it all down in verses along with the rest of the story of Zembla. Of course, the conspiracy is too good to be true, is actually as theatrical as it is imaginary and partakes of Kinbote's persecution mania in real life. His homosexuality does sometimes cause the feelings of disapproval or of hostility he is ready to recognize in other people's attitudes toward him. These feelings are, however, more often motivated by his aggressive personality and by his irrepressible madness. In fact, as Kinbote is writing and living again his past with no past in the cottage in Cedarn, Utana (or in a madhouse?), he is gradually breaking down and giving the reader hints about the real state of his mind and thus about his special unreliability as a narrator. He candidly relates the episode in which a woman in a grocery store tells him: " 'You are a remarkably disagreeable person. I fail to see how John and Sybil [Shade] can stand you,' and, exasperated by my polite smile, she added: 'What's more, you are insane.' "[51] At Wordsmith University in New Wye, the notion of Kinbote's insanity is common, as even a mimeographed letter from the English department states that he "is known to have a deranged mind."[52] Out of his persecution mania, Kinbote also tells the reader of his commentary about a "brutal anonymous note saying: 'You have hal-----s real bad, chum,' meaning evidently 'hallucinations,' although a malevolent critic might infer from the insufficient number of dashes that little Mr. Anon [the alleged anonymous writer], despite teaching Freshman English, could hardly spell."[53] Kinbote is at least correct in being perplexed about the number of dashes, which in fact are rightly filled if one substitutes "halitosis." Thus Kinbote's defensive interpretation provides another clue that supports the reader's doubts about his sanity. His mentioning throughout the commentary that he is tortured by excruciating headaches[54] is a further hint of his impending mental breakdown. Kinbote almost gives the game away at the end of the commentary, as he did in the problem of the Gradus-Grey identity:

> Yes, better stop. My notes and self are petering out. . . . My work is finished. My poet is dead.
> "And you, what will *you* be doing with yourself, poor King, poor Kinbote?" a gentle young voice may inquire.
> God will help me, I trust. . . . I may assume other disguises, other forms, but I shall try to exist. . . . I may pander to the simple tastes of theatrical critics and cook up a stage play, an old-fashioned melodrama with three principles: a lunatic who intends to kill an imaginary king, another lunatic who imagines himself to be that king, and a distinguished old poet who stumbles by chance into the line of fire, and perishes in the clash between the two figments. Oh, I may do many things. . . . I may huddle and groan in a madhouse.[55]

In his usual theatrical fashion, Kinbote tells the reader the truth by reducing it to a project for a soap opera. When he mentions that he "may huddle and groan in a madhouse," even the Cedarn cottage disappears, and we envision a shabby mental institution where a logorrheic madman is building worlds of words for a silent audience of fellow inmates, as his self is "petering out."

Certainly there is some method in this madness. If we reject this last hint about the asylum, which reduces everything to a lunatic's fantasy, and accept as true at least the basic facts (Shade is killed because he is mistaken for Goldsworth, and his poem is edited by Kinbote), we are still supried by the promptness and detachment shown by Kinbote when Shade is shot. He does not waste a second; he leaves the body lying in the grass, hurries in the house, conceals the envelope containing the manuscript of the poem (which he "happened" to carry for Shade) at the bottom of a closet, dials 11111 for an ambulance, returns with a ridiculous but apparently thoughtful glass of water "to the scene of the carnage."[56] Everything is so perfect that it seems to have been planned and mentally rehearsed quite a few times. Could Kinbote also have "inverted" the truth about his talks with Jack Grey, rather than having made them up completely? While it is unlikely that he could have been allowed interviews with the lunatic after the murder, it is not altogether impossible that he could have talked with him before the murder and arranged Jack Grey's escape from "Zembla" (the asylum) rather than his own. He could have told him to come to the judge's house at a certain time to kill Goldsworth, perhaps even promising to bloodthirsty Jack Grey that he, Kinbote, would be with the judge, in front of his house, in order to make the assassin's task easier. The resemblance between Shade and Goldsworth, the fact that Kinbote was living in the judge's house and that Shade had been invited for dinner by Kinbote and was in front of the rented house can be seen as mere chances (quite a few, though) or as the elements on which a perfect murder has been built.

Another suspicious series of details is the following: "The armed gardener [Kinbote's gardener, who had clubbed down the killer with a spade] and the battered killer were smoking side by side on the steps . . . The gardener took the glass of water I had placed near a flowerpot and shared it with the killer, and then accompanied him to the basement toilet, and presently the police and the ambulance arrived."[57] Someone who has just hurt an assassin watches out, does not smoke or share with him a glass of water, or take the assassin to the bathroom, unless everything has been prearranged.

The fact that even this third version of the murder, which does not clash with the second, but rather completes it, as it explains puzzling details (the glass of water, the behavior of the gardener, the too many coincidences), is not impossible—there is not enough evidence for it or against it—makes *Pale Fire* even more tantalizing and gives it an unexpected "turn of the screw" of planned and lunatic wickedness. It would not be the first time that a loony fan of a celebrity shifts his aim from adoration to assassination. But Kinbote has indeed some reasons to have Shade killed. It is the only way in which he can snatch the manuscript from the poet and at the same time be given permission to edit it. In fact it is easy for Kinbote to take advantage of Sybil's sorrow and confusion and to play on his alleged (and vain) heroic defense of the poet as related by the gardener:

> [B]ut Shade's widow found herself so deeply affected by the idea of my having "thrown myself" between the gunman and his target that during a scene I shall never forget, she cried out, stroking my hands: "There are things for which no recompense in this world or another is great enough." That "other world" comes in handy when misfortune befalls the infidel but I let it pass of course, and indeed, resolved not to refute anything, saying instead: "Oh, but there *is* a recompense, my dear Sybil. It may seem to you a very modest request but—give me the permission, Sybil, to edit and publish John's last poem." The permission was given at once, with new cries and new hugs, and already next day her signature was under the agreement I had a quick little lawyer draw up.[58]

When (and if) Kinbote planned the murder, he was certain that Shade's poem was about Zembla. To become the editor of the work seemed to him the only way to make the poem his own, to link his name forever with the poem and its artistic eternity. But "Pale Fire" has nothing to do with Zembla, and Kinbote has to cover up his murder in order not to get caught and not to show that he had someone killed for nothing, which would make him not only a lunatic but a fool as well. The Zemblan fantasy could even be considered a way to distract the reader from seeing Kinbote's involvement in the murder (which in a nonfantastic account of the facts would come almost as a natural connection) and to cancel its evidence by overburdening the killing with romantic and "inverted" details: Gradus is not Jacques d'Argus sent by the Shadows to kill Charles the Beloved but Jack Grey sent by Kinbote to kill his beloved Shade.

It would be nice to prove that Kinbote by his pseudocommentary—in which he imagined that the murder was not planned by him but by the Zemblan regicidal organization (the Shadows)—made one neat package of both his Zemblan fantasy and his guilt for Shade's useless death at the same time. Unfortunately, I cannot find for this theory the kind of chronological evidence which Christina Tekiner[59] finds to demonstrate that all that happens in Nabokov's *Lolita* after Humbert gets the letter from Lolita is a fruit of his imagination and thus he stops being a memoir writer to become an artist, for he creates the last nine chapters out of his inability to deal with reality, with a pregnant, older Lolita. In this sense, reading the manuscript of Shade's poem would have on Kinbote the same effect that Lolita's letter had on Humbert. Unable to deal with the reality of the poem, he would set himself to distorting it, creating for it a new reality through his pseudocommentary, through his imagination.

It is worth remembering that Oedipa also became an "artist" because of an unexpected letter from a law firm in which she found out that "she, Oedipa, had been named executor, or she supposed executrix, of the estate of one Pierce Inverarity."[60] The unexpected contents of letters and manuscripts (think also of the mysterious Aristotle codex in *Il nome della rosa*) play an important role in anti-detective fiction, which in turn often involves the hunt for lost (the Aristotle codex in *Il nome della rosa*), corrupted (the Scurvhamite version of *The Courier's Tragedy*) or complete books (Calvino's ten novels in *Se una notte d'inverno un viaggiatore*). Books, letters, and manuscripts inside the fiction testify to the special concern for literary matters of the anti-detective novel, which is in the metafictional category a "book conscious of its bookness."

Like *Se una notte d'inverno un viaggiatore* and *The Crying of Lot 49*, *Pale Fire* has both a deconstructive and a metafictional aspect, although the second is predominant. It proves itself a deconstructive anti-detective novel as it offers a "double solution": the fantastic and irrational one Kinbote tries to impose on the reader and the plausible and rational one the reader-detective reconstructs through Kinbote's slips. The third possibility I mentioned goes along with the deconstructive aims of *Pale Fire* since it poses a disturbing alternative to the second version just as the reader becomes ready to accept it as the solution.

In *Pale Fire,* as in *Se una notte d'inverno un viaggiatore,* there is not a detective but an anti-detective who complicates the mystery in the text thanks to his literary job, which, rather than complicating, was instead supposed to clarify the text. In fact Kinbote takes advantage of his role as editor and commentator to distort the truth; Marana is not a translator of but a "traitor"[61] to texts as he corrupts and forges them. His "opposite," the He-Reader, trying in vain to read a complete book, certainly elicits a sympathetic response from the real reader, who experiences the same frustration. No He-Reader or She-Reader within the fiction is present in *Pale Fire,* in which the real reader is also the detective. As detection shifts from murder in the text to "murdered" (distorted, forged) texts, and as the reader is forced reluctantly to fulfill both the role of victim (he is deprived of the pleasure of the text) and the one of detective (he must "seek it") at the same time, we enter the realm of metafictional anti-detective fiction.

The focus of the novel is no longer the relation among the characters, as it is in conventional novels, but rather the one among the writer, the reader, and the text. In fact the writer makes the reader continuously self-conscious about his fictional creation and even addresses himself directly to him. In *Se una notte d'inverno un viaggiatore* the various narrators of Calvino's unfinished novels remind the reader continuously that he is reading fiction and so does Calvino himself in the introductions to the unfinished novels, as he plays with the personal pronouns. In *Pale Fire* Kinbote reminds the reader continuously that he is reading fiction by his absurd notes to "Pale Fire," which is a poem, a "fiction" onto which he is trying to impose another "fictional truth," his commentary, in which he addresses himself to the real reader.

In the metafictional category the anti-detective novel becomes mainly 'assassination" of texts and "hide-and-seek" between the writer and reader. The detective game is rarefied and intellectualized to such an extent that it becomes the sophisticated ritualization of the timeless game between writer and reader present in any good novel. The roles of the murderer and of the detective are here played mainly outside the fiction by the writer and by the reader respectively. The text is the "corpse," as it is mutilated ("translated" by Marana) or disfigured ("edited" by Kinbote). The reader can bring the text-corpse "back to life" by solving the mystery, that is, by piecing together its unfinished parts (the titles which compose a "solution" in *Se una notte d'inverno un viaggiatore*) or by making sense out of the distortion imposed on it (Kinbote's commentary). In both cases, the corpse is no longer within the text, but is the text itself; consequently the main relation between detective and murderer is not within the text but outside it, since the reader's role is to reconstruct the corpse that the writer offers him.

Largely, the game is again between the creative side of M. Dupin (the writer who creates and "murders" the fiction) and his resolvent side (the reader, who tries to "resurrect"—and thus also to "recreate—the murdered fiction by making sense out of it). The Poesque duality here becomes the polarization of the relation between writer and reader, between the fiction-maker and his active recipient.

6

The Detective Unbound

What is the future of anti-detective fiction? We saw how its three categories interact and sometimes merge, giving life to a "fiction of possibilities," while conventional detective fiction always ends up being a "fiction of certainty."

Until a decade ago anti-detective fiction could easily be considered the postmodern exploitation of a subgenre, the product of that typically avant-garde process that absorbs and regenerates literary "pariahs." Now, after at least a twenty-year span of anti-detective fiction, the process appears more articulate, drawing not only from an avant-garde revaluation of low genres, but from an awareness that the only possibly vital fiction today is allusive fiction, a fiction of potentialities. The time for easy affirmation seems long gone. Anti-detective fiction denies what the reader is accustomed to expect, justice and a happy denouement; it tantalizes and confuses him by proliferating clues and by nonsolution; or even plays prestidigitation games with him as it denies him heartfelt involvement, reassurance, and escape from reality by reminding him continuously that fiction is only fiction.

It could be said that this is a literature of negation much more than one of affirmation and that eventually even the reader will become a negative (nonexistent) counterpart in too-rarefied fictional games performed by heartless authors. Yet it seems safe to consider anti-detective fiction more a literature of possibility than one of negation. The only adequate solution to a life of possibility is the acceptance of it, of total suspension, since to "solve life" is to accept the mystery within it. Our own is of course no time of certainty, as the possibility for total annihilation has never before been so real. To ask literature for certainty is to relegate it to the role of the sleeping pill, which good fiction by definition cannot accept.

As the He-Reader in Calvino's *Se una notte d'inverno un viaggiatore* puts it, "the best we can expect is to avoid the worst," that is, the best we can do is not to consider the worst a certainty, but only a strong possibility. The "worst as a strong possibility" is the revised oxymoron from which anti-detective fiction and contemporary fiction generally draw their precarious lives.

It should in fact be clear by now that good contemporary fiction and anti-detective fiction are for the most part the same thing, and contemporary fiction is the ultimate exploitation of "cheap" nineteenth-century detective fiction. Any recent good novel that holds the attention of the reader through suspense, undermines his expectations, and offers a revelation (often unpleasant), is largely drawing on anti-detective fiction's techniques. These techniques are in turn the inversion of detective fictional techniques, that is, the postmodern negation of the centeredness and reassurance typical of the genre. In turn the detective novel, which existed in seeds much before Poe catalyzed it (think of the *Newgate Calendar,* of the Gothic tales, of Voltaire's *Zadig*), is the vital core of man's rational exorcism of the mystery of life through evocation of the unexplainable (the "irrational" moment) and its subsequent explanation (the "rational"moment)—again, M. Dupin's creative and resolvent forces.

This double concern, which is shown in the rational and irrational currents, always merging and intersecting in detective fiction, remained vital until the early twentieth century. In fact the years during and after World War II proved a fundamental turning point in the Western World: man gives up his pretense of reassuring and explainable mystery and does not any more expect to "solve" it (existentialism, *nouveau roman*). The "irrational" current of detective fiction, after the zenith reached by the best examples of the hard-boiled (Hammett, Chandler), degenerates again into mass media and trash fiction, while the rational current represented by the old-fashioned British mystery, Agatha Christie-style, seems to have by now become a literary dead end. It is saved by what it still epitomizes, which is fictional order, tightly structured plot, centralization—in other words, all that postmodernism denies. So it is chosen as the perfect genre to be subverted and "decapitated" (that is, deprived of a solution) by the postmodern imagination and, paradoxically, the apparent dead end is turned into a new life by the wreckage of the formula. In fact the most important literary movement now visible, the ironic, intellectual fiction of Borges, Pynchon, and Calvino is the ultimate result of the apparent *cul-de-sac* of the old-style British mystery. Thus the Poesque rules, codified in the British mystery, once severed from the "genre-centralization" and subsumed into the "free circuit" of literature, have proved to be still vital and capable of new and original combinations.

We have here a sort of cyclical situation that can be summarized this way:

1) Seeds of detective fiction anterior to Poe are part of man's needs for reassurance and explanation of mystery, that is, closely connected with life and death, basic concerns of the human mind.

2) Poe catalyzes and codifies the irrational and rational attitudes toward mystery in his new invention, the detective story, in which the rational explanation of the mystery supersedes the exorcism of mystery through "irrational" reevocation (typical, for example, of the Gothic tales).

3) The rational and irrational currents interact in detective fiction and one dominates the other according to the moral and social concerns of each epoch (e.g., Victorian morality and positivism: stereotyped and puzzle-like British detective fiction).

4) Postmodernism does the opposite of what Poe did 100 years ago: it decentralizes and deconstructs the old rules that already had been undermined by the hard-boiled school and by Naturalism. The "detective fiction machine" is either renewed and undermined at the same time (*A ciascuno il suo*), or subverted (*The Crying of Lot 49*), or transcended (*Pale Fire*), and

at times even totally pulled apart and used piece by piece (any good fiction taking advantage of detective-novel techniques such as mysterious death of a character, suspense, an unreliable narrator, the search for a mysterious object—think for example of John Hawkes' *The Blood Oranges*). One may go so far as to say that whenever there is an unreliable narrator (and in contemporary fiction there is almost always an unreliable narrator), there is potential or actual anti-detective fiction, that is, a fiction that in an original way exploits and subverts conventional detective-novel techniques. In fact detective-fictional rules, precisely because severed from the "genre-centralization," are restored to fiction in general and become the ground on which authors may write literary detective fiction. Thus paradoxically, contemporary literary fiction is the result of the wreckage and decentralization of the "low" detective novel's code. To some extent, any good contemporary fiction is basically anti-detective fiction, the ultimate "grinding" (inversion or even "pulverization") of the Poesque rules.

5) We go back to the beginning. The detective and detective-like concerns are no longer constricted within a set of rules (Poe). Anti-detective fiction restores and assimilates them to twentieth-century man's acceptance of the nonlogical in everyday life. Once decapitated by the nonsolution, detective rules no longer epitomize a genre but a contemporary attitude toward life as a mystery to be accepted. This will be so until these rules are eventually subsumed, reinterpreted, recycled (codified?) by a new epoch, a new attitude toward life and its mystery.

Notes   Bibliography   Index

Notes

1. THE DEVELOPMENT OF THE DETECTIVE NOVEL AND THE RISE OF THE ANTI-DETECTIVE NOVEL

1. See Leonardo Sciascia, "Appunti sul 'giallo'," *Nuova Corrente* 1 (June 1954), pp. 28–29, in which Sciascia distinguishes a logical and an emotional type of detective novel, connecting the former to Poe and the latter to the Gothic novel. All Italian, French, German, Russian, and Spanish titles are noted throughout this book in their original languages. A published English translation, if it exists, is given in parentheses or in a note the first time the title is mentioned.

2. A. E. Murch, *The Development of the Detective Novel* (London: Peter Owen, 1958), p. 26. Although more than twenty years old, Murch's book is still one of the best works on this subject. I am indebted to it for valuable information on the forerunners of the detective novel.

3. See Murch, p. 18.

4. See Murch, p. 19.

5. Edgar Allan Poe, "The Murders in the Rue Morgue," in *The Short Fiction of Edgar Allan Poe*, ed. Stuart Levine and Susan Levine (Indianapolis: Bobbs-Merrill, 1976) p. 180.

6. Poe, p. 180. Italics mine.

7. A similar division emphasizing the clash between the rational and the irrational side of Poe's personality is the one made by Julian Symons, who in *The Tell-Tale Heart* (New York: Harper & Row, 1978) distinguishes between a "Logical Poe" and a "Visionary Poe" (pp. 173–179).

8. See Robert Louis Stevenson, "The Strange Case of Dr. Jekyll and Mr. Hyde" (1886), in *The Works of Robert Louis Stevenson,* Tusitala Edition, vol. 5 (London: Heinemann, 1927).

9. "When I [Jekyll] know how he [Hyde] fears my power to cut him off by suicide, I find it in my heart to pity him," Stevenson, p. 73.

10. Poe, "The Purloined Letter," *Short Fiction,* p. 232.

11. Poe, p. 231.

12. Poe, p. 210.

13. Joseph Wood Krutch, *Edgar Allan Poe* (London: Alfred A. Knopf, 1926), p. 118

14. D. H. Lawrence, *Studies in Classic American Literature* (Harmondsworth: Penguin Books, 1977), pp. 70, 74.

15. In the 1840s Poe subjected the concept of mystery to the kind of logical deconstruction that Marx during the same period applied to the social structure (*The Communist Manifesto,* 1848). Both of them show "how it works," but Poe, by making logic out of mystery, creates order and reassurance (in fact as he

deconstructs it he demythologizes it). Marx, on the other hand, reveals by logic the system of exploitation of the capitalistic state. His deconstruction is thus an accusation against the bourgeois ruling class, the prelude to that social disorder (the working class revolution), the fear of which is supposedly just what the detective novel unconsciously exorcised in its predominantly bourgeois readers during the 1920s and the 1930s.

16. Poe was almost certainly not aware of Baudelaire, who was soon going to publish his revolutionary *Les Fleurs du Mal,* (1857) with its strikingly Poesque identification of the lying artist and the "hypocrite lecteur." Baudelaire translated and made Poe's work popular in France. In 1848, his first translation, "La révélation mesmerique," was published in *La liberté de pensée.*

17. In fact the publication history of the feuilleton began itself in melodramatic conflict. The original project of Emile de Girardin to publish a new daily that would print novels in serials with the financial help of Dutacq, owner of the newspaper *Le Droit,* fell through. The two men ended up publishing separately on the same day, July 1, 1836, two dailies (see Angela Bianchini, *Il romanzo d'appendice* [Turin: Edizioni Rai Radiotelevisione Italiana, 1969], pp. 12–13). The simultaneous publication of *Presse* by Giradin and *Siècle* by Dutacq immediately set off a long journalistic fight to secure the best available authors to write feuilleton serials. Writers like Balzac, Sand, and Dumas were some of the best paid and most popular.

18. Antonio Gramsci, *Quaderni del carcere,* vol. 3 (Turin: Einaudi, 1975), p. 2134. Translation mine.

19. A good description of Holmes' dual nature, so similar to Dupin's, is given by Watson in the following passage:

> My friend was an enthusiastic musician, being himself not only a very capable performer but a composer of no ordinary merit. All the afternoon he sat in the stalls wrapped in the most perfect happiness, gently waving his long, thin fingers in time to the music, while his gently smiling face and his languid, dreamy eyes were as unlike those of Holmes, the sleuth-hound, Holmes the relentless, keen-witted, ready-handed criminal agent, as it was possible to conceive. In his singular character the *dual nature* alternately asserted itself, and his extreme exactness and astuteness represented, as I have often thought, the reaction against the poetic and contemplative mood which occasionally predominated in him. . . . Then it was that the lust of the chase would suddenly come upon him, and that *his brilliant reasoning power would rise to the level of intuition,* until those who were unacquainted with his methods would look askance at him as on a man whose knowledge was not that of other mortals. (From "The Red-Headed League" in *The Penguin Complete Sherlock Holmes,* Harmondsworth: Penguin, 1981, p. 185; italics mine.)

20. *The Ways of the Hour* is a forerunner of the French *roman judiciaire* and has characteristics of both the mystery novel and the social novel, of which Cooper was so fond in his later production. It is the story of a rich woman, unjustly accused of a double murder, who wants to be acquitted by the popular jury (the jury system had just been introduced in the United States) without having to defend herself personally, although she could easily prove her inno-

cence. The consequence of her whimsical belief in the unreliable jury system (here is Cooper's polemical point) is a death sentence. At the end, as she finally decides to defend herself, the reader realizes she is insane. Both mystery and trial are geared to the social purpose of the novel, that is, Cooper's claim that a popular jury is so ineffective as to be unable to recognize insanity from sanity and that, even worse, only a crazy woman could entrust her life solely to its good functioning. *The House of the Seven Gables* is a romance in which a family curse, mystery, and strange deaths play an important part, but no detection presents itself: Judge Pyncheon's long stillness in the armchair produces little suspense and less detection, as the reader understands immediately that the Judge is dead. In "Benito Cereno" Captain Delano is supplied with sufficient clues to allow him to make a classical detection; that is, he gets clues that might allow him to realize that the *San Dominick* has been taken over by its slaves; but the Captain's innocent nature, if not bluntness of mind, makes him unable to see evil and draw the logical conclusions, notwithstanding those suspenseful moments in which the revelation seems about to burst through. Even earlier in the American tradition, we encounter potential situations for the detective exercise. For example, James Fenimore Cooper's *The Deerslayer* (1841) anticipates a state of affairs similar to that in Poe's "The Purloined Letter" (1845). Deerslayer and his friend Chingachgook look for the key to a mysterious chest—which supposedly hides proofs of Judith's identity—in one of the most obvious places, that is, the pocket of a ragged dress belonging to Hetty, Judith's sister. The cunning Indian Chingachgook and Deerslayer know that the obvious place is a perfect hiding spot, as the refined Judith would never think of laying a hand on coarse clothes during her search for the key (see *The Deerslayer*, New York: Signet, 1963, pp. 196–98). Deerslayer's technique of finding clues of Indian presence through his observation of nature and objects (e.g., the "classical" broken twig, p. 25, or an Indian moccasin floating on the lake, p. 318) is obviously a form of detection based on the inductive principle. But no crime is involved, and the moment is tangential to the main business of the novel. In the five "Leatherstocking Tales," which range from 1823 to 1841, Deerslayer (alias Natty Bumppo, alias Hawkeye, alias Trapper, alias Leatherstocking, alias Pathfinder) defines himself as a prototype of the detective. Like future heroes of the detective-novel genre from Dupin (who emerged as a literary creation in 1841) to Sherlock Holmes to Philip Marlowe, Deerslayer, the "scout," is a bachelor. His exclusive devotion to the forest as a source of endless "natural detections" is equivalent to the detective's obsessive devotion to his job.

21. Marjorie Nicolson, "The Professor and the Detective," *The Atlantic*, April 1929, p. 485.

22. Nicolson, p. 486.

23. Michael Holquist, "Whodunit and Other Questions: Metaphysical Detective Stories in Post-War Fiction," *New Literary History* 3 (Autumn 1971) 147. Michael Holquist's remarkable essay is, along with William V. Spanos' "The Detective and the Boundary," *Boundary 2*, 1(Fall 1972), p. 1, one of the pioneering contributions in the field of the anti-detective novel (which Holquist calls metaphysical detective novel).

24. Nicolson, "The Professor and the Detective," p. 487.

25. Nicolson, p. 490.

26. Julian Symons, *The Detective Story in Britain* (London: Longmans, 1962), p. 22.

27. Walter Benjamin, "Paris, die Hauptstadt des XIX. Jahrhunderts," *Illuminationen, Ausgewählte Schriften* (Frankfurt am Main: Suhrkamp Verlag, 1961), pp. 193, 194. Translation mine.

28. Raymond Chandler, "The Simple Art of Murder," *The Atlantic*, December 1944, p. 58.

29. W. M. Frohock, *The Novel of Violence in America* (Dallas: Southern Methodist University Press, 1958), pp. 21–22.

30. Raymond Chandler, "The Simple Art of Murder," p. 59.

31. Dashiell Hammett, *The Continental Op*, ed. by Steven Marcus (New York: Random House, 1974), p. xx.

32. Dashiell Hammett, *Red Harvest* (London: Cassell, 1974), p. 165. John G. Cawelti offers an insightful and stimulating interpretation of Hammett's *Red Harvest* in his impressive *Adventure, Mystery, and Romance* (Chicago: University of Chicago Press, 1976), a study of literary formulas that, concerning detective fiction, anticipates some of the arguments developed in this and in the following chapter.

33. Edward Margolies, "The American Detective Thriller and the Idea of Society," *Dimensions of Detective Fiction*, ed. Larry N. Landrum, Pat Browne, Ray B. Browne (Bowling Green, Ohio: Bowling Green University Popular Press, 1976), p. 84.

34. Loris Rambelli, *Storia del "giallo" italiano* (Milano: Garzanti, 1979), p. 33. Translation mine. The following significant passage from this valuable work (the only history of the Italian detective novel and the source of a good deal of my information on the subject) further explains Varaldo's technique: "Varaldo sensed, perhaps without even realizing it, that the main characteristic of the *giallo* is irony: since the author of detective novels states that the detection will unfold according to logic, he actually knows very well that he will have to resort to some trick in order to cause the opportune intervention of chance and knows that in the tide of the described details many will be useless and actually even misleading: it will be up to the reader to detect them" (Rambelli, p. 40; translation mine).

35. Rambelli, pp. 115–17.

36. The *neorealismo* was a cultural movement born after World War II which yielded good results, especially in cinema (e.g., Vittorio De Sica's films such as *Sciuscià*, 1946, and *Ladri di biciclette*, 1948) and in fiction (e.g., Beppe Fenoglio's *I ventitré giorni della città di Alba*, 1952, and, to a certain extent, Italo Calvino's first novel, *Il sentiero dei nidi di ragno*, 1947). The *neorealismo* stressed episodes of the partisan and popular Resistance against the German occupation, the harshness of Italian reality after the devastation of the war, and the necessity for a social and political message in art—an art that also would evoke a rediscovery of lyricism in the poverty of everyday life.

37. As Rambelli points out in his *Storia del "giallo" italiano*, this attempt to publish collections of literary detective novels, although significant as a proof of the crisis present in the publishing market of the "serious novel," has been

mostly unsuccessful; such was the case of the short-lived collection "Il Rigogolo" (Milan: Rizzoli, 1968) edited by Raffaele Crovi. Instead, isolated high-quality detective novels presented as "straight novels" (e.g., *La donna della domenica* by Carlo Fruttero and Franco Lucentini, Milan: Mondadori, 1972) have had a remarkable commercial success.

Another interesting and successful experiment was conducted in 1980 when the magazine *Panorama* commissioned some Italian celebrities—men of culture, judges, politicians, managers—to write detective stories related to their lives and professions. In the form of booklets, the detective stories were added to the weekly issues of the magazine itself; the title of this unusual collection of *gialli*—which went on for a few weeks—was "i gialli verità" [detective stories of truth] in order to emphasize their "fictional true report" common character. This episode could be considered merely as an original device to increase sales (altogether a late-late sophisticated version of the idea behind the *Newgate Calendar* reports: the "true" account), but I see in it also a proof of the persistent view of the detective story as divertissement for intellectuals. I also see it as an indication of the vitality of the genre and of the lasting cryptic tendency "to improve upon it" by having detective stories written by prestigious nonprofessionals, either "serious novelists" or politicians.

A more popular and playful approach to the detective novel has been recently offered by "Giallosera" [The evening detective story], a television program broadcast in spring 1983 by RAI, the Italian television network. A host introduced a detective story situation set in a hotel, asking two candidates in the studio and the television audience at home to find out who the culprit was. Then a film acting out the situation was shown and stopped a moment before the house detective (played by the host) unravelled the mystery. At this point, the two candidates and the television audience were asked to guess who the murderer was. Afterwards the filmed denouement of the story followed and showed who was right and who was wrong.

38. The *nouveau roman* is, in a typical French way, one of the most precisely theorized literary movements of the century. The emphasis is on the silent presence ("being there" rather than "becoming") of things and surfaces, and on their antisymbolical and antimythical (thus antimodernist) "thingness." The *nouveau roman* tries to describe things and their "still action" on enviroment and men, not implying any symbolical or mythical meaning in these descriptions. The detective-like atmosphere of many of these novels (Robbe-Grillet's *Les Gommes, Dans le labyrinthe, La Jalousie, Le Voyeur*) should somehow replace the action and stimulate some interest in the reader. At the same time the stress on bare surfaces and objects (which may become clues, "detective objects") and a sort of camera-eye detached and analytical third-person narrator (very careful in avoiding any description of feelings—only things matter) should attack the traditional (or even modernist) novel conceived as "experiment in depth," as an attempt at essence (symbolical meaning), and rather "establish the novel on the surface . . . [thus] the novel becomes man's direct experience of what surrounds him without his being able to shield himself with a psychology, a metaphysic, or a psychoanalytic method in his combat with the objective world he discovers." (*Two Novels by Robbe-Grillet, Jealousy & In the*

Labyrinth, Introductory Essay by Roland Barthes [New York: Grove Press, 1965], p. 25). All this is very interesting from a theoretical point of view but, once written, the *nouveau roman* is often disappointing for the reader, an experiment in form and surfaces with frequently little substance and less life.

39. *Les Gommes* (Paris: Les Editions de Minuit, 1953) reminds one of Oscar Wilde's "Lord Arthur Savile's Crime" (1887), in which a palm reader predicts to Lord Arthur that he shall commit murder and Lord Arthur in fact ends up killing the palm reader. I do not know if Robbe-Grillet took the idea for *Les Gommes* from Wilde's short story. There are, however, two basic differences: Lord Arthur is not a detective and the plot is more a light parody of a crime story than a serious and intentional exploitation of the detective fiction genre. Also Wilde's "The Portrait of Mr. W. H." (1889), narrating the attempt to discover the identity of the mysterious W. H. to whom Shakespeare addressed his sonnets, is more a fascinating "Borgesian" case of scholarly detection than a true detective story.

40. William V. Spanos in his original essay "The Detective and the Boundary: Some Notes on the Postmodern Literary Imagination" (*Boundary 2*, 1 [Fall 1972], pp. 147–68) has been the first to use this term, describing the anti-detective novel as "the paradigmatic archetype of the postmodern literary imagination . . . the formal purpose of which is to evoke the impulse to 'detect' and/or to psychoanalyze in order to violently frustrate it by refusing to solve the crime (or find the cause of the neurosis)" (p. 154).

41. Tzvetan Todorov, *The Poetics of Prose* (Oxford: Basil Blackwell, 1977), p. 43. Original title: *Poétique de la prose* (Paris: Editions du Seuil, 1971).

2. TOWARD A DEFINITION OF THE ANTI-DETECTIVE NOVEL

1. Jurij N. Tynjanov, "Literaturnyj Fakt," in *Poetika, Istorija Literatury, Kino* (Moscow: Nauka, 1977), p. 262. Translation mine. This essay was originally published with a slightly different title in the magazine *Lef* in 1924, and subsequently in a collection of essays by Tynjanov, *Archaisty i novàtory* (Leningrad: Priboj, 1929).

2. Thomas S. Kuhn, *The Structure of Scientific Revolutions* (Chicago: University of Chicago Press, 1970).

3. See Ihab Hassan, "POSTmodernISM, A Paracritical Bibliography," *New Literary History* 3, no.1 (Autumn 1971), p. 11.

4. See John Barth, "The Literature of Replenishment," *The Atlantic*, January 1980, p. 66.

5. See for example the following articles: Ihab Hassan, "POSTmodernISM, A Paracritical Bibliography"; John Barth, "The Literature of Replenishment"; Gerald Graff, "The Myth of the Postmodernist Breakthrough," *Tri-Quarterly* 26 (1975); William Spanos, "The Detective and the Boundary: Some Notes on the Postmodern Literary Imagination," *Boundary 2* 1, no. 1 (Fall 1972); Michael Holquist, "Whodunit and Other Questions: Metaphysical Detective Stories in the Post-War Fiction," *New Literary History* 3, no. 1 (Autumn 1971).

6. Existentialism as the philosophical discovery and acceptance of the limits of human reason, of the void, and the *ante litteram* postmodernism as literary application of existentialism do not even claim to substitute for the modernist code. The void is no longer shielded by a mythological system (modernism), which justifies itself by struggling against a materialistic middle-class morality; in fact the bourgeois ethos is by now as broken as the modernist mythology. There is no moral system or center on which to rely. Man senses what in existential terms has been called the death of God, the absence of any purpose in the universe. The choice now is between stoic endurance of nothingness—of a total freedom that is also suffering and dread because it is not soothed by any "mythical" reassurance (God)—and self-annihilation that comes from clinging to anesthetic worship of a neopositivistic technological society. For a detailed discussion of existentialism see William Barrett, *Irrational Man: A Study in Existential Philosophy* (New York: Doubleday, 1958).

7. See Michael Holquist, "Whodunit and Other Questions."

8. William V. Spanos, "The Detective and the Boundary," p. 167.

9. These five definitions stress two main aspects of postmodernism as it has developed in the last fifteen years. The first aspect is still closely connected with existentialism as the postmodernist philosophy; the second shows how post-modernism has lately found more articulated (and less strictly existential) paths of growth and self-awareness. 1) Black humor and new gothicism stress the acceptance of the existential void through a nihilistic "dark laughter." Nothing-ness is everything and thus comic and tragic at the same time; the dark laughter is a saving attitude because, as long as you laugh at what cannot be either ordered or foreseen, you are alive and coping with it in a nonself-destructive way—this seems to be the most that an unreliable twentieth-century writer can promise his reader. 2) New fiction, metafiction, and fabulation stress the playful mistrust of the writer (and often of the narrator) for his literary medium; the problem of the relationship linking writer-narrator-characters-reader; the laying bare of the fictional techniques that sometimes become the content of the fiction itself; and the sheer pleasure for its own sake of telling unreliable stories.

10. Jurij Tynjanov, "Literaturnyj Fakt," p. 259.

This statement by Tynjanov recalls one made by William Barrett in *Irrational Man:* "Every age projects its own image of man into its art" (p. 52). Also, Barrett argues that recent art is "concerned, in any case, simply with the de-struction of the traditional image of man," so that nothingness has become "one of the chief themes in modern art literature" (p. 54). These general observa-tions, when applied to our topic, explain the postmodern destruction of the traditional image of the detective as a detached and successful man. In fact, as we will see, the detective of the anti-detective novel gets emotionally involved in the mystery and often fails to solve it. The detective novel structure itself is destroyed in the anti-detective novel which, in the deconstructive category, offers no solution: nothingness, acceptance of the mystery, becomes its chief theme. Indeed Barrett's work shows throughout that existentialism, as a phi-losophy stressing the limits of human reason and the consequent acceptance of "nothingness," prepares for the nonsolution of the anti-detective novel.

11. See part 2 of note 9.

12. The Freudian adaptation of the Oedipus myth may be used to illustrate this concept of time in detective fiction. Theoretically conceived, the Freudian construct recalls the Dupin paradox: the detective and the criminal depend upon, or "invent" each other. The Freudian construct might be expressed as follows: to the detective, to find (and perhaps kill) the culprit is to find (and perhaps kill) a father, since the fiction in which he exists is generated by a crime, and without a criminal the detective would not exist otherwise. The fiction does indeed end when the detective finds the "father"; the quest has been fulfilled and, after his descent into the past, the detective comes back into the present to explain to a skeptical audience his successful reconstruction of things past.

13. See Guido Carboni, "Un matrimonio ben riuscito? Note sul giallo d'azione negli USA," *Calibano* 2 (Rome: Savelli, 1978), p. 118.

14. See for example Ana Maria Barrenechea, *Borges, the Labyrinth Maker* (New York: New York University Press, 1965).

15. Michel Butor, *Passing Time,* translated from the French by Jean Stewart (New York: Simon & Schuster, 1960), p. 3. Original title: *L'emploi du temps* (Paris: Les Editions de Minuit, 1956). Italics mine. One of the very few *nouveaux romans* in which "form and surfaces" do not suffocate "substance and life."

16. Claude Ollier's *La Mise en Scène* (Paris: Les Editions de Minuit, 1958) is not available in English. Alain Robbe-Grillet's *La Jalousie,* published by Les Editions de Minuit in 1957, has been translated into English (*Two Novels by Robbe-Grillet, Jealousy & In the Labyrinth* [New York: Grove Press, 1965]).

17. "La muerte y la brújula," "La ruinas circulares," "El jardín de senderos que se bifurcan," "La forma de la espada" belong to the collection of short stories *Ficciones* (Buenos Aires: Editorial Sur, 1944), published in English under the same title (New York: Grove Press, 1962).

18.*Dans le labyrinthe* by Alain Robbe-Grillet was published by Les Editions de Minuit in 1959; for English translation see note 16.

19. "Abenjacán el Bojarí, muerto en su laberinto" belongs to the collection of short stories *El Aleph* (Buenos Aires: Editorial Losada, 1949), published in English under the title *The Aleph & Other Stories* (New York: Dutton, 1979).

3. THE INNOVATIVE ANTI-DETECTIVE NOVEL

1. See Luigi Cattanei, *Leonardo Sciascia* (Florence: Le Monnier, 1979), p. 6.

2. Leonardo Sciascia, "Appunti sul 'giallo,' " *Nuova Corrente* 1 (June 1954), p. 28. Translation mine. Unless otherwise noted, all the translations from the Italian in this chapter are my own.

3. Leonardo Sciascia, "La carriera di Maigret," *Letteratura 2,* no. 10 (July-August 1954), pp. 73–75.

4. Leonardo Sciascia, "Letteratura del 'giallo,' " *Letteratura 2,* no. 3 (May-June, 1953), p. 66.

5. Leonardo Sciascia, "Letteratura del 'giallo,'" p. 66.

6. See Norman Lewis, *The Honored Society* (New York: G. P. Putnam's Sons, 1964), pp. 34–43.

7. Conversation of Jole F. Magri with Leonardo Sciascia quoted in the introduction by Jole F. Magri to Leonardo Sciascia, *A ciascuno il suo* 5th ed. (Turin: Einaudi, 1977), p. vi.

8. It may well be that Sciascia would refuse the definition "postmodern" for himself and for his work. In his novels, as in the case of many other talented writers, there are also traditional and modern (as opposed to postmodern) tendencies that, if isolated and stressed, could give way to other possible critical judgments. To note how approximate labels and definitions are one need only remember that, within anti-detective fiction, Sciascia is "innovative" in *A ciascuno il suo* while he becomes "deconstructive" in *Todo modo*. In the case of Calvino it seems easier to individuate a pattern of postmodern preoccupations, as it is with most writers who are concerned with metafictional impulses. Eco's studies on mass media, semiotics, and the role of the reader in narrative structures make his postmodern concerns especially evident.

9. The epigraph from Poe in the opening page of the novel is in Italian.

10. Leonardo Sciascia, *Le parrocchie di Regalpetra* (Bari: Laterza, 1956), p. 11.

11. Leonardo Sciascia, *A ciascuno il suo*, p. 37. Italics mine.

12. See for example the following passage: "Concerning his private life, he was considered [by the people in the village] the victim of the exclusive and jealous affection of his mother: and it was indeed true" (Sciascia, p. 41).

13. Sciascia, *A ciascuno il suo*, pp. 43, 112.

14. Sciascia, p. 112.

15. Sciascia, p. 134.

16. The novel's symbolism is reminiscent of Moravia's *The Time of Indifference* (*Gli indifferenti*, 1929), in which the speculator Leo marries Carla, the beautiful daughter of his longtime lover Mariagrazia, obtaining also the reluctant acquiescence of Michele, Carla's brother, and of Mariagrazia herself. The novel is a subtle parody of the bourgeoisie's compromise with the fascist regime, which obtained respectability through the bourgeois acceptance and in return guaranteed privileges and social security to the upper-middle class.

17. Sciascia, *A ciascuno il suo*, p. 83.

18. Sciascia, p. 134.

19. Sciascia, p. 140.

20. For a treatment of the alien in Gardner's fiction see Susan Strehle, "John Gardner's Novels: Affirmation and the Alien," *Critique, Studies in Modern Fiction*, 8 (December 1976), pp. 86–96.

21. John Gardner (1933–1982), *The Sunlight Dialogues* (New York: Knopf, 1972), p. 670.

22. Gardner, *The Sunlight Dialogues*, p. 123, last line of chapter 2.

23. Gardner, p. 579.

24. Gardner, p. 229.

25. Gardner. p. 272.

26. John Gardner, *Nickel Mountain* (New York: Knopf, 1973), pp. 139–41.

27. John Gardner, *The Sunlight Dialogues*, p. 442.

28. Gardner, p. 518.

29. Gardner, pp. 556–63.

30. Gardner, pp. 571–76.
31. Gardner, p. 392.
32. Gardner, p. 449.
33. Gardner, p. 627.
34. See Gardner, p. 249.
35. Gardner's statement in a conversation between Stefano Tani and the novelist, November 1980.
36. Gardner, p. 463. "The time is out of joint" is from *Hamlet,* I. 5. 188.
37. In the Italian edition (*Il nome della rosa,* Milan: Bompiani, 1980) the pattern is not only present in the book, but also *on* the book: the map of an actual labyrinth is printed on the jacket, while on the interior of the book cover there is a complete map of the monastery in which the library building has the same shape as the labyrinth on the outside cover. Library and labyrinth are thus associated immediately at a visual—and almost unconscious—level by the reader. (The American edition does not have the map of the labyrinth on the jacket.)
38. Umberto Eco (b. 1932), *The Name of the Rose,* translated from the Italian by William Weaver (New York: Harcourt Brace Jovanovich, 1983), p. 492.
39. Eco, p. 492.
40. This is definitely a concept that occurs throughout literature (e.g., "What's in a name? That which we call a rose by any other name would smell as sweet" Shakespeare, *Romeo and Juliet,* II. 2. 43–44).
41. Eco, p. 502. Italics mine.
42. Eco, p. 492.
43. See an outline of the writer/reader relation in Calvino's novel in the description of the metafictional category (Chapter 2, pp. 43–44).
44. "La biblioteca de Babel" belongs to the collection of short stories *Ficciones* (Buenos Aires: Editorial Sur, 1944).
45. Eco, pp. 500, 501.
46. See A. E. Murch, *The Development of the Detective Novel* (London: Peter Owen, 1958), p. 256.
47. See Murch, p. 256.

4. THE DECONSTRUCTIVE ANTI-DETECTIVE NOVEL

1. Friedrich Nietzsche, *Beyond Good and Evil,* trans. Helen Zimmern (London: George Allen and Unwin, 1967), p. 97.
2. Leonardo Sciascia, *Todo modo* (Turin: Einaudi, 1974), p. 4. All the translations from the Italian in this chapter are my own. Italics mine.
3. Sciascia, p. 4–5.
4. Sciascia, pp. 47–48.
5. *Democrazia Cristiana,* which has governed Italy for more than thirty years, is never named in *Todo modo,* just as the word *Mafia* is never named in *A ciascuno il suo.* The connection between religion and political power that Sciascia brings to light in the novel through don Gaetano, however, makes

blatantly clear which party he is talking about. *Democrazia Cristiana* still, at least theoretically, stresses a religious commitment and claims as its origins the Catholic populist movement (the so-called *Partito popolare*) before Mussolini.

6. Sciascia, p. 27.

7. Sciascia, p. 12.

8. Edgar Allan Poe, "The Murders in the Rue Morgue," in *The Short Fiction of Edgar Allan Poe,* ed. Stuart Levine and Susan Levine (Indianapolis: Bobbs-Merrill, 1976), p. 180.

9. Sciascia , pp. 17–18, 20.

10. Sciascia, p. 99.

11. Sciascia, p.69.

12. Sciascia, pp. 107–8.

13. Sciascia, p. 110.

14. Sciascia, pp. 115–16.

15. Sciascia, p. 117.

16. Sciascia, pp. 122–23.

17. Agatha Christie, *And Then There Were None* (New York: Dodd, Mead, 1940).

18. Sciascia, p. 120.

19. Sciascia, p. 108.

20. Agatha Christie, *The Murder of Roger Ackroyd* (London: Collins, 1926).

21. Sciascia, p. 108.

22. Sciascia, p. 110.

23. Sciascia, pp. 115–16. Italics mine.

24. A partly similar although less circumstantial interpretation is given by Claude Ambroise in *Invito alla lettura di Sciascia* (Milan: Mursia, 1978), pp. 166–67.

25. Sciascia, pp. 115–16. Italics mine.

26. Sciascia, p. 117. Italics mine.

27. Sciascia, p. 4.

28. Sciascia, p. 12.

29. Sciascia, p. 107.

30. Sciascia, p. 108.

31. Sciascia, p. 108.

32. Sciascia, p. 4.

33. Sciascia, p. 4.

34. Sciascia, p. 69.

35. Sciascia, pp. 77–78. Italics mine.

36. Sciascia, pp. 17–18.

37. Sciascia, p. 99.

38. Sciascia, p. 117.

39. Eco, *The Name of the Rose,* p. 87.

40. Sciascia, pp. 4–5.

41. Thomas Pynchon (b. 1937), *The Crying of Lot 49* (Philadelphia: Lippincott, 1966), p. 76.

42. Pynchon, p. 171.

43. Pynchon, p. 171.

44. Pynchon, p. 126.

45. Pynchon, p. 119.

46. Pynchon, p. 9.

47. Pynchon, p. 109.

48. Pynchon, p. 90.

49. Pynchon, p. 171.

50. Pynchon, p. 82.

51. Pynchon, pp. 170–71.

52. For this concept of the "marvelous" as a phenomenon that implies a supernatural intervention, see Tzvetan Todorov, *The Fantastic, a Structural Approach to a Literary Genre* (Ithaca: Cornell University Press, 1975). Original title: *Introduction à la littérature fantastique* (Paris: Editions du Seuil, 1970).

53. Pynchon, *The Crying of Lot 49*, p. 183.

54. Pynchon, p. 182.

55. William Hjortsberg was born in Manhattan in 1941. He is the author of three other novels (*Alp*, 1969; *Gray Matters*, 1971; *Toro! Toro! Toro!*, 1974), all characterized by simultaneous and labyrinthine plots and subplots, a playful and macabre sense of humor, and a predilection for the fantastic and the exotic. He also wrote a novella, *Symbiography* (1973), which has a science fiction plot. *Falling Angel* marks a development from a light to a deeper conception of fiction in his career.

56. William Hjortsberg, *Falling Angel* (New York: Harcourt, Brace Jovanovich, 1978), p. 7.

57. Hjortsberg, p. 4.

58. Jack Sullivan, "Grotesque & Villains," *The New York Times Book Review*, 4 February 1979.

59. Hjortsberg, *Falling Angel*, pp. 77–78.

60. Hjortsberg, pp. 138–39.

61. Hjortsberg, pp. 156–57.

62. Hjortsberg, p. 196.

63. Hjortsberg, p. 130.

64. Hjortsberg, p. 155.

65. Hjortsberg, p. 227.

66. Hjortsberg, p. 228.

67. Hjortsberg, p. 34.

68. Hjortsberg, p.1. Italics mine.

69. Hjortsberg, pp.242–43.

70. Hjortsberg, p. 177.

71. Hjortsberg, p. 172.

72. Pynchon, *The Crying of Lot 49*, p. 160.

73. Pynchon, p. 124.

74. Pynchon, p. 124.

75. Hjortsberg, *Falling Angel*, pp. 238, 239.

76. Pynchon, *The Crying of Lot 49*, p. 171.

77. Tzvetan Todorov, *The Fantastic, a Structural Approach to a Literary Genre* (Ithaca: Cornell University Press, 1975), pp. 41–42.

78. Todorov, pp. 169–74.

79. I do not analyze *Quer pasticciaccio brutto de via Merulana (That Awful Mess on Via Merulana,* trans. William Weaver [New York: George Braziller, 1965]) here because of chronological reasons (it was published in 1946) and because it has already been extensively analyzed as a detective novel (e.g., see the recent article by JoAnn Cannon, "The Reader as Detective: Notes on Gadda's *Pasticciaccio," Modern Language Studies* 10 [Fall 1980]). Gadda's novel describes the shabby routine of a police commissioner in Fascist Italy in the late twenties, a sexual murder, and the inability of police to make sense out of the "awful mess."

5. THE METAFICTIONAL ANTI-DETECTIVE NOVEL

1. The structure of Calvino's novel seems evocative of the one of *Statements,* a novel described in Borges' short story "Examen de la obra de Herbert Quain" ("Analysis of the Work of Herbert Quain"), published in *Ficciones.*

2. Calvino's *Se una notte d'inverno un viaggiatore* (Turin: Einaudi, 1979) came out in English in a translation by William Weaver (*If on a winter's night a traveler* [New York: Harcourt Brace Jovanovich, 1981]). I disagree with Weaver's clumsy translation of *lettore* as "the Reader" and of *lettrice* (*lettrice* is the feminine correspondent to the masculine *lettore*) as "the Other Reader," since it misses the crucial masculine/feminine opposition present in the two Italian nouns. I will quote, however, from Weaver's translation, since it is the only one published. Nevertheless, throughout the text, I am going to refer to the *lettore* as "He-Reader" and to the *lettrice* as "She-Reader," while Weaver's translation ("the Reader" and "the Other Reader") will of course remain in the quoted passages.

3. Italo Calvino (b. 1923), *If on a winter's night a traveler,* translated by William Weaver (New York: Harcourt Brace Jovanovich, 1981), p. 27.

4. Calvino, p. 4.

5. Calvino. p. 4.

6. Calvino, p. 30.

7. Calvino, p. 32.

8. Calvino, p. 159.

9. Note the parodical assonance between "Silas Flannery" and "Sean Connery," the name of the actor who played Ian Fleming's James Bond.

10. Calvino, p. 189.

11. Calvino, pp. 169, 170, 171.

12. Calvino, pp. 240, 241. Italics mine.

13. Calvino, pp. 10, 11, 12.

14. For an exhaustive study on the theory of narration and the notion of point of view, which are only peripheral concerns in this work, it would be helpful to see Gérard Genette's structuralist "classic," *Narrative Discourse* (Ithaca: Cornell University Press, 1980). Original title: "Discours du récit," a portion of *Figures III* (Paris: Editions de Seuil, 1972).

15. Calvino, *If on a winter's night a traveler,* p. 141.

16. Calvino, p. 141.

17. Calvino, p. 155.

18. Unlike English, in Italian the second person plural (*voi*) differs from the second person singular (*tu*).

19. Calvino, *If on a winter's night a traveler*, p. 132.

20. Remember the following passage: "What are you like, Other Reader? It is time for this book in the second person to address itself no longer to a general male you [the He-Reader], perhaps *brother and double of a hypocrite I* [Calvino]" (Calvino, p. 141; italics mine).

21. Calvino, pp. 197–98.

22. Calvino, p. 161.

23. Calvino, p. 162.

24. Calvino, p. 215.

25. Thomas Pynchon, *The Crying of Lot 49* (Philadelphia: Lippincott, 1966), p. 156.

26. Calvino, *If on a winter's night a traveler*, pp. 235, 236.

27. Calvino, p. 259.

28. Calvino, p. 3.

29. Calvino, p.26.

30. Calvino, p. 3.

31. Vladimir Nabokov, *Pale Fire* (New York: G.P. Putnam's Sons, 1962), p. 81.

32. Nabokov, pp. 214, 215.

33. Nabokov, p. 315.

34. Nabokov, p. 238.

35. Nabokov, p. 238.

36. Nabokov, p. 238. Italics mine.

37. Nabokov, p. 20.

38. Nabokov, p. 86.

39. From the entry on Vladimir Nabokov by John V. Hagopian in *Dictionary of Literary Biography*, vol. 2: *American Novelists since World War II* (Detroit: Gale Research Co., 1978), p. 360.

40. Hagopian, p. 361.

41. Pynchon, *The Crying of Lot 49*, p. 82.

42. Nabokov, *Pale Fire*, p. 296. Italics mine.

43. Nabokov, p. 183. See especially Mary McCarthy's penetrating interpretation of *Pale Fire* ("A Bolt from the Blue," *The New Republic*, 4 June 1962).

44. Nabokov, p. 299.

45. See Nabokov, p. 267.

46. Patrica Merivale, "The Flaunting of Artifice in Vladimir Nabokov and Jorge Luis Borges," *Wisconsin Studies in Contemporary Literature* 8 (Spring 1967), p. 308.

47. Nabokov, *Pale Fire*, p. 212.

48. Nabokov, p. 33.

49. Nabokov, p. 69.

50. Nabokov, pp. 28, 29.

51. Nabokov, p. 25.

52. Nabokov, p. 195.

53. Nabokov, p. 98.
54. See Nabokov, pp. 107, 189, and 194.
55. Nabokov, pp. 300, 301.
56. Nabokov, p. 295.
57. Nabokov, p. 295.
58. Nabokov, p. 298.
59. Christina Tekiner, "Time in Lolita," *Modern Fiction Studies* 25 (Autumn 1979), p. 3.
60. Pynchon, *The Crying of Lot 49*, p. 9.
61. In Italian *traduttore* (translator) and *traditore* (traitor) are very similar words. Ironically, Marana's role in the novel fits perfectly the assonance between the two nouns. Furthermore, Marana recalls the Italian *marrano* (traitor) and Ermes, Marana's first name, is in Greek mythology the name of the god of thieves.

Bibliography

Ackerman, James S. "The Demise of the Avant Garde: Notes on the Sociology of Recent American Art." *Comparative Studies in Society and History* 10 (1969), pp. 371–84.

Ambroise, Claude. *Invito alla lettura di Sciascia*. Milan: Mursia, 1978.

Auden, W. H. "The Guilty Vicarage." *Harper's*, May 1948.

Bader, Julia. *Crystal Land: Artifice in Nabokov's English Novels*. Berkeley: University of California Press, 1972.

Barbolini, R. "Le istituzioni del romanzo poliziesco." *Il Verri* 8 (1977), pp. 127–54.

Barrenechea, Ana Maria. *La expresión de la irrealidad en la obra de Jorge Luis Borges*. Mexico City: Fondo de Culture, 1957. English edition: *Borges: The Labyrinth Maker*. Edited and translated by Robert Lima. New York: New York University Press, 1965.

Barrett, William. *Irrational Man: A Study in Existential Philosophy*. Garden City, N.Y.: Doubleday, 1958.

Barth, John. *Letters*. New York: G. P. Putnam's Sons, 1979.

———. "The Literature of Replenishment." *The Atlantic*, January 1980, pp. 65–71.

Barthes, Roland. *Le plaisir du texte*. Paris: Editions du Seuil, 1973.

Barzun, Jacques, ed. *The Delights of Detection*. New York: Criterion Books, 1961.

Benjamin, Walter. "Paris, die Hauptstadt des XIX. Jahrhunderts." In *Illuminationen, Ausgewählte Schriften*. Frankfurt am Main: Suhrkamp Verlag, 1961.

Benvenuti, Stefano and Gianni Rizzoni. *Il romanzo giallo*. Milan: Mondadori, 1979.

Bianchini, Angela. *Il romanzo d'appendice*. Turin: ERI/Edizioni Rai Radiotelevisone Italiana, 1969.

Bloch-Michel, Jean. *Le présent de l'indicatif*. Paris: Gallimard, 1963.

Blok, Anton. *The Mafia of a Sicilian Village, 1860–1960*. New York: Harper & Row, 1975.

Borges, Jorge Luis, and Adolfo Bioy Casares. *Seis problemas para don Isidro Parodi*. Buenos Aires: Editorial Sur, 1942.

Borges, Jorge Luis. *Ficciones*. Buenos Aires: Editorial Sur, 1944.

———. *El Aleph*. Buenos Aires: Editorial Losada, 1949.

———. "Sono un cavaliere dell'Ordine Giallo." *L'Espresso*, no. 52, 28 December 1980, pp. 50–59.

Brecht, Bertolt. "Kehren wir zu den Kriminalromanen zurück!" and "Glossen über Kriminalromane." In *Gesammelte Werke 18: Schriften zur Literatur und Kunst 1*. Frankfurt am Main: Suhrkamp, 1967.

————. "Über die Popularität des Kriminalromans" and "Über den Kriminalroman." In *Gesammelte Werke 19: Schriften zur Literatur und Kunst 2*. Frankfurt am Main: Surhkamp, 1967.

Butor, Michel. *L'emploi du temps*. Paris: Les Editions de Minuit, 1956.

Calvino, Italo. *Se una notte d'inverno un viaggiatore*. Turin: Einaudi, 1979.

————. *Una pietra sopra: discorsi di letteratura e società*. Turin: Einaudi, 1980.

Cameron, Ian, and Robin Wood. *Antonioni*. New York: Praeger, 1971.

Cannon, JoAnn. "The Reader as Detective: Notes on Gadda's *Pasticciaccio*." *Modern Language Studies* 10 (Fall 1980), pp. 41–50.

————. *Italo Calvino: Writer and Critic*. Ravenna: Longo Editore, 1981.

Cappabianca, Alessandro. "Appunti sul poliziesco cinematografico." *Filmcritica*, Rome, September-October 1971, pp. 379–82.

Carboni, Guido. "Un matrimonio ben riuscito? Note sul giallo d'azione negli USA." *Calibano* 2. Rome: Savelli, 1978, pp. 109–37.

Cattanei, Luigi. *Leonardo Sciascia*. Florence: Le Monnier, 1979.

Cawelti, John G. *Adventure, Mystery, and Romance*. Chicago: The University of Chicago Press, 1976.

Ceccaroni, Arnaldo. "Per una lettura del 'Pasticciaccio' di C. E. Gadda." *Lingua e Stile* 5 (1970), pp. 57–85.

Champigny, Robert. *What Will Have Happened: A Philosophical and Technical Essay on Mystery Stories*. Bloomington: Indiana University Press, 1977.

Chandler, Raymond. "The Simple Art of Murder." *The Atlantic*, December 1944, pp. 53–59.

Charney, Hanna. "Pourquoi le 'Nouveau Roman' Policier?" *The French Review* 46 (October 1972), pp. 17–23.

Christie, Agatha. *The Murder of Roger Ackroyd*. London: Collins, 1926.

————. *And Then There Were None*. New York: Dodd, Mead, 1940.

Copi, L. M. "Il detective come scienziato." In *Introduzione alla logica*. Bologna: Il Mulino, 1964.

Couturier, Maurice. "Nabokov's Performative Writing." In *Les Américanistes: New French Criticism on Modern American Fiction*. Ed. Ira D. Johnson and Christiane Johnson. Port Washington, N.Y.: National University Publications-Kennikat Press, 1978.

Cranston, Maurice. "Fine del romanzo poliziesco?" *Minerva* 1 (1948), pp. 9–11.

Cremante, Renzo, and Loris Rambelli, eds. *La trama del delitto. Teoria e analisi del racconto poliziesco*. Parma: Pratiche Editrice, 1980.

Crispolti, C. "Origini e sviluppo del racconto 'giallo' ." *La Fiera Letteraria*, 29 August 1969, pp. 6–7.

D'Amore, B. "Analisi logica del romanzo poliziesco." *Rendiconti* 24 (1972), pp. 305–20.

De Lauretis, Teresa. *Umberto Eco*. Florence: La Nuova Italia, 1981.

Del Buono, Oreste. "Il romanzo popolare." In *Almanacco letterario Bompiani 1968*. Milan: Bompiani, 1968.

Del Monte, Alberto. *Breve storia del romanzo poliziesco*. Bari: Laterza, 1962.

De Vecchi Rocca, Luisa. "Apoteosi e decadenza del romanzo poliziesco d'azione." *Nuova Antologia* 506, no. 2024 (August 1969), pp. 532–40.

Eco, Umberto. "Le strutture narrative in Ian Fleming." In *L'analisi del racconto*. Milan: Bompiani, 1969.

———. "L'industria aristotelica." In *Almanacco Bompiani 1972*. Milan: Bompiani, 1972.

———. *Il nome della rosa*. Milan: Bompiani, 1980.

Frohock, W. M. *The Novel of Violence in America*. Dallas: Southern Methodist University Press, 1958.

Gabutti, Diego. "Il giallo americano." *Alfabeta* 15/16 (July/August 1980), pp. 16–17.

Gadda, Carlo Emilio. *Quer pasticciaccio brutto de via Merulana*. Milan: Garzanti, 1957.

Gardner, John. *The Sunlight Dialogues*. New York: Knopf, 1972.

———. *Nickel Mountain*. New York: Knopf, 1973.

Graff, Gerald. "The Myth of the Postmodernist Breakthrough." *Tri-Quarterly* 26 (1975).

Gramigna, Giuliano. "Come si scrive un romanzo poliziesco: il sogno di Robinson." *Il Caffè* 2 (1971), pp. 3–10.

Gramsci, Antonio. "Romanzi polizieschi." In *Quaderni del carcere*. *Quaderno* 21 (17) [1934–1935]. Turin: Einaudi, 1975.

Grossvogel, David I. *Limits of the Novel: Evolutions of a Form from Chaucer to Robbe-Grillet*. Ithaca: Cornell University Press, 1968.

———. *Mystery and Its Fictions: From Oedipus to Agatha Christie*. Baltimore: The Johns Hopkins University Press, 1979.

Hagopian, John V. "Nabokov, Vladimir." *Dictionary of Literary Biography*, vol. 2, *American Novelists since World War II*. Detroit: Gale Research Co., 1978.

Hammett, Dashiell. *The Continental Op*. Ed. Steven Marcus. New York: Random House, 1974.

———. *Red Harvest*. London: Cassell, 1974.

Hassan, Ihab. "The Dismemberment of Orpheus." *The American Scholar* 32, no. 3 (Summer 1963).

———. "POSTmodernISM, A Paracritical Bibliography." *New Literary History* 3, no. 1 (Autumn 1971), pp. 5–30.

Haycraft, Howard. *Murder for Pleasure: The Life and Times of the Detective Story*. New York, 1941.

Heath, Stephen. *The Nouveau Roman: A Study in the Practice of Writing*. London: Elek Books, 1972.

Hirsch, E. D. *Validity in Interpretation*. New Haven: Yale University Press, 1967.

Holquist, Michael. "Whodunit and Other Questions: Metaphysical Detective Stories in Post-War Fiction." *New Literary History* 3, no. 1 (Autumn 1971), pp. 135–56.

Hjortsberg, William. *Falling Angel*. New York: Harcourt Brace Jovanovich, 1978.

Iser, Wolfgang. *Der Akt des Lesens*. Munich: Wilhelm Fink, 1976.

Jameson, Fredric. "On Raymond Chandler." *The Southern Review* 6, no. 3 (July 1970), pp. 624–50.

———. "Magical Narratives: Romance as Genre." *New Literary History* 7, no. 1 (Autumn 1975), pp. 135–63.

Kracauer, Siegfried. "Der Detektiv-Roman." In *Schiriften 1*. Frankfurt am Main: Suhrkamp Verlag, 1971.

Krutch, Joseph Wood. *Edgar Allan Poe*. London: Knopf, 1926.

Kuhn, Thomas S. "Comment." *Comparative Studies in Society and History* 11 (1969), pp. 403–12.

———. *The Structure of Scientific Revolutions*. 2d ed. Chicago: The University of Chicago Press, 1970.

Lacassin, Francis. *Mythologie du Roman Policier*. Vols. 1 and 2. Paris: Union Générale d'Editions, 1974.

Landrum, Larry N., Pat Browne, and Ray B. Browne, eds. *Dimensions of Detective Fiction*. Bowling Green, Ohio: Bowling Green University Popular Press, 1976.

Laura, Ernesto G. *Storia del giallo da Poe a Borges*. Rome: Edizioni Studium, 1981.

Lehan, Richard. *A Dangerous Crossing: French Literary Existentialism and the Modern American Novel*. Carbondale and Edwardsville: Southern Illinois University Press, 1973.

Levine, June Perry. "Vladimir Nabokov's *Pale Fire:* 'The Method of Composition' as Hero." *The International Fiction Review* 5, no. 2 (July 1978), pp. 103–8.

Lewis, Norman. *The Honored Society*. New York: G. P. Putnam's Sons, 1964.

McCarthy, Mary. "A Bolt from the Blue." *The New Republic* 4 (June 1962), pp. 21–27.

Macdonald, Ross. "The Writer as Detective Hero." In Francis M. Nevins, Jr., ed. *The Mystery Writer's Art* (Bowling Green, Ohio: Bowling Green University Popular Press, 1970), pp. 295–305.

Mangel, Anne. "Maxwell's Demon, Entropy, Information: *The Crying of Lot 49.*" *Tri-Quarterly* 20 (Winter 1971), pp. 194–208.

Merivale, Patricia. "The Flaunting of Artifice in Vladimir Nabokov and Jorge Luis Borges." *Wisconsin Studies in Contemporary Literature* 8, no. 2 (Spring 1967), pp. 294–309.

Murch, A. E. *The Development of the Detective Novel*. London: Peter Owen, 1958.

Nabokov, Vladimir. *The Real Life of Sebastian Knight*. Norfolk: New Directions, 1941.

———. *Lolita*. New York: G. P. Putnam's Sons, 1955.

———. *Pale Fire*. New York: G. P. Putnam's Sons, 1962.

Narcejac, Thomas. *Une Machine à Lire: Le Roman Policier*. Paris: Denoël/Gonthier, 1975.

Nicolson, Marjorie. "The Professor and the Detective." *The Atlantic*, April 1929, pp. 483–93.

Olderman, Raymond M. *Beyond the Waste Land: The American Novel in the Nineteen-Sixties*. New Haven: Yale University Press, 1972.

175 Bibliography

Ollier, Claude. *La Mise en Scène*. Paris: Les Editions de Minuit, 1958.
Palermi, Maria Gabriella. "Dal romanzo sensazionale al romanzo poliziesco." *Nuova Antologia* 524, no. 2095 (July 1975), pp. 379–89.
Palmer, Jerry. *Thrillers, Genesis and Structure of a Popular Genre*. London: Edward Arnold, 1978.
Pifer, Ellen. *Nabokov and the Novel*. Cambridge: Harvard University Press, 1981.
Poe, Edgar Allan. *The Short Fiction of Edgar Allan Poe*. Ed. Stuart Levine and Susan Levine, Indianapolis: Bobbs-Merrill, 1976.
Poggioli, Renato. *Teoria dell'arte d'avanguardia*. Bologna: Il Mulino, 1962.
Pynchon, Thomas. *The Crying of Lot 49*. Philadelphia: Lippincott, 1966.
Rambelli, Loris. "Acculturazione di un genere letterario: il detective, l'analista italiano." *Lingua e Stile* 10, no. 1 (1975).
———. "Il filosofo e i 'Detektivromane.' " *Lingua e Stile* 11, no. 1 (1976), pp. 141–50.
———. *Storia del "giallo" italiano*. Milan: Garzanti, 1979.
Rabkin, Eric S. *Narrative Suspense*. Ann Arbor: University of Michigan Press, 1973.
Rank, Otto. *The Double, A Psychoanalytic Study*. Chapel Hill: The University of North Carolina Press, 1971.
Robbe-Grillet, Alain. *Les Gommes*. Paris: Les Editions de Minuit, 1953.
———. *Le Voyeur* . Paris: Les Editions de Minuit, 1955.
———. *La Jalousie*. Paris: Les Editions de Minuit, 1957.
———. *Dans le labyrinthe*. Paris: Les Editions de Minuit, 1959.
———. *Pour un nouveau roman*. Paris: Les Editions de Minuit, 1963.
Santucci, Antonio. "Per una storia del romanzo giallo." *Il Mulino* 2 (December 1951), pp. 78–86.
Sarraute, Nathalie. *L'ere du soupçon*. Paris: Librairie Gallimard, 1956.
Scaringi, Carlo. "Riscrivono la cronaca con l'inchiostro giallo." *Radiocorriere TV*, 5/11 December 1976, pp. 131, 133.
Scholes, Robert. *Fabulation and Metafiction*. Urbana: University of Illinois Press, 1979.
Sciascia, Leonardo. "Letteratura del 'giallo.' " *Letteratura* 1, no. 3 (May-June 1953), pp. 65–67.
———. "Appunti sul 'giallo.' " *Nuova Corrente* 1 (June 1954), pp. 23–24.
———. "La carriera di Maigret." *Letteratura* 2, no. 10 (July-August 1954), pp. 73–75.
———. *Le parrocchie di Regalpetra*. Bari: Laterza, 1956.
———. *Il giorno della civetta*. Turin: Einaudi, 1961.
———. *A ciascuno il suo*. Turin: Einaudi, 1966.
———. *Todo modo*. Turin: Einaudi, 1974.
———. "Breve storia del romanzo giallo: 1) E l'investigatore fu." *Epoca*, 20 September 1975, pp. 66–72.
———. "Breve storia del romanzo giallo: 2) L'inchiesta è aperta." *Epoca*, 27 September 1975, pp. 60–66.
———. *La scomparsa di Majorana*. Turin: Einaudi, 1975.
———. *Candido ovvero un sogno fatto in Sicilia*. Turin: Einaudi, 1977.
———. *L'affaire Moro*. Palermo: Sellerio, 1978.

Šklovskij, Viktor B. *O teorii prozy.* Moscow-Leningrad: Krug, 1925.

Sorani, Aldo. "Conan Doyle e la fortuna del romanzo poliziesco." *Pégaso* 2, no. 8 (August 1930), pp. 212–20.

Spanos, William V., ed. *A Casebook on Existentialism.* New York: Thomas Y. Crowell, 1966.

———. "The Detective and the Boundary: Some Notes on the Postmodern Literary Imagination." *Boundary 2* 1, no. 1 (Fall 1972), pp. 147–68.

Stevenson, Robert Louis. *The Works of Robert Louis Stevenson.* Tusitala Edition. Vol. 5: *The Strange Case of Dr. Jekyll and Mr. Hyde.* London: Heinemann, 1927.

Strehle, Susan. "John Gardner's Novels: Affirmation and the Alien." *Critique, Studies in Modern Fiction* 18, no. 2 (December 1976), pp. 86–96.

Sullivan, Jack. "Grotesque & Villains." *The New York Times Book Review,* 4 February 1979.

Symons, Julian. *The Detective Story in Britain.* London: Longmans, 1962.

———. *Bloody Murder.* London: Faber & Faber, 1972.

———. *The Tell-Tale Heart. The Life and Works of Edgar Allan Poe.* New York: Harper & Row, 1978.

Tekiner, Christina. "Time in *Lolita.*" *Modern Fiction Studies,* Vladimir Nabokov number, 25, no. 3 (Autumn 1979), pp. 463–69.

Todorov, Tzvetan. *Introduction à la littérature fantastique.* Paris: Editions du Seuil, 1970. English edition: *The Fantastic, a Structural Approach to a Literary Genre.* Ithaca: Cornell University Press, 1975.

———. *Poétique de la prose.* Paris: Editions du Seuil, 1971. English edition: *The Poetics of Prose.* Oxford: Basil Blackwell, 1977.

Tynjanov, Jurij N. *Poetika, Istorija Literatury, Kino.* Moscow: Nauka, 1977.

Varaldo, Alessandro. "Dramma e romanzo poliziesco." *Comoedia* (July 1932), pp. 9–10.

Williams, Carol T. " 'Web of Sense': *Pale Fire* in the Nabokov Canon." *Critique, Studies in Modern Fiction* 6, no. 3 (Winter 1963), pp. 29–45.

Wilson, Edmund. "Why Do People Read Detective Stories?" *The New Yorker* 20, no. 35, 14 October 1944, pp. 73–75.

———. "Who Cares Who Killed Roger Ackroyd? A Second Report on Detective Fiction." *The New Yorker* 20, no. 49, 20 January 1945, pp. 52–58.

———. " 'Mr. Holmes, They Were the Footprints of a Gigantic Hound!' " *The New Yorker* 20, no. 1, 17 February 1945, pp. 73–78.

INDEX

Existentialism: and the detective as
the intellectual's hero, xi, xii; rise
of, 39; in relation to postmodernism, 39; philosophical notion of,
161 n.6; 161 n.9, 161 n.10

Farrell, James Thomas, 22
Faulkner, William: mentioned by
Sciascia, 54
Feuilleton: rise and characteristics
of, 15–16, 155 n.17; and the
"dime novel," 19, 25; and the
hard-boiled, 25; and the post-
WWII degeneration of detective
fiction, 26, 27
Fleming, Ian: James Bond, 26, 73
Folgore, Luciano: *La trappola colo-
rata,* 28–29
Freda, Riccardo, 30
Frohock, W. M., 22

Gaboriau, Emile: *L'Affaire Lerouge,*
16, 17, 37
Gadda, Carlo Emilio: *Quer pasticciaccio brutto de via Merulana,* xv,
33–34, 38, 110, 166 n.79
Gardner, John, 32
—*The Sunlight Dialogues:* as an innovative anti-detective novel, 42,
43, 52; explicated, **62–68;** Clumly
as a doomed detective in, 63, 67–
68; and the Sunlight Man as an
alien, 63; related to *A ciascuno il
suo,* 63, 67; and frustrated
reader's expectations, 64–65, 68;
and *Nickel Mountain,* 64–65; and
duality detective-criminal, 65; and
existential identity, 66
Gide, André: *Les caves du Vatican,*
85, 86, 87
Gothicism: rise of, 2; and Poe's detective story, 7, 37, 149, 150, and
the feuilleton, 16; and the hard-
boiled, 25, 27; and the involution
of detective fiction, 54; and
Falling Angel, 99
Gramsci, Antonio, 16–17, 32

Hammett, Dashiell: and the mythic
private detective, xi, xii; and the
hard-boiled, 22; and differences
with anti-detective fiction, 23–24;
and Italian version of, 29
Hawkes, John, xii, 151
Hawthorne, Nathaniel: *The House
of the Seven Gables,* 18, 156 n.20
Hemingway, Ernest, xiv, 22; mentioned by Sciascia, 54
Hjortsberg, William, 32, 165 n.55
—*Falling Angel:* as a deconstructive
anti-detective novel, 42, 43, 76,
77–78; as a "marvelous" novel,
97, 108–9; and satanism innovat-
ing the hard-boiled, 99, 107–8; explicated, **99–109;** and duality
detective-criminal, 102–3; and the
devil in *Todo modo,* 103, 110–11;
and Angel as doomed detective,
103; and the Oedipus myth, 103–
4; and names, 105; and conspiracy
against the detective, 106–7; and
its irrational solution compared to
nonsolution in *The Crying of Lot
49,* 107–8; and frustrated reader's
expectations, 108; and American
optimism contrasted with Italian
anti-detective fiction, 111–12
Holquist, Michael, 19–20
Hubbard, P. M., 27

Johnson, Samuel, 1
Joyce, James, 39

Kafka, Franz, 39; "Die Verwand-
lung," 108–9
King, Stephen, 99
Knox, Ronald, 20
Krutch, Joseph Wood, 10
Kuhn, Thomas: *The Structure of Sci-
entific Revolutions,* 37

Labyrinth, theme of the: in the *nouveau roman,* 47, 48–50; in Borges,
50; in *Il nome della rosa,* 70; in *Se
una notte d'inverno un viaggiatore,*
129

Stefano Tani, born in 1953 in Florence, Italy, holds a *laurea* in American Literature from the Università degli Studi di Firenze, an M.A. in English Literature from Drew University, and a Ph.D. in Comparative Literature from the State University of New York at Binghamton. He has taught English Literature at the Università degli Studi di Trieste, and is currently teaching American Literature at the Università degli Studi di Pescara.